12.28.23

OPHIE'S GHOSTS

Justina Ireland

BALZER + BRAY
An Imprint of HarperCollins*Publishers*

Balzer + Bray is an imprint of HarperCollins Publishers.

Ophie's Ghosts
Copyright © 2021 by Justina Ireland
All rights reserved. Printed in the United States of America.
No part of this book may be used or reproduced in any manner
whatsoever without written permission except in the case of brief
quotations embodied in critical articles and reviews. For information
address HarperCollins Children's Books, a division of HarperCollins
Publishers, 195 Broadway, New York, NY 10007.
www.harpercollinschildrens.com

Library of Congress Control Number: 2020951009
ISBN 978-0-06-291589-4

Typography by Molly Fehr
21 22 23 24 25   PC/LSCH   10 9 8 7 6 5 4 3 2
❖
First Edition

For all the names we never knew

Prologue

OPHELIA HARRISON JOLTED AWAKE, HER HEART pounding with terror. It was the middle of the night, and her room was dark. Dark enough that she shouldn't have been able to see her father standing at the end of the bed, but she could.

"Ophie, you got to wake up. Get up, girl."

Ophie's father hadn't gotten home before she'd fallen asleep, and at first Ophie thought she was imagining her daddy standing there—he was still in his checkered work shirt and dungarees, sleeves rolled back to reveal deep brown arms her mama always said were just as strong as John Henry's.

But rubbing her eyes didn't clear the vision, so she knew she wasn't dreaming. "Daddy, what's happening?"

"Something bad, Ophie, but you ain't got time to

fret. Get up and go get your mama, and find the coffee can I keep under the floorboards. Third one from the door, the one with the squeak. Then meet me outside."

"Why can't you get it?" Ophie asked. She knew she shouldn't act so petulant, but she wanted to go back to sleep, not run around in the middle of the night looking for noisy floorboards.

An icy chill entered the room, and Ophie wrapped her arms tight around herself. Even though it was November in Georgia, the weather had been unseasonably warm, enough so that Ophie wore just a thin nightgown. Still, the window wasn't open, and it had been cozy a few moments before.

Ophie's father shook his head; if he noticed the sudden cold, he didn't show it. "I know you ain't back-talking me. What I tell you?"

Ophie sighed. "Get Mama and the coffee can from the front room." Ophie had only once talked back to her father in her twelve years. The result had been a week of mucking out the chicken coop. It wasn't a mistake she aimed to make again.

"Good girl. Now get."

Ophie rubbed her eyes once more, climbed out of the tiny bed her father had built for her when she was born, and went to wake her mother.

When Ophie pushed open the door to her parents' bedroom she was startled to find her mother awake. Almost as surprised as Mama was.

"Ophelia Harrison, where was that knock?" she asked.

"I didn't knock. Daddy said I should get you and the coffee can from the living room and meet him outside."

Ophie didn't wait for her mama. The strangeness of her daddy's appearance and the late hour conspired to sink a peculiar anxiousness into Ophie's bones. Now that she was fully awake, cold dread unfurled in her chest, making it hard to breathe. It was like that sudden chill in her bedroom had settled in right under her heart, lodged into her like an icy splinter. She couldn't explain the nervous feeling to her mama. There wasn't time. Instead, she ran to the living room and started pressing the floorboards near the door.

"Ophie!" Mama hurried into the living room. Their house wasn't big, only three rooms, really, and by the time Ophie knelt down to wedge her fingers in the small gap between the third and fourth floorboards from the door, her mama stood over her, pulling her robe tight. When she spoke, her words shook. "Are you and your daddy having a go at me?"

"No, Mama. And we've got to hurry." The board

lifted up with a creak, and sure enough, underneath was a coffee can. Ophie pulled it out of the hole, and Mama grabbed it up right quick.

"What's this? Who put this here?"

"I did; we got to move." Daddy stood next to the front door. Like before, Ophie could see him clear as noontime. There was something amiss; Ophie knew it, but the dread in her chest shifted to bone-numbing fear, and she couldn't stop to think about what was happening.

It was at that moment that she heard the far-off sound of a car approaching, and Daddy's face shifted, a combination of rage and sadness twisting his features. "Y'all need to get outside. Ophie, take Mama to your hiding spot. Go through the back door. Hurry now!"

"But what about you?" Ophie asked, fear causing sudden tears.

"Ophie?" Mama asked, confused. "What in the Lord's name is going on?"

"Don't worry about me," Daddy said, ignoring Mama completely. "Go! Go on now!"

The urgency in Daddy's voice was enough to spur Ophie into movement. She grabbed Mama by the wrist and pulled her toward the back of the house, putting all her weight into tugging her mother along with one hand.

Mama sighed in exasperated confusion but kept walking, the coffee can cradled in her arm. "Ophie, what are you doing? The middle of the night ain't no time for pretend." Her words were stern, but the expression on her face wasn't anger. It was fear.

Ophie huffed out her annoyance. "I ain't playing! Didn't you hear Daddy? He said I should take you to my hiding spot."

Mama opened her mouth to say something, but the far-off car engines grew louder in their approach. Mama clamped her mouth shut and let Ophie pull her along out the door, the screen slamming shut behind them.

The moon was high in the sky, painting the woods beyond their back door in silver and shadow. There were no electric lights where Ophie's family lived— though the nearby town had electricity, the power company didn't consider rural Negroes to be a priority—and Ophie hadn't had time to stop and light an oil lamp. Luckily, she didn't need to see to find her hiding spot. Her body knew the way, knew the roots and rocks to step over and the low branches to duck under. She rushed straight between two knotty pines, the thick undergrowth in between the trees swallowing the sounds of her and Mama's footsteps. The sharp pine needles poked at Ophie's bare feet, filling the night air with their clean scent, and something small and scurrying ran across the path in front of them, but Ophie barely noticed. The dreadful knot of cold fear in her chest chilled her arms and legs, urgent pinpricks that pushed her forward.

And all the while, the cars drew closer, headlights glowing somewhere out on the road, enough to brighten the gloom.

Faster, Ophie. Hurry up now, girl. Ophie swore she could hear her daddy's voice, even though he was still back at the house, waiting on whatever had put such a fright in him.

Ophie's favorite hiding spot wasn't all that far beyond the tree line. She'd found it on the way to the wide, muddy, sluggish creek where Daddy liked to fish on hot days. The oak had fallen over long ago, most likely during one of the violent thunderstorms that ran across Georgia in the summer, and at one point some creature had dug out a burrow amongst the roots. The critter was long gone, but Ophie made frequent visits to the spot, most especially when Mama got to hollering at her about some chore or another.

When Ophie showed Daddy her hidey-hole, he'd laughed. "You can't just run off to a hole in the ground. You're going to end up bit, or worse." So he'd helped Ophie plant marigolds around the outside of the burrow to keep the snakes away. And then he'd brought home scrap wood from the rail yard and built an elevated floor, sturdy enough that sometimes Ophie liked to stomp the boards, pretending it was a fine dance floor or a stage.

But that night, there was no pretending. Ophie slowed, letting go of her mama's hand only long enough to feel for the armlike branch that marked the entrance to the burrow. Once she found it, she stepped around to where she'd built makeshift steps.

But Mama hesitated. "What about snakes, Ophie? And the mosquitoes are already eating me alive. I don't know what's got into you, but we can't go running out into the woods like this in the middle of the night. I don't care what your daddy said. We need to go back and find him."

There was a quaver to Mama's voice that Ophie had never heard before, and she laid a calming hand on her mother's arm.

"It's safe, I promise. Daddy helped me fix it up." The pinprick feeling now felt like icy bugs crawling up and down Ophie's skin, and she yanked hard on Mama's hand. "You gotta get down here, quick. *Please.*"

Maybe it was Ophie's tone, or maybe it was the strange thickness in the air finally seeping into her mother, but whichever it was, Mama climbed into the hole after Ophie.

Headlights cut through the night, tangling in the trees closest to the yard, as several cars pulled into the grass, the rowdy sounds of men echoing through the still night. Ophie couldn't tell what they were saying, and she couldn't see much of anything past the roots of the oak tree, but she caught enough of it that she knew these were the white men in town her mama and daddy had warned her about. Not many Negroes she knew could afford a car, after all—just the pastor, and Dr. Hamilton, who came down once a week from Atlanta to take care of all the sick colored folks. But Ophie mostly knew who it was by the words the men were saying: words that were unkind at their heart, the kind of words that bruised and jabbed just by being spoken. The men in her yard, yelling and laughing, were the kind of white men who had beat up Tommy Williams just because he accidentally looked the wrong way at a white lady from Atlanta. After they'd pummeled Tommy they'd dropped him off in the woods near Ophie's house, most likely because they'd figured no one would find him. But Daddy had found him, brought him home, and they'd pressed a cool, wet rag to Tommy's bruises and stitched up a cut over his eye while the boy tried not to cry.

Ophie had been anxious before, the kind of feeling she sometimes got when Miss Anders—the nice, light-skinned teacher from up north—gave them a timed test. But now? Now fear dug sharp talons into Ophie, chilling her blood and making her shiver. Because nothing good could come of running afoul of the bad men in the yard.

Any objections Mama might have had to hiding were long gone. She crouched in the hidey-hole, wrapping strong, warm arms around Ophie, pulling her near and squeezing her hard. "Stay where you are, don't make a sound, Ophelia," she breathed. "You hear me? If those men find us, we are dead."

Mama's voice was strong and steady, but Ophie could feel the way her mother trembled. She leaned back into her mother's soft strength and tried to hold on to her, tried to give her as much support as she could.

But Ophie was so scared that it took everything she had not to burst into terrified tears.

After several heartbeats came the sound of glass breaking and loud whoops. The scent of burning wood, usually so comforting when Daddy lit a fire on cold days, drifted through the forest. The snap and crackle of fire slowly grew louder than the voices of the men, a roar of consumption, followed by thick smoke that twined sinuously through the treetops, illuminated by the headlights from the cars and the flickering of flame. Where Ophie and her mother huddled, the air was still clear and sweet, even as the acrid scent of burning wood began to taint it.

Ophie squeezed her eyes shut and startled at a small touch on her forehead. Standing outside of the hidey-hole, looking down like he always did when he came to fetch her for supper, was Daddy, a sad smile on his face.

"They'll leave soon, Ophie. Don't be scared. You did good, girl. You and your mama'll be safe here until the sun comes up. You get some sleep now."

Ophie shook her head, unsure how she was supposed to sleep after all that had happened, but within moments a powerful drowsiness weighed her down, and she found herself yawning widely.

And before she knew it, she was fast asleep.

Ophie woke to the sound of voices. She was stiff and cold, and it took a long, fumbling moment for her brain to remember where she was. Once she did, she shot up in the hidey-hole. Her mama and the coffee can were both gone, and for a moment she feared the worst.

That's when the sound of voices came through the trees—both her mother's and the pastor's. As Ophie picked her way out of the woods she saw them in the yard; the pastor and his wife were standing near their big car, holding Ophie's mama in a comforting embrace. Mama didn't like the pastor all that much—both he and his wife were originally from Atlanta, and Mama said they asked for too much in tithing and did too little shepherding. But Ophie always liked the way the pastor's deep bass rumble voice read the Scripture, and the way his wife always closed her eyes as her husband read. It made Ophie feel that maybe some of those Bible words were actually true, even if she didn't entirely believe they were meant for her.

But Ophie's gaze was quickly drawn away from them and to the house. The house that Daddy bragged about building with his own two hands after he married Mama. The house where they spent Christmas and Sunday dinners and where Ophie slept and argued and cried and did all the messy business of growing up. *Her* house.

The house was gone, a smoking ruin left in its wake.

"Ophelia, honey, come over here with your mama," called the pastor's wife. She was a big woman, and Ophie's impression of her had always been of glamour, even as she taught the children about Jesus in Sunday school. Usually she wore sharp red lipstick that highlighted her dark skin and matched her Sunday suit; that day she wore no makeup, her face was streaked with tears, and she wore a regular housedress.

Ophie made her way over to where the pastor had his head lowered next to the car. At first she thought he was praying, but then she realized that he, like his wife, was crying.

"What happened?" Ophie asked, forgetting her manners. A creeping gloom unfurled in her chest, the same kind of bleak feeling she got when she'd broken a rule and knew her mama was fixing to be cross with her. "Why did those men burn down our house? And where's Daddy?"

Mama shook her head and looked away. She wasn't crying, but she had a look of despair and anger and something else, an emotion that Ophie didn't have a name for. The sight of her made Ophie feel panicky, and her own eyes prickled with tears.

"What's happening?" Ophie asked again, even as she began to dread the answer.

The pastor came over and dropped down onto one knee. "I'm very sorry, Ophelia. Your daddy has gone to Heaven to be with Jesus. He was a good man, and a brave man, and some cowards in this town killed him because of it."

"I don't understand," Ophie said. The pastor must have been mistaken. She'd just seen Daddy the night before when he came into her room to wake her up and tell her to get her mama. Unless . . . "Did they . . .

did they get him when they came to burn down the house?"

The pastor shook his head and rubbed his hand over his face before resting it on Ophie's arm. "No, they got hold of him last night on his way home from the rail yard. He voted yesterday morning, and those men didn't like that, so they . . ." The pastor trailed off, and from the expression on his face, Ophie didn't want to know what those men had done to her daddy.

She remembered Tommy Williams. And other names, people she hadn't met but whose names she'd heard whispered in her home and at church: Mary Turner, Obe Cox, Paul Jones. Colored folks who'd broken some unspoken rule, gotten uppity and acted above their station, and paid the price for such an error with their lives.

And here was the pastor telling Ophie she could add her own daddy to that list.

"Can't we call the sheriff?" Ophie asked, setting aside for the moment the strange memory of her daddy from the night before. How could those men do something like this, destroy someone's house in the dead of night, and get away with it? It was more than just unfair: it was a whole new kind of awful.

It wasn't right.

The pastor shook his head but looked to Ophie's

mama as he answered. "If we go to the authorities they'll just say he was a bootlegger. Or worse." The pastor did not say what the worse was, and Mama pressed her lips into a pale pink line at the pastor's words.

"We should go," the pastor's wife said, putting a small bit of distance between her and Ophie's mama. "There's no telling whether those men will come back to admire their handiwork."

The pastor nodded. He rose and opened the passenger-side door to the back seat of his car. "We'll take you to our house and get you fed and cleaned up. We have some extra clothes that we've collected that should fit the two of you. It might be a good idea to get out of town."

Ophie slipped inside, and he shut the door after her. She was covered in mud and scratches from their flight through the woods, but neither the pastor nor his wife seemed to mind much. Mama slid into the seat next to Ophie as the pastor held the door open on the opposite side. Usually Ophie would be excited to ride in such a fancy car, but all she could think about was her daddy and the way she could see him clearly among the shadows of her dark house, almost as if he'd been glowing with his own light.

Normal people didn't glow like that.

"We can head up north," Mama said after a long moment, once everyone was settled inside. "Robert was saving money to leave Georgia, and we have enough to get us there. He has kin up in Pittsburgh, so when we get to the train station I can send them a wire to let them know we're coming."

"You might want to take the train out of Atlanta," the pastor's wife murmured.

"But what about Daddy? I saw him," Ophie said to her mother, quiet enough that the pastor and his wife couldn't hear over the sound of the engine as it started up.

Mama gave Ophie a sharp look. "I don't know what happened last night, and I don't want to know. You did not see your father, Ophelia, and that is enough of that! You are going to leave off talking about it right this moment, and you won't ever talk about it again. Understood?"

"But Mama—"

"Promise me, Ophelia."

Ophie opened her mouth to argue, but all her objections died on her tongue. Her mother's eyes glittered, and she'd started shaking. She wasn't crying, not yet, but she was moments away from falling apart, and Ophie didn't want to be the one to break her fragile control.

"I promise."

The pastor said something then, but Ophie stopped listening to the conversation around her. She was trying to puzzle out the mystery of seeing her father the night before. Had she imagined it? Dreamed it?

She looked out the window. Standing in the front yard in his work clothes was her daddy. His hands were in his pockets, and he looked sad and wistful, and maybe a bit faded, like something had leeched most of the color from him. Ophie raised her hand to the glass, waving to him or reaching for him, she didn't know.

But it didn't matter, because her daddy raised one hand in return, smiled at her, and disappeared into sparkling sunlight.

I love you, Ophie. Be a good girl for your mama.

As the car pulled out of the yard and onto the road, Ophie fell back against the seat and let the tears she'd been holding back finally fall.

When she was twelve, Ophelia Harrison saw her first ghost.

And it was the last time she saw her father.

The Pennsylvania Railroad

THE PENNSYLVANIA RAILROAD, OR THE PENNSY AS she was known to her friends, was a proud, strong train line. *The Standard Railroad of the World,* that was what folks called her. And it was a name she lived up to. Pennsy's length eclipsed that of her sisters, the Union Pacific in the west, the Topeka and Santa Fe in the middle of America. Pennsy's only competition was her older sister, the New York Central, which had twice as much track.

But she didn't have Pennsy's reach. Pennsy sent her engines all over the East Coast, as far south as Florida and then all the way up to Boston. Pennsy's thousands of miles of track crisscrossed the United States. Every day she opened her arms and welcomed riders aboard.

And it was her rails that ferried hopeful colored folks away from the clutches of Jim Crow in the South and into new opportunities in northern cities like Philadelphia, Chicago, and New York. If colored folks were only allowed to sit in certain train cars, well, that was the work of Jim Crow, not Pennsy, and once north of the Mason-Dixon Line people were free to sit where they liked. Pennsy was a true and loyal friend, and if you had the funds she was happy to take you wherever you might like to go.

But the living were not the only ones to be found on the greatest railroad in the nation.

Ghosts congregated thickly along Pennsy's corridors, pulled along by the bright shining lives of the living. Pennsy didn't mind the dead, because they left her passengers alone. And it wasn't like folks could see them, lined up along the track, waiting for who knew what. Poor, dead boys in army uniforms from every era, their pale skin even whiter in death, clung to bridges and passenger cars, their grasping fingers reaching out for the memory of life. Hollow-eyed women and children, the casualties of a million cruelties, ran after Pennsy's engines as they sped past. But they never quite got anywhere, because Pennsy never slowed down for them. They were no concern of hers, and so the dead were doomed to watch the train rush past, forgetting them just as quickly as the rest of the world had.

As Ophie and her mother traveled from Atlanta to Washington, DC, on the Birmingham Special, Pennsy enfolding the wounded pair in the embrace of her passenger car seats, the dead took notice. They met the girl's eyes as she stared out the window at them, they felt her gaze like sunshine on a spring day, warm and comforting, and for a moment they were seen. They existed once again.

It was a heady feeling, and every specter wanted more.

And so, as Pennsy's Birmingham Special sped Ophie and her mother north, the ghosts noticed. They watched the sad-eyed colored girl as she went, and their whispers carried on the wind, sharing the joy of her regard, the news traveling from spirit to spirit so that, when Ophie and her mother disembarked in DC, the dead welcomed them. They pressed in close, reaching toward the little girl who could see.

Pennsy, ever busy, always on a schedule, rushed the little girl and her mother through Union Station so that they could catch their next train.

As Ophie and Mrs. Harrison boarded the Capital Express to Pittsburgh, the dead of the nation's capital grieved. They were, after all, a city of the best ghosts. In their lives they had been men of importance and ladies of standing. They spent their days hoping and yearning for someone who could see them, a connection to the world of the living, for it was rare that such folks came along anymore. Once, the city had a number of spiritualists, real and pretend, but the capital had lost its penchant for séances and the paranormal. Now, the people were more concerned with lawmakers lining their pockets at the expense of their constituents. The Teapot Dome scandal preoccupied the living, but the dead had their own concerns. And so the spirits left Union Station as Ophie's train left Washington, DC. There were better places to haunt.

As Ophie fell asleep the dead whispered, their ghostly voices carrying along Pennsy's tracks over the distance, winding through autumnal forests and mountains, over rivers and through towns. The dead knew where Pennsy's engine would take the girl who could see, and if they couldn't follow her, the least they could do was to tell of her arrival.

As the Capital Express pulled into Pittsburgh, a city of steel and iron, coal and power, Pennsy unloaded her charges onto the platform, bidding them farewell as the Steel City opened strong arms to welcome the newcomers.

But the dead of the city were only concerned with Ophie. They watched her passage and awaited what would come next.

The dead were very good at waiting.

Chapter 1
Three months later

"LET'S GO, OPHELIA. TIME TO GET UP."

Ophie opened one eye and groaned. The room was still dark. It seemed unnatural to wake up before the sun, but that was exactly what she was doing.

It was her first day working with her mother at Daffodil Manor, and Ophie didn't want to go. Not because she wanted to lie about in bed, like no-good Aunt Helen did. But because she didn't want to work. She wanted to go to school, to read and write and learn her arithmetic. But Mrs. Harrison had put an end to that yesterday, when a housemaid position at the manor had come available.

"We're living on charity," she'd said when Ophie had gotten home from school, "and I will not have us overstaying our welcome. Pittsburgh is expensive, and we're never going to make enough to move out of your Aunt Rose's house with me doing folks' hair like I did back in Georgia. So we have to make a few sacrifices. For me, that means working at Daffodil Manor. For you, that means leaving school and doing the same."

It hadn't been a row like it would have been once upon a time. Mrs. Harrison had just very quietly told Ophie what was what, and that had been the end of it. Even so, the unfairness of it all burned in Ophie's chest as she dragged herself from the warm cocoon of the bed she shared with her mother and made her way to the basin to wash her face.

While she did, Mrs. Harrison kept up a constant stream of chatter, giving Ophie endless reminders about what the day would entail. "When you first meet Mrs. Caruthers, the lady of the house, you're gonna curtsy, just like we practiced. Whenever she gives you a command you say yes'm and you never, ever say no, you got that? These are good people, Ophie, with nice things. You need to be careful not to take advantage of their kindness."

Ophie nodded and swallowed a huge yawn. "I know, Mama."

Mrs. Harrison pursed her lips and waved Ophie over. "Let me redo those braids, since we have a bit of time."

Ophie sat on the cold floor and let her mother tug at her hair as she considered the day before her. She still didn't understand how it was that the Carutherses were being *kind* by giving her a job. Wouldn't it be much kinder for them to just pay Mama more money and let Ophie stay in school?

It was one of those things Ophie had started to notice a lot more since her daddy's passing. People had a curious way of double-talking around things, saying the opposite of what common sense would dictate. The Carutherses were "good people" with "nice things" . . . so did that mean Ophie and her mama weren't good people? Ophie knew better than to ask such a thing, to wonder why it was that all the grown folks said nice things about people even when they were lies. She just took it as part of the unspoken rules of life, the same as *don't back-talk elders* and *clear off the sidewalk for white folks to get by*. Things that had always existed, that she couldn't question or argue, any more than she could argue with the rain. But it seemed like there were even more of them now that they were in a new town, which was unfair. It wasn't as if they got to leave any of the old ones behind.

Ophie stared at the wall in front of her while her mama continued to speak. It was all things she'd heard before, after all; Mama was repeating it because she was nervous. Ever since they'd left Georgia, Mrs. Harrison had been wound up tight as a top, and Ophie was loath to set her spinning. So she nodded and yes'm'd right up until her mother finally sighed, the last braid laid down tightly against Ophie's scalp.

"Get dressed and meet me downstairs once you've used the privy," Mama said, picking up a hand mirror and double-checking her own hair, which was as neat and tight as Ophie's. And then Mrs. Harrison was gone.

Ophie finished pulling on her new dress, all black like the rest of the household staff at Daffodil Manor, along with heavy stockings and her shoes, which pinched just a bit. She needed new ones, but, like so many things in her life, new shoes were expensive and would have to wait. If she'd been back in Georgia she could have run around barefoot, shoes only necessary on Sundays. But Pittsburgh was cold, and walking barefoot was not an option.

After using the toilet—Aunt Rose had indoor plumbing, thankfully, even if she didn't have electricity—Ophie tiptoed downstairs to the kitchen. Aunt Rose and the rest of the house were all asleep, and it would do nothing but cause strife to wake them. There had been enough tight-lipped conversations since Ophie and her mother had appeared on Aunt Rose's doorstep. While the older woman had been happy to see them, the rest of the family—Aunt Helen and the insufferable cousins—had been less excited to have their lives complicated by two more mouths to feed. That was the reason Ophie's mama had taken a position at Daffodil Manor. It had been the first work she could find.

"It's 1923, for goodness' sake," Mama had grumbled one night as she scanned the newspaper, looking for jobs and finding very little. Even though women had the vote, there were still many who believed a woman's place was in the home, and for a colored woman with few options, that meant taking care of someone else's home.

So Ophie, ever conscious of the precarious state of their lives since Daddy had died, held her breath as she moved through the quiet house to the kitchen, where a cold biscuit and a glass of water waited for her. Mama said nothing as Ophie ate, but Ophie had gotten used to her mama's silences. Before Daddy had died, Mama had been brighter; now the light had gone out of her. Ophie chewed the biscuit and drank the glass of water, and once she'd broken her fast Mama gave a nod.

"All right, then, let's go. We don't want to miss the trolley."

After putting on heavy coats, Ophie's a few sizes too big ("So you'll have some room to grow," Mama had said), they walked quickly to the trolley stop. It was a short trip down and around the block. Aunt Rose's house was in a nicer part of the city, the place where respectable colored folks lived, as the elderly woman liked to brag. Ophie wasn't quite sure what that meant, but she figured it had something to do with the nice yards behind each row home, even if the plants were currently buried beneath several inches of snow.

Pittsburgh was cold.

Stupid cold.

Ophie tucked her head inside the collar of her coat as much as she could and prayed for the trolley to hurry. They waited a few feet away from the stop, toward the back of the group, because the city crowds still made Mama a little bit nervous. Ophie shivered and looked around at the people gathered: housekeepers like her mother wearing black uniforms that peeked out from below the hem of their jackets; steelworkers heading to the mills that belched steam on the outskirts of the city, their lunch boxes weighed down with the day's meal; and men wearing sharp suits who were most likely up to no good. Mostly everyone was colored, and the few white folks who were gathered in amongst the group seemed oblivious to the differences of their skin.

"Ophelia, you're going to muss your hair. Stop squirming. You can't go before Mrs. Caruthers looking a fright." Mama pulled Ophie toward her so she could triple-check the handiwork of the braids she'd painstakingly laid into Ophie's crinkly, curly hair.

"It's cold," Ophie said, pulling away. "Mrs. Caruthers isn't going to hire me if I freeze to death."

"And if you keep talking back like that you're going to see what it feels like to go to bed without dinner. You hear me?"

"Yes'm," Ophie said, rounding her shoulders and trying once more to pull her coat up around her ears. Even now, three months after leaving Georgia, Ophie still found Pittsburgh strange. February in their small town of Darling, Georgia, was chilly, but the sun still rose every morning to remind everyone that spring was on its way. But Pittsburgh was gray and sad, the sun nonexistent and the clouds fluffy with unshed snow. The weather wasn't the only different thing Ophie had noticed. Everything about the gloomy town seemed odd. From the trolleys that everyone used to get around to the department stores that offered a dizzying assortment of ready-made clothes, city living was different. Back in Darling, people were always talking about trying to find work, maybe heading up to Atlanta to see what the possibilities were. In Pittsburgh, the factories hummed with activity, and Negro men filed into work daily with their lunch buckets. Skyscrapers poked at the gray sky with skeletal fingers, and politicians promised big things coming to the Steel City.

The biggest thing that had come through recently had been a snowstorm that drifted up huge piles of fluffy white snow. The walks had been cleaned since the night before, but there were still a few slick spots near the trolley stop. Ophie watched as a white lady with smooth blond hair accidentally stepped on one, her heels skidding dangerously. A nearby Negro man caught her arm, steadying her, and she thanked him laughingly. He tipped his hat at her and turned back around to wait for the trolley. Ophie expected someone to yell at him, but mostly no one seemed to notice. She frowned, wondering if maybe some of the old rules didn't apply in Pittsburgh after all.

"Most likely passing light," Mama said, her voice low, as she caught Ophie watching the woman. "Not a lot of white folks in this part of town, but plenty of passing folks."

Ophie nodded. Colored folks with pale skin—light enough to look white—but not white according to another one of the unspoken rules. There had been a girl back in Georgia with light brown hair and freckles, and everyone had always stared at her whenever she went anywhere, thinking maybe she had gotten lost and ended up in the colored school. One day she disappeared, and the story was that she had run off to California to be a movie star. But Mama said she'd probably just moved to Atlanta and told everyone she was white.

Ophie could understand why someone would want to do that, even though she couldn't imagine abandoning her people. The more Ophie thought about it, the harder it seemed to be colored, to have to think before doing anything, to wonder if the white folks looking at her meant her harm. No one came and burned someone's house down in the middle of the night if that person was white.

A dinging bell dragged Ophie from her musings and back to the icy day. The trolley trundled toward them, only half full since most of the factory men caught an earlier car. Ophie stood back, letting all the other folks, especially the white-looking ones, get on before she clambered aboard. When he'd dropped them off at the train station, the pastor had told Mama that Jim Crow didn't rule the North, but from what Ophie had seen, Old Jim still held some sway here in Pittsburgh. And even if the pastor was right, and the North was different than the South . . . well, Ophie and her mama were just the same. They knew firsthand how white people acted when colored folks broke the unspoken rules, forgot their place.

And there was a chance that not all the pale-skinned

folks at the stop were passing light.

Ophie's mama settled into a seat near the back, and Ophie squeezed in next to her. An elderly Negro lady sitting on the opposite side of the car gave them a gap-toothed smile. There were a few folks standing in the aisle, and she leaned around them to talk.

"Going to school?" she asked, whistling curiously as she spoke.

"Good morning, Miss Alice," Ophie's mother said. "And, no, not today. Today we are going to work." Mama straightened a little as she said the last word, and she smiled down at Ophie. "She starts her first job today."

Ophie fought to keep the pout off her face. She wished right then that she was back home with her cousins, getting ready to head off to the Frederick Douglass School for Negro Children. And considering that Ophie *never* wanted to be around her cousins, that was saying something about how much she already missed school.

Miss Alice leaned forward into the trolley aisle, causing a man to adjust slightly to give her the space, and shook her head. "Working already? That's a big responsibility for such a little thing," she said, clucking her tongue.

"Ophelia can do it," Mama said, her voice respect-ful but containing the hint of an edge. Mama didn't like it when folks questioned her choices, and Miss Alice was treading dangerous ground.

The older woman leaned back and nodded. "Oh, no doubt, my dear, most definitely," she said, adjusting her flowered bonnet and sucking at her teeth. "You're lucky to have such a good girl. I ain't heard from my own girls since they both ran off with those fellas of theirs."

Miss Alice launched into a story, and Ophie stopped paying attention. She had more than enough to occupy her thoughts at the moment.

Such as the young female ghost sitting next to Miss Alice, casting the old woman baleful looks.

Ever since the night she saw her daddy back in Georgia, Ophie had seen ghosts everywhere. At least, that's what she figured they had to be. Some days she wondered if maybe her brain was sick and she was just imagining the people no one else could see, the ones who floated through buildings and light posts like they weren't even there. But here she was, nearly three months later, and the apparitions hadn't gone anywhere.

Sometimes they even talked to her if they caught her looking.

At first, she'd been scared. But the ghosts didn't seem to want to hurt her, so Ophie began to study them. And she soon found they were just as varied and different as living folks. Some of them were sad, sobbing piteously. Others were happy, trying to knock off the hats of living folks who passed by. The worst ghosts were the angry ones, the ones who still bore the scars of their violent ends: gunshot wounds, bruises, bones that bent the wrong way and made Ophie feel ill if she stared for too long.

Most days, Ophie tried to ignore the ghosts, because she didn't know what else she was supposed to do. It had been easy to talk to her daddy, because she hadn't known that he was dead. But since that night, Ophie had learned how to tell the difference between a ghost and a living person. Most ghosts were slightly translucent, and if she looked hard enough she could see right through them. There was also a slight sparkle to the spirits if she looked closely, and different ghosts had different-colored sparkles. Ophie figured it was based on their mood: most happy ghosts glimmered yellow, while sad ghosts like the one sitting next to Miss Alice were outlined in shimmering blue. Angry ghosts had a deep purple aura that scared Ophie, and she tried to avoid looking at those ghosts as much as possible. While riding on the train to Pittsburgh, Ophie had seen a ghost outlined in a deep, stormy gray that shaded to black. That ghost had scared Ophie so badly that she'd hidden her face in her mother's shoulder, and she'd been relieved when they'd left the train station at Harpers Ferry.

Ophie watched the ghost standing next to Miss Alice and wondered if it was one of her long-gone daughters. The colored girl wore a dress made of calico, old-fashioned and ugly. Her hair was loose, the curls wild and free about her head. Tears left shimmering trails down her deep brown cheeks, and every now and again she reached out toward Miss Alice, as though trying to get her attention.

"What does your daughter look like?" Ophie asked all of a sudden, interrupting whatever Miss Alice had been on about.

"Ophelia," Mama said. "That is very rude."

"Oh, young girls are just like that! You can't change a leopard's spots," Miss Alice said, even though Ophie wasn't impulsive. Well, not usually. It was just that the ghost next to Miss Alice looked like she had something she wanted to tell the old woman, and Ophie couldn't help but think that Miss Alice's sad tale of abandonment and this girl's ghost were somehow linked.

But then the trolley stopped and Ophie's mother was pulling her toward the door.

"This is our stop. See you tomorrow, Miss Alice!" Mrs. Harrison called as they exited, leaving the old woman and her ghostly companion behind.

"Ophelia, please do not encourage that woman," Mama said once the trolley doors had closed. "She's like to talk my ear off enough as it is without you egging her on. Now, let me get one last look at you before we head to Daffodil Manor." She stepped around the group of women who had also gotten off at the stop, most of them domestics as well, and while they all set off up the hill, Mama held Ophie back, fussing over her one last time.

Ophie shivered and watched as the trolley pulled away. She felt unsettled, like she'd missed a chance to do something good, and now she wasn't sure when she would get another opportunity to tell Miss Alice about the sad ghost who seemed connected to her.

But then, she told herself, she wasn't sure she even should. After all, if someone had told her that her daddy's ghost was sitting next to her and she couldn't see him, would she believe them?

Probably not.

So instead of saying anything, Ophie just bit her lip and followed her mother along the sidewalk, up the hill, in the direction of Daffodil Manor.

Chapter 2

THE TROLLEY STOP WAS ON A QUIET BLOCK WITH A few stores, lots of trees, and freshly cleared sidewalks, but it was another twenty minutes to the Carutherses' family mansion. As they walked up the hill, Ophie tried to give herself a pep talk:

This is going to be a good thing for me and Mama.

After a few weeks we'll have enough money to move into our own apartment.

We can't spend the rest of our lives relying on charity.

Maybe once we get a little comfortable, maybe then I can go back to school!

But as they reached the long, winding drive that led to the Carutherses' house, Ophie couldn't shake her overwhelming sense of dread. She'd never seen a house like that before, and the way it loomed made her feel small and insignificant. It seemed more like Doom Manor than Daffodil Manor, since there wasn't a flower in sight, just imposing gables and a wrought iron fence.

Ophie's nervousness must have shown on her face, because Mama reached out and squeezed her hand encouragingly. "You get used to it," she said. "There are lots and lots of rooms, and I got lost all the time my first week. Why, Mrs. Caruthers has rooms that she doesn't even use, if'n you can believe that."

Ophie couldn't believe that. What was the point of having a room if it was never even used? They'd used every single inch of space back in their tiny house in Georgia, and Aunt Rose's house was full to the brim (mostly with hateful cousins). Aunt Helen and the cousins had acted cold and rude from the moment Ophie and her mama arrived in town, because it meant less space for them. But they'd left their home in South Carolina and come north because it was no longer safe, same as Ophie and her mama, so it wasn't like the cousins and their mama should be throwing stones.

But entire rooms that never got used? Rich white folks really were something else.

When they reached the top of the drive, they didn't go up the front walk like Ophie expected. Instead, Mama led her around the side.

"This is where the help goes in and out. Don't let me catch you trying to go in the front door," Mama said. "That's for guests and such."

As they walked along the path, they passed an elderly black man shoveling the walk. "Well, hello, there. I see Mrs. Caruthers's new caretaker is here, and just in time, too."

"Morning, Henry," Mama said, then dropped her voice so low that Ophie could barely make out the words. "How is *she* this morning?"

"Hungry as a bear and twice as mean," Henry said with a laugh. And then to Ophie he said, "Good luck in there, young miss. You'll need it."

Ophie's mother gestured for her to follow, and Ophie was left wondering whether the man had been joking in that way old people sometimes did.

She would find out soon enough.

They entered through a small room off the kitchen, where they took off their shoes. It was a relief to free her cramped toes.

"These are house shoes," Mama said, handing Ophie a pair made of soft cloth that she took from off a small shelf. "Mrs. Caruthers doesn't like anyone tracking mud and dirt onto her carpets, so whenever you arrive you'll switch out your shoes for a pair of these. Understood?"

Ophie nodded, but she was only half listening. A

young Negro boy watched her balefully from the corner, and Ophie was about to say hello to him when he faded away from sight. She blinked; it was always a bit of a shock when she didn't realize someone she was looking at wasn't real right away.

A house with a ghost. Just what she needed.

Ophie quickly laced up the house shoes, tying them as tight as possible. They were several sizes too big, but still better than her regular shoes, and as she followed her mother they made a curious slapping noise on the tile of the kitchen floor.

"Oh-ho-ho, who do we have here?" asked a large Negro woman tending a pot on the stove. Sweat beaded on her dark skin, and she mopped at her face with the edge of her apron.

"Carol, this is Ophelia, my daughter," Mama said, a small shake in her voice. "Ophelia, Miss Carol here is the head of the household, and the cook."

"Oh, that's only half right. Mr. Richard actually oversees the household staff. That's Mrs. Caruthers's son. You'll meet him a little later. But I am the cook, and you'll mind me when you fetch Mrs. Caruthers's trays. You can call me Cook. I try to look out for folks here. Help them stay out of trouble."

Mama smiled uncertainly, and Ophie tried the curtsy they'd practiced.

"It's nice to meet you, ma'am," she said. The movement was strange with the slipperiness of the house shoes, but she managed to sink down and return to her standing position without falling.

Cook laughed, a deep booming sound. "Well, all right, then. I think she'll do." She turned off the burner on the stove—it was a gas stove, very fancy—and scooped the contents of the pot into a painted bowl sitting on a tray, next to a vase that held a single daffodil. It was still much too cold for flowers, and Ophie wondered where it had come from. It was a luxury to have something so beautiful when the weather was so ugly.

"Ophelia, why don't you grab that tray and take it up to Mrs. Caruthers. Your mama will show you which room it is. I have to see to getting the lunch together. Mr. Richard is having guests today, and cold beef just will not do."

Ophie's stomach growled at the smell of cinnamon and maple syrup that wafted off the oatmeal as she lifted the tray. She'd eaten breakfast, but her biscuit didn't compare to the breakfast set out for Mrs. Caruthers.

"This way," Mama said, her voice quieter than usual. "And do not drop that tray." There was an urgency to Mama's voice that Ophie hadn't heard since Georgia, and she squared her shoulders and gripped the tray as hard as she could.

Ophie followed her mama down the hall and tried to keep the tray balanced as she marveled at the house. Every hallway and room, it seemed, was lit up with electric lights; Ophie had never known anyone who actually had electricity in their house. The soft yellow glow cast by the wall sconces seemed impossibly luxurious. They passed a room with a huge piano and another with a dining table, each sight a spectacle, before turning and heading up a set of stairs that made Ophie's thighs ache.

"It gets easier," Mama murmured, and then she was rapping loudly on a door on the right side of the hallway.

"Enter," came a gravelly voice, and Mama opened the door, gesturing for Ophie to follow her.

The temperature of the room was the first thing Ophie noticed. The heat was intense, like a summer day, and on the heels of the heat came a stink that made Ophie want to cover her nose. It smelled of mint and liniment and unwashed body with another odor that Ophie couldn't quite place but wasn't at all good. Mama had said Mrs. Caruthers was in failing health, but Ophie hadn't understood what that meant until she had stepped into the room.

"Ma'am," Mama said, her shoulders rounded and her eyes downcast. This was a version of her mother that Ophie had seen only a few times, usually when white folks were around. "This is my daughter, Ophelia. She's here to help see to your needs."

"Who hired her?" the old woman demanded, struggling upright in the bed. She wore a nightcap, and wispy bits of white hair escaped around the edges. Her pale face was sallow and deeply lined, her blue eyes watery and narrowed. "The last thing I need is some pickaninny stealing my jewelry while I sleep."

Ophie stilled her expression to blankness and gripped the increasingly heavy tray tighter. She'd heard the slur before, and worse besides, but it always felt like a slap to her face when she did. Now she understood why Mama had been so cautious, why she'd spent so much time talking about how kind and good the Carutherses were.

Mrs. Caruthers was a rattlesnake.

Not literally, of course. But Ophie had learned that the best way to survive in this world was to treat white folks, especially important white folks, the same way she treated snakes: cautiously, and with respect, whether or not they deserved it.

Ophie knew all about snakes. Back in Georgia, there were many different kinds of snakes. A rattlesnake often warned a body before it struck, but a cotton-mouth might attack before folks even knew it was there. And some snakes weren't venomous at all and spent their days eating crickets and mice and finding a nice sunny rock to lie on. The thing with a snake was a body was never sure what kind they were until it was too late, so it was best to be cautious around all of them until it was known whether it was a copperhead or a garter snake.

Mrs. Caruthers had shown her true nature early, and so, even if Ophie was nervous, it was something of a relief to know already what sort of creature she was dealing with.

Ophie sank down into a curtsy, tricky with the heavy tray and the slippery shoes. "Good morning, ma'am. I brought your breakfast," she said, struggling back to standing and lifting the tray a little higher. Her arms screamed from the effort, but her grip was steady.

There'd be no snakebites for Ophie.

Mrs. Caruthers stared at the girl. Her mouth puck-ered in displeasure, but then her eyes flicked to the tray. "Well, fine," the old woman snapped. "Hurry up and hand it over. You're letting it get cold."

Ophie stepped forward and gently set the tray in the woman's lap. There was a sharp rap at the door, and it opened, the visitor not waiting to be invited in.

"Mother! I see you've already met young Ophelia!"

A dashingly good-looking man with dark tousled curls stepped into the room, his hat in his hand. His pale cheeks bore two spots of color, and his suit jacket had a few snowflakes here and there, revealing that he was most likely returning home rather than heading out. He looked like a prince from a fairy tale, and Ophie noticed that he did not wear the house shoes like she and her mother did, instead tracking dirty snow slush across the carpets.

"Richard, did you hire another colored girl? I specifically told you that I didn't want any more Negro help at Daffodil Manor."

"And yet you fired the Polish woman I hired before her first day was over," he said, his chiding tone playful and indulgent. He set his hat upon a nearby chair and leaned in to drop a kiss on Mrs. Caruthers's wrinkled cheek before straightening.

"Her English was repugnant," Mrs. Caruthers sniffed before taking a large bite of oatmeal.

"Ah, but I trust young Ophelia's English is satisfactory?"

When Mrs. Caruthers didn't argue he clapped his hands and snapped his fingers.

"Aces, then, it's settled. Ophelia will be here with you during the day while I'm working and help you out with whatever you need."

"I need you here with me," the old woman said, and her son sighed.

"I know, Mother, but you and I both know I need to make a living. But I won't be going into the offices today; I'll be just downstairs in the study if there's anything you need. Also, do remember that I have those people coming for the luncheon today—in fact, some of them should be arriving soon—so the rest of the help will be tied up with that."

"I don't want you hiring any more servants, Richard. They aren't worth the cost. And they steal."

Richard laughed, oblivious, it seemed, to how his mother's words hit the people beside him. A muscle twitched in Mama's cheek, and Ophie reached out for her hand. Mrs. Harrison squeezed it for a split second before releasing it.

"Mother, your humor is as dry as the Sahara. Please don't forget that Mr. Carnegie's man is coming over tomorrow night to talk about that new library they're building. I hope you'll feel up to joining us. Like Father always used to say, we have a duty to contribute to the legacy of this city." Richard grinned. As dour as his mother was, he was anything but.

He turned his beaming grin onto Ophie. "Welcome to Daffodil Manor, Ophelia. I'm certain you'll do amazing things here." Ophie half wondered if he somehow hadn't noticed that she'd be looking after an old woman who already didn't seem to like her. What was amazing about that?

As suddenly as he'd arrived, Richard Caruthers grabbed his hat and disappeared.

"Well, then," Mrs. Caruthers said, her mouth full of oatmeal. "Do not just stand there like a statue. Fetch me a pot of tea."

Mama swallowed and smiled, just the slightest bit, so Ophie did the same, and curtsied again, before leaving to head back to the kitchen.

The two of them walked in silence. Ophie knew she should be happy. Now she and Mama both had positions with one of the richest families in Pittsburgh, and before they knew it, they would be able to afford to move into their own little place. No more charity.

But Ophie wasn't happy. Instead, she felt like she'd just been handed a rattlesnake. And she had no idea what to do with it.

Daffodil Manor

THE BIG HOUSE ON THE HILL COULD FEEL A CHANGE in the air. It wasn't spring—that was still weeks away, and the trees surrounding the house were still deeply asleep. And it wasn't anything to do with the people who lived there; most of his rooms, after all, remained locked up tight, furniture draped with sheets, dust settling into thick layers as the sparse household staff struggled to keep up.

No, whatever was about to happen had nothing to do with the Carutherses.

The house sighed and settled into itself. Daffodil Manor was lonely. It would like a new family to run through its massive halls, children to climb on the grand staircase, mothers to chide them and fathers to play hide-and-seek through the many rooms. But instead, only a solitary widow and her adult son occupied the house. The days of them spending leisurely afternoons in the library before a roaring fire and dinners in the dining room with friends and family were long gone.

But even though Daffodil Manor was lonely, the house was not alone. There was the staff: Cook, who prepared the food, and Mr. Henry, who kept the house in good repair. And the new additions, the girl and her mother, cleaning and helping as the owners saw fit.

And there were, of course, the ghosts.

There were more dead people than living in Daffodil Manor. Many lives had been lived and lost in the grand old house, and ghosts roamed the upstairs hallway and prowled the attic, their spectral fingers trailing icy memories along the walls that turned the house chill and damp.

There was old Mr. Edward Caruthers, who still worked on accounts in the study, his pursuit of profit continuing even after the heart attack that took his life. One of the closed-off bedrooms held the ghost of Alvin Caruthers, still wearing his service uniform and drinking to numb the pain of a heart broken by a war fought in trenches. The dining room contained Elvira Caruthers, a wayward daughter who cared more about gossip than chewing her food before swallowing and who had died before she could create her own branch of the family line. There were dozens of forgotten cousins, young and old alike, and even a servant girl who had been careless while cleaning a high window and had plunged onto the flagstones below, her blood long washed away but her spirit still trying to reach that one last spot in the uppermost corner of the hallway windows. And then there was poor Colin, a colored boy who had come to the manor as a child. He had died long ago in Virginia, but his bondage had carried on into his death, so that his spirit was forced to follow the mistress of the manor when she moved north.

Daffodil Manor felt the dead within it begin to move, more alert than they had been in a very long time. And as a small Negro girl and her mother descended the grand staircase and entered the kitchen, the house finally, finally understood the change in the air.

The dead were restless. And the little girl was the reason why.

Justice, a voice said, a newer ghost in the house stretching phantom limbs and reaching out. She was stronger than all the rest, and angry. The house shied away from the presence, timbers creaking as it settled into its foundation.

Yes, change was coming. The house just hoped it would be for the better.

Chapter 3

OPHIE BALANCED THE TEA TRAY, WINCING EVERY time the dishes rattled the least little bit. As Cook handed her the tea service, which was somehow even heavier than the oatmeal tray, she'd made certain to warn Ophie that the dishes were valuable. "These were given to the missus by President Theodore Roosevelt, so be careful." Ophie didn't know how that frail old woman knew Teddy Roosevelt, but she could heed a warning. She would not drop that tea service.

So as Ophie walked through the house she held her arms stiff as she could and took her time. The dishes seemed impossibly fragile, the china thinner than a cracker and painted with brightly colored elephants. Every movement set the cups and saucers to tinkling in warning. As sour as Mrs. Caruthers was about oatmeal, Ophie didn't want to see how she acted if one of her dishes got chipped.

Ophie's slow pace through the house gave her time to study her surroundings a bit more than she had earlier that morning. The kitchen exited directly into a grand dining room, the wood heavy and dark. The air smelled of furniture polish and long-ago meals seasoned with garlic and onions. Ophie counted sixteen chairs as she walked through! She tried to imagine a meal with that many people and couldn't. There were only eight people in Aunt Rose's house, and every meal was as overcrowded as the 6:00 a.m. trolley, cramped and uncomfortable. Sixteen people at dinner didn't sound very fun, even with such fancy dishes to eat off of.

Beyond the dining room was a grand foyer, the floor inlaid with a very pretty gray stone that reminded Ophie of the train station in Atlanta. It seemed much too fancy to have in a house, and Ophie thought of the plain polished wood floor in Aunt Rose's parlor. When Ophie had seen the floor in her aunt's house, she'd thought it the finest floor ever, and that that was what it meant to live in the northern states. This, however, was something else entirely, and Ophie shivered as the cold stone leeched the warmth from her toes through the thin material of her house shoes.

Singing echoed down the hall, and Ophie's heart lifted a little. It was her mama's work song, which meant that she was cleaning somewhere off in that direction. Ophie hadn't heard her sing since the Better Days, which was what she'd come to think of the time before Daddy died. Once upon a time, Mama would sing while washing laundry or cooking dinner or any of a million chores that had to be done around the house. "Singing makes the work go faster," she'd always say. Even though the Carutherses' house was cold and unwelcoming, hearing Mama sing warmed the place a tiny bit.

"Where is my tea?" came a shout from the top of the stairs, the strident voice silencing the singing and ending Ophie's happy reverie. "Where has that girl gotten to?"

"You'd better hurry, chickadee. She hates when her tea is cold."

Ophie turned, too fast, and the cream in the little pitcher sloshed, sinking into the doily underneath. It was hardly noticeable, and Ophie had other problems, anyway.

Where had that friendly voice come from?

Ophie stood alone at the bottom of the stairs. The scent of lilac filled the air, and that's when she saw a length of blue skirt flash at the edge of the landing, just beyond where Ophie could see. Someone was walking down the hallway, toward the bedrooms. Ophie frowned. Was there someone up there besides Mrs. Caruthers? Did Richard have a sister Cook hadn't told her about? Or had one of the guests for his luncheon already arrived?

"Hello?" Ophie called. "Is there someone up there?"

"Yes! And I'm waiting for my tea!" came Mrs. Caruthers's angry cry.

Ophie began to climb the stairs. By the time she reached the top, her thighs burned and her arms trembled. The tray rang and sang like chimes. If the entirety of her job was going to be carting heavy trays to and from the kitchen, she would have to get stronger.

The door to Mrs. Caruthers's room swung open as Ophie approached, the seemingly frail old woman standing on the other side like an ill omen. The hair on Ophie's arms raised in alarm, and she swallowed thickly past her fear. She could and would do this.

"What took you so long?" Mrs. Caruthers demanded, shuffling back to the bed. Ophie didn't know what to tell the woman. It seemed like anything she said would be wrong, so she said nothing.

Ophie followed Mrs. Caruthers into the room, setting the tea service on the small table next to the bed. The oatmeal tray was on the floor next to the bed, the bowl clean and not a crumb of toast remaining. Even the small pot of jam looked to have been licked clean. Mrs. Caruthers was apparently not a woman to waste food.

Ophie reached for the breakfast tray. She figured that since her job seemed to consist of taking trays hither and thither she would be expected to take the empty breakfast setting back to the kitchen. But Mrs. Caruthers let out an impatient sigh that stilled Ophie's hands.

"What are you doing?" Mrs. Caruthers said, leaning back against the bed pillows and crossing her arms.

Ophie blinked, her brain searching for an answer that wouldn't provoke the woman any further. "I was taking this back to the kitchen, ma'am."

"You can do that after you fix my tea. Just the way I like it."

This was a trap. Ophie could sense it. The woman seemed to think Ophie was a mind reader. How was she supposed to know how the woman liked her tea? Ophie didn't even know anyone who drank tea, at least not like this. Mama had always put the leaves in a mason jar with sugar and water and left it in the sun until it was as brown as Ophie's skin. After, they'd cool it down with ice if they could afford it, a perfect summer treat. Daddy had also liked coffee, strong and black with lots of sugar. "Dark and sweet, just like me," he'd always joked.

Sudden tears pricked Ophie's eyes, hot and unwelcome. A lump welled up in her throat from nowhere, just like it always did whenever she thought of her daddy. But she couldn't cry now, not in front of this mean old rich woman.

"Don't cry, chickadee. I'll walk you through it."

Standing in the doorway, wearing a grand gown of deepest blue with a dramatic red scarf to set it off, was the most beautiful woman Ophie had ever seen. Her reddish-brown hair fell over her shoulders in waves, her pale skin flawless and luminous. She seemed to be dressed more for a fancy ball than a luncheon, but Ophie knew very little about rich people. Richard had been very nicely dressed when he had met them earlier. Maybe rich people always looked fancy, even when just waking up.

And it wasn't like Ophie was going to turn away any help she could get.

"Well?" said the old woman.

"Calm down, Mrs. Caruthers," the lady said, smooth and sweet as cream. "You're going to lose what's left of your hair if you're not careful. I'm just trying to show your new maid how you prefer your tea."

"I can do it," Ophie said, trying to reassure the

elderly woman. It wouldn't do to get fired on her first day like the Polish woman Mr. Richard had talked about.

Mrs. Caruthers looked like she was going to complain again but thought better of it, and just wrinkled up her mouth instead. "Go on, then."

"Okay, first you're going to want to pick up the teapot," the fancy lady said, and Ophie did so. "Yes, just like that. Hold the lid, it likes to jump off sometimes."

Ophie followed the woman's instructions, pouring the tea into the cup and then preparing it just how Mrs. Caruthers apparently liked it: two cubes, a generous splash of cream. She stirred it carefully so that the spoon didn't hit the sides, and at the end the young woman snapped her fingers, just like Richard had earlier. "Such a smart girl! You're doing fantastic."

"Why are you looking at me like that?" Mrs. Caruthers demanded, but Ophie had no idea what the woman meant. She glanced at the younger woman, but she just shrugged and winked at Ophie, as though Mrs. Caruthers was somehow the joke.

Perhaps the old woman was a bit confused about things. It sometimes happened with old folks.

So Ophie pushed aside the strangeness—the whole manor was odd, really—and carefully handed Mrs.

Caruthers her tea, the delicate cup balanced upon its equally fine saucer.

"Don't forget your curtsy," said the beautiful woman.

As Mrs. Caruthers raised the cup, Ophie sank into a deep curtsy, eyes downcast as her heart pounded while she waited for the inevitable rebuke. But none came.

"That is all, Olivia," Mrs. Caruthers said.

Ophie didn't bother correcting the woman. She just gathered up the breakfast tray and fled the stuffy, smelly room.

Out in the hallway, Ophie turned to thank the beautiful lady who'd helped her, but she was nowhere to be seen.

"Excuse me?" Ophie said, as loud as she dared. She didn't want to anger Mrs. Caruthers again. "Miss?"

No answer came. But Ophie wasn't quite alone.

At the end of the hallway stood the ghost of the Negro boy she'd seen down in the kitchen when she'd first arrived. He was shirtless, a pair of threadbare pants his only attire. His eyes were sad, like he felt sorry for Ophie, but his outline was too faint for her to pick out what color it might be.

A chill ran along Ophie's arms, skittering down her skin and leaving goose pimples in its wake. She stood there, waiting for the ghost to say something, anything.

He had come to find her, after all. Or at least, that's how it felt to Ophie. But the boy said nothing. Instead, after a long moment he turned toward the stairs and disappeared.

But not before Ophie saw the seeping, bloody welts crisscrossing his back.

Chapter 4

RELIEF FLOODED THROUGH OPHIE THE MOMENT she and her mother left Daffodil Manor and lasted the entire trolley ride and the walk from their stop to Aunt Rose's house. Her first day of trying to keep Mrs. Caruthers happy, a task that Ophie now understood to be impossible, was finally at an end. She hadn't even gotten a break during lunch—she had wanted to peek into the room where Richard was entertaining guests to try and spot the woman in the blue dress, but Mrs. Caruthers's demands dashed that hope. And all the while she was running up and down that blasted staircase she couldn't stop thinking about the ghost boy in the house, whether she'd be seeing him every day from now on. It wasn't right to have a ghost walking around the house like that. What was he doing in such a fancy house, anyway? The whole thing made Ophie deeply nervous, like a thunderstorm that rolled in too fast, the threat of a tornado swirling in its dark clouds.

It had been a long day, and now all she wanted was dinner and bed.

Ophie entered the house, leaving her shoes by the door. She then slipped her feet into her soft, warm slippers, the ones Mama had handsewn for her. All her fear and distress drained away, and even though Aunt Rose's house wasn't really home, and there were too many other people under the roof for Ophie to ever truly relax, in that moment she felt more herself than she had all day.

"Ophelia, I'm very proud of you," Mama said, her voice low and heavy with the same exhaustion Ophie felt. "You did good."

"Thank you," Ophie said.

"Auntie Rose is out traveling today, so why don't you go stoke a fire in the hearth. Looks like those good-for-nothing cousins let it go out once more." Mama's voice went low at the end, so Ophie knew that last part hadn't been meant for her. She made her way into the parlor while Mama went to the kitchen to put something together for supper, even though it would most likely be lean. It was the middle of the week, and no one would have any money for food for a couple more days, when their meager wages were collected. For now, it would be a meal of leftover Sunday ham and cold biscuits. That was, if the cousins hadn't cleaned out the icebox once again.

Ophie started a fire in the fireplace, and she took a moment to warm her hands and enjoy the heat after the chill of the day. The sun set early in winter, but a little light still filtered in through the lace curtains Aunt Rose had crocheted long ago when she and her husband had first been married. Like the rest of the parlor, the curtains were a bit dusty and a bit worn, but well loved and comfortable. The room boasted a fine area rug that kept off the chill of the wooden floor, and a leather wing chair that had been gifted to Aunt Rose's husband when he left his job at the post office. There were various other wooden chairs and rockers for the rest of the family to sit in, but only Aunt Rose sat in that brown leather wing chair. It was her house, after all, and her prerogative, a phrase she used often when anyone wanted to sass her.

Ophie couldn't wait to grow up and have her own prerogative.

She was starting to doze in front of the fire, the warmth and comfort conspiring to make her eyelids heavy, when the front door slammed. All her lethargy fled as the sound of giggles and running feet echoed down the hallway and into the parlor.

The cousins were home.

When they'd first arrived at Aunt Rose's house after the fraught train ride up from Atlanta, Ophie had been excited at the idea of more family to spend time with. For all her life it had been just her, Mama, and Daddy. Daddy's aunt Rose and the rest of his family all lived up north, and Mama's people were dead and gone long before Ophie had been born. It wasn't that she had been lonely, mostly just that she'd been excited to live with other kids. She'd never much liked the way Mama and Daddy seemed to have secret conversations right over her head, always talking past her in a language of their own. Maybe, for once, Ophie could be the one to have secrets. It seemed natural that she and her cousins would be fast friends.

But all those tiny hopes and dreams had died a violent death upon arrival.

There were three of them. Muriel was eleven, a year younger than Ophie. Next was Agnes, who was ten, and right behind was Eloise at nine. All the girls bore the shadow of their parents in a nose here or a pouted lip there. They looked nothing like Ophie, but Ophie hadn't much minded that. Blood was blood.

Unfortunately, the cousins were more interested in *drawing* blood, especially after they were forced to give up their bedroom to Ophie and her mother. They now slept on the floor of their parents' room. This turn of events had been objected to most vocally by their mother, Ophie's aunt Helen. Uncle Alfred—who was actually Ophie's cousin and Rose's son, a bit of gnarled family tree that Ophie didn't quite understand—was indifferent to Ophie and her mother, but Aunt Helen resented their sudden arrival. The one time Ophie made the mistake of calling her "auntie" she'd been met with a rebuke. "Child, I can assure you that we are in no way related."

Muriel, Agnes, and Eloise absorbed all their mother's spite and directed it back at Ophie magnified by a thousand. It seemed terribly unfair that her one chance at connection had been dashed so thoroughly before it even began. And while Ophie knew that the cousins couldn't truly hate her—she'd barely exchanged two words with them before they'd declared war—it didn't make the constant backbiting or tiny pinches any more bearable.

The cousins were very good at being very, very bad.

That's why Ophie was tensed in the parlor, waiting to see if the cousins would descend upon her like one of the seven plagues the pastor back in Darling always talked about. Truth be told, Ophie would've far preferred a swarm of locusts.

"Hey, Ophelia," Muriel said as she slinked into the parlor, her sisters close behind. All three of them wore matching pink dresses and smart black shoes that they had left on—an act of defiance they'd get a scolding for if Aunt Rose wasn't out.

Ophie climbed to her feet, not saying anything, just giving up the warmth and comfort of her spot nearest the fireplace without a fight. She'd tried standing her ground in the beginning, but three against one was never a fair fight, and she'd quickly learned her lesson.

"Mama said Ophelia doesn't go to school anymore because she's stupid," cackled Eloise. "Are you stupid, O-feel-yah?"

"She looks pretty stupid to me, sitting here staring at the fire like a dope," Muriel said, moving ever closer to where Ophie stood.

Anger made Ophie's mouth go dry, but she held her tongue. Mama was concerned about charity, about earning what she got by pulling her own weight, not making a fuss, and being kind to others. Neither the cousins nor their mother shared the same attitude. The dresses they wore were new, and not only did they get to go to school, but they'd also been to the picture show twice since Ophie and her mother had arrived. The cousins had so much and yet they still went out of their way to cause Ophie grief.

Ophie watched as a chunk of slush on Eloise's shoe fell onto the clean wood floor and said nothing. She clenched her fists and tried to remember that she was working so that she and Mama could find someplace else to live. A place far away from the cousins and their pretty but spiteful mother.

"What do you think, Aggie?" Eloise said, trying to goad her older sister into action. Agnes said nothing, but her massive frame blocked the only exit, and the set of her jaw promised a world of hurt. Agnes wasn't a good student like her sisters. She was sullen and mean and had trouble keeping her letters correct. Ophie had tried to help her, and the result had been a vicious slap without any kind of warning. Muriel and Eloise might know how to land a verbal jab so that it laid open all of Ophie's secret hurts, but it was Agnes Ophie truly feared. Emotional pain she was used to, but physical pain was another matter entirely.

Ophie cast her eyes around the room for something to distract the cousins before they could get started on her when she noticed an eerie light out in the garden, just beyond the lace curtains. It looked like a lantern, except that it was a deep blue. Ophie squinted as it made its way down the barren paths.

"Do you see that?" she asked. The cousins turned toward the window.

"See what?" Muriel demanded, hands on hips.

But Ophie already realized what it likely was, and was moving toward the window, the cousins and their petty cruelties forgotten for the moment. It was chilly away from the fire, the leaded glass not doing much to keep winter at bay, and when she pulled the filmy curtain to the side and looked out, she spied a man. He was dark and smiling, and he waved to Ophie cheerily. He was so lifelike that Ophie waved back. She was so focused on the man in the garden that she didn't notice Agnes walk up behind her, and it was not until she felt the hands in the middle of her back, shoving her forward, her nose knocking painfully into the glass, that she remembered to be afraid.

"There ain't nothing out there," Agnes growled, her hot breath too close.

"What do you girls think you're doing?"

Aunt Rose stood in the doorway to the room. She leaned heavily on her cane, and she still wore her traveling coat. The scowl on her dark brown face made it clear that she'd sensed trouble and had come into the parlor after entering the house.

Agnes stepped away from Ophie just as quickly as she'd approached. Ophie's shoulders sagged with relief.

"We're not doing anything, Aunt Rose. But Ophie is telling lies. She said she saw someone out in the garden, but there ain't anyone there," Eloise said, sniffling as she worked up some tears.

"There *isn't* anyone there; *ain't* is improper," Aunt Rose said. "And keep those crocodile tears where they are, missy, I saw Agnes shove Ophie. You're all up to your nasty old tricks again, and I have had about enough of it. You girls go put on your house shoes, and after that you can get a rag and clean up the mess you just made, tracking that slush all across my nice floors."

The girls looked down at their shoes. "Yes'm," they said before slinking out.

No one talked back to Aunt Rose.

Ophie tried to follow the cousins out of the parlor, but Aunt Rose stopped her with a heavy hand on her shoulder. "What exactly did you see outside, Ophie?"

Ophie opened her mouth, and in that moment, she longed for nothing more than to tell Aunt Rose. To tell her about all of it. The crying girl on the trolley, the sad boy at the Carutherses' mansion, the happy old man out back who cast the bluest light. But when she tried to talk, the words died in her throat, and all she remembered was the way her mama had snapped at her back in Georgia.

"You did not see your father, Ophelia, and that is enough of that!"

Ophie said nothing, just shook her head and

squeezed past Aunt Rose as she headed to the kitchen to see if her mother needed any help with supper.

After the meal, which was a warm, flaky biscuit, canned green beans Aunt Rose had brought home courtesy of a friend, and a thin slice of ham, the cousins disappeared without a word, not even a thanks, and Mama clucked her tongue as she cleared dishes off to the sink.

"Etta, don't you worry about those, I'll get them," Aunt Rose said, shuffling toward the sink.

Mama nodded and sighed. "You'd think they'd at least offer to wash up since they had nothing to do with the cooking," she said in a low voice.

Aunt Rose shook her head. "Can't change a leopard's spots, and no sense in trying. I'm just glad they've finally learned that we share at the dinner table."

"I suppose we should be thankful that Alfred came home for dinner instead of going to one of the jazz clubs," Mama said.

Aunt Rose chuckled. "Sure enough. Now we won't have to listen to Helen chew him out for his tomcatting in the middle of the night."

Mama and Aunt Rose laughed, and as Aunt Rose began to run water to wash the plates, Ophie tugged on her mama's sleeve.

"Can we play checkers before you go to bed?" she

asked. Back in Georgia, when Daddy had still been alive, they would end every evening with a rousing game of checkers. When Ophie was little she would sit on Mama's lap and watch, and when she got old enough to play she would take turns playing either her mama or daddy.

But after the journey north the evening games had disappeared, and Ophie sorely missed those better days. She would do just about anything to see her mama smile like she always did when she crowed, "King me!" Ophie wouldn't even be cross about losing. Anything to see a glimmer of the woman Ophie had once known.

Mama's expression shuttered as she rubbed her lower back. "Not tonight, Ophelia, I think I'm going to head on up to bed. I appreciate you washing up, Rose."

"No problem, no problem at all," the old woman said.

Ophie watched her mama go but remained behind to help Aunt Rose clean up the dishes. Sounds of laughter came from the parlor as the cousins and their parents listened to one of the radio shows, and Ophie's heart burned with the injustice of it all. But she had nowhere to direct her upset, so she put it into cleaning up the kitchen.

After the last dish had been dried, Aunt Rose turned and looked at Ophie. She had a way of asking complicated questions without saying a word. But when she spoke, all she said was, "Ophelia, would you be a dear and go and get my coat?"

It wasn't what Ophie had been expecting. "Yes'm?"

"Get your coat as well, dear. And your boots. We're going to step outside for a moment."

Ophie's momentary relief melted away, and she went to fetch their coats with a heavy heart. It was cold outside, and most likely Aunt Rose was going to ask her to accompany her on a walk. All their previous walks had been less about exercise and more about Aunt Rose asking Ophie endless questions, a gentle inquisition that always left Ophie feeling uncomfortable and vaguely out of sorts. They always seemed to talk about matters Ophie would rather not think about, like her daddy, or not going to school, or the cousins and their viciousness; and after a day spent with a demanding old white woman, Ophie just wasn't up to another trial. But she also knew better than to disrespect her elders, so she pulled on her boots before taking Aunt Rose's coat and her own off the hook and making her way back to the kitchen.

When she got there Aunt Rose waited, a small bag and a nail in her hand. The bag was tied off so Ophie couldn't see what it contained, but Aunt Rose held both out to Ophie. "Put these in your pocket, girl, and follow me."

Ophie did as she was told, dropping it in the pocket of the maid's uniform she still wore, and walked behind Aunt Rose, out the back door that led to the small rear yard. She didn't go any farther than the porch, though, causing Ophie to stop short next to her.

The ghost man she'd seen before dinner was standing in the middle of a particularly large snowdrift next to the path her uncle had shoveled a few hours ago, bent over a spindly bush as though he were sniffing it. After a moment, the ghost man turned toward them and half walked, half floated toward the porch, stopping suddenly at the edge.

"You see him," Aunt Rose said.

It wasn't a question, and Ophie was afraid. Not because of the ghost, but because now someone knew her secret. She thought for a moment about lying, but this was Aunt Rose. It would be no use.

"Yes'm," Ophie whispered.

They stood in silence as the man made to walk up onto the porch; each time he did, he seemed to hit into an invisible wall. After a few tries, he frowned and left to busy himself in a ghostly way about the garden.

"Haint blue," Aunt Rose said, pointing to the pale

blue painted on the underside of the porch's overhang. Ophie had noticed the same soft blue paint on the windowsills. "It keeps the ghosts from coming into the house."

The man waved to Aunt Rose, who waved back.

"You know him?" Ophie asked, unable to keep the surprise from her voice.

"Yes. That is my husband, George. Passed away four years ago. He pops in every once in a while to check on his garden. He's waiting for me." Aunt Rose said it so plainly, like she was talking about the best kind of lye soap, and Ophie felt the tiniest bit of her nervousness break away.

"I see them everywhere," she said, her voice hoarse. It was terrifying to share such a personal truth, much more frightening than the dead themselves.

Aunt Rose nodded slowly.

Ophie didn't know what she wanted to ask until the words came out of her mouth. "What . . . what do they want?"

"Lots of folks with unfinished business that think sticking around is going to help them fix it," Aunt Rose said. "You have your monthlies?"

Ophie shook her head. "Not yet. Mama said she got hers when she was close to my age, though." Menstruation was not something that Ophie looked forward to; she understood the monthly ritual of bleeding but was rather happy not to have one more hassle in her life. Wasn't it enough to be able to see dead people?

Aunt Rose pursed her lips. "The sight doesn't usually start until after a girl starts to blossom, but I suppose the shock of what happened to your daddy could have brought it on. Let's go back in the warm. I'm sure you have questions."

Ophie did, so many in fact that they tripped over each other in her brain. Aunt Rose could see ghosts, too! That meant Ophie wasn't the only one. It also meant that when Mama got mad at Ophie for making up stories it was because she wasn't like Ophie and Aunt Rose. Mama couldn't see the ghosts who crowded around the living as they went along their daily tasks. But since Aunt Rose could, Ophie now had someone who would believe her. Someone who could help her.

They walked back inside the warm house, and Ophie put their coats and boots away while Aunt Rose busied around the kitchen. When Ophie returned, there was milk warming on the stove and a big bottle of honey on the table. The cousins tried to slink in; Aunt Rose shooed them away, but not before they realized that Ophie was getting a treat of warm milk with honey and cinnamon and they were not. There would be grief for that, but Ophie didn't care. She was just so glad to know that she wasn't alone in her visions of the dead that she reckoned the inevitable revenge would be worth it.

Once Ophie was settled with her warm mug of milk, Aunt Rose sat down as well. "So, I figure the best way to go about this is for you to tell me what questions you have and I'll answer them best as I can."

"Do you see a lot of ghosts?" Ophie asked, blowing at her milk and inhaling the cinnamony scent.

Aunt Rose smiled gently. "Yes, almost daily. I try to go out once or twice a week and help them that I can. There are folks who know what I can do and sometimes they ask for help as well. Those green beans you ate at dinner came from a friend who's being haunted by her son. Clearing out the dead keeps the city from getting too clogged. That has been the job of the women in our family for hundreds of years. Back before white people bought Negroes and brought them to America, our ancestors were responsible for talking to the dead. The women in our family were respected and were consulted whenever a loved one died."

"So they were important?" Ophie asked. All she had ever seen were Negroes treated like bothersome pests by white folks, and to imagine that there had once been a time when colored women were able to live their lives in a different way, to be sought out and respected for their abilities, well . . . that was strange and wonderful. And just about as unexpected as seeing the dead.

"They surely were, Ophelia. They communicated with the dead for folks. They kept villages safe from haints and made sure everyone passed on when it was their time."

"Is that what you do now?"

Aunt Rose nodded. "When I go on my walks, I check to see if there are any dead in our neighborhood who have yet to move on. For some of them that means reminding them they're dead; for others it means listening to their stories. Most folks just want someone who will hear them, who will see them. The dead are no different."

Ophie sipped at her milk, which was warm and sweet and creamy. Even as she was eager to finally learn about this strange power she had, the milk was by far the best part of her day, and Ophie was going to enjoy it. "What happens if no one helps the ghosts?" Ophie asked after finally swallowing.

Aunt Rose sighed. "Well, the way my mama used to tell it is that a city with too many ghosts can get to be a miserable place. All that negative energy builds up; there can be accidents, or worse. Wars, killing, people just generally being awful to one another. Those kinds of things can come to pass because of too many haints milling about. But that isn't your business just now. You, Ophelia, first need to learn how to protect yourself from the dead."

"Why? Are they dangerous?"

"Yes."

The answer drew Ophie's gaze away from her milk and into the dark, lined face of her great-aunt. Her expression had gone hard, and Ophie leaned back in her chair, her full attention on Aunt Rose's next words.

"You listen to me, child, and you listen well. The dead are cold, greedy things. They are shallow, they are selfish, and they only care about themselves."

All the mirth had drained from Rose's face, and Ophie shivered as a draft found its way around the windows and twirled through the kitchen. She gulped her milk and licked the sweetness from her lips.

"But you said that you helped the dead," Ophie said, a little bit confused.

"Helping them is sometimes necessary to move them along to the afterlife, but you should never, ever trust a haint. You keep iron and salt in your pockets at all times—" She gestured at Ophie's apron pocket, which still held the nail and the little pouch Aunt Rose had given her before the walk. "That way they can't take hold of your body, which some of the more powerful ones will try to do. Never leave out sweets, especially someplace that doesn't have any haint blue to keep them out. The dead love sweets. And you never, ever make a ghost a promise, otherwise they'll be as persistent as fleas. And if you're ever attacked, you just find salt or iron. That'll banish them but good."

"Is *banishing* different from passing on?" Ophie asked.

Aunt Rose nodded. "Many ghosts are shells of their former selves—needy, but not really a threat. But sometimes a haint can become so angry that you can't help them; all you can do is banish them so they don't hurt anyone else. But that's not something you need to worry about just yet. You're too young to be dealing with these sorts of things on your own. When you get a bit older, I'll send for Sarah—that's your older cousin—to come and teach you the way of negotiating with the dead. For now, you just leave them haints alone." Her expression softened a little. "I know this is all a bit much, and that you likely have more questions than I have answers. I just wanted you to know that you aren't alone, Ophelia. You understand?"

"Yes'm." Ophie took another big gulp of her milk. Ghosts were real; they could even hurt her. . . . It was a scary thing, but it also made her feel special. Someday—soon, maybe—Ophie wouldn't have to feel so helpless around the spirits she saw every day. She could speak to them, listen to them, maybe even fix things for them. She could be self-assured and confident like Aunt Rose.

Ophie thought of her mama then. The way she looked so empty at the end of the day, her expressions hollow like a ghost; the way she cried softly at night when she thought Ophie had fallen asleep; the broken heart that it seemed like nothing could mend. She was a shadow of the mama Ophie had grown up with, the best parts of her destroyed with a single act of violence. If Ophie couldn't help her, maybe there was *someone* she could help.

And maybe, by helping the haints, Ophie could learn how to fix her mama.

"Well, that's enough chatter for one night," Aunt Rose said, standing. "Finish up that milk and get to bed, I know you and your mama have a long day tomorrow. How was your first day of work?"

"Fine," Ophie said. She'd almost forgotten that every day would be another day stepping and fetching for Mrs. Caruthers, and it made the last few sips of milk taste sour.

"Well, I'm sure it will get better," Aunt Rose said, patting Ophie's shoulder reassuringly before heading out of the room.

Ophie tipped back her mug to get the last few drops of milk and sighed.

Tomorrow, and a return to Daffodil Manor, would come entirely too soon.

Pittsburgh

∞

PITTSBURGH WAS A RESILIENT, ROUGH-AND-TUMBLE city. His arms were forged of steel, his backbone was the railroad, and in his veins was the coal that powered them both. The people who made their homes within his limits came from some of the hardest, meanest places on earth. Throughout the years, Pittsburgh had welcomed all—anyone who wanted to work hard could come to the confluence of the Allegheny and Monongahela Rivers. And come they did. Scottish, Irish, Hungarians, and Polish all made their way to the city to build new lives. Now colored folks like Ophie and her mother, historically in bondage, exercised the freedom they did have to make their way to the city, escaping the chokehold of Jim Crow.

Yes, people came to Pittsburgh not to relax but to work. This was not Philadelphia, with its Brotherly

Love and polite political history. Pittsburgh was a city that had once sparked a rebellion, a place where one had to scrabble and scrape and fight for a chance at prosperity. And fight they did. After the Revolutionary War, Pittsburghers built their opportunities from whiskey and farming, then they broke their backs on coal and the railroad. Now the residents of the city forged an American dream of steel girders, fashioning opportunity with fire and iron.

And if the living of the city were hardy and tough, the dead were even more so.

Pittsburgh's dead crowded along the trolley routes and clogged the streets. They flitted in and out of homes where the residents didn't know how to protect themselves, spoiling milk and bread left out overnight, chilling skin and taking the warmth for their own. The ghosts of Pittsburgh were many and varied. Natives who had lost their lives in the white man's push across the continent rubbed elbows with runaway slaves who never tasted freedom until their last breath. Men of consequence and means, who had made their fortunes exploiting laborers in their factories, drifted along next to those who had lost their lives toiling on those same factory machines. There were men and women, children and elderly, of all colors and ethnicities, whispering in a dozen languages stories of heartache and spite, a perfect ghostly mirror to the living of the city.

As Ophie made her way in and around the streets with her mother, she saw them all. And the dead saw her.

Soon enough, they told themselves, she would help them. They just had to be patient.

Chapter 5

OPHIE'S SECOND AND THIRD DAY AT DAFFODIL Manor were much the same as her first. She arrived, changing out her too-tight shoes for the slippery house shoes. She brought Mrs. Caruthers her oatmeal, and then her tea, huffing and puffing up and down the stairs. Then a lunch tray, and then an afternoon tea tray. Then there was helping the old woman to the lavatory and back, and anything else she decided she wanted or needed. Hours of being at a sour old white woman's beck and call, and then finally a trolley ride back home, dinner, and sleep just so she could do it all over again. She didn't see the ghost of the young boy, at least, for which she was thankful. After talking with Aunt Rose, she wasn't sure what she would say to him if she did.

By the fourth day of working at Daffodil Manor, Ophie knew that she would never, ever have a good day again. She wanted to cry from the boredom and awfulness of it all, and the injustice that the cousins got to spend their days going to school and seeing other kids and doing the learning that Ophie longed to be doing. There wasn't a lot of excitement in being a servant, and the only thing she had learned in the past few days was that Mrs. Caruthers liked to complain about *everything*.

It was so unfair. And she still hadn't seen the glamorous lady who'd helped her on her first day again, the lone bright spot in the whole gloomy week. No one had mentioned there being any other Carutherses in the house aside from Mrs. Caruthers and Richard, so she couldn't have been his sister or cousin. But the woman had spoken to Mrs. Caruthers like they'd met before. Ophie reckoned she was a friend of Richard Caruthers, which meant she was probably rich, too. Had she gone on a fantastic trip somewhere? The radio was always talking about people of consequence traveling around the world by steamer. What if she was gone and Ophie would never see her again, never discover who she was? The mystery of it poked at Ophie, combining with her overall displeasure at waiting on Mrs. Caruthers to put her in a fine snit.

On her fourth day at Daffodil Manor, Ophie brought down the breakfast tray to find Cook waiting for her. The old colored woman leaned a hip against the prep table that cluttered the center of the kitchen. A mound of dough sat off to the side, rising in the warm kitchen.

"Come get yourself a snack, child, you are too skinny by half," Cook said, setting out a plate and a glass of milk. "I made shortbread."

Ophie cleared Mrs. Caruthers's breakfast tray, placing each bowl in a nearby sink as she'd been shown, before joining Cook at the prep table. Square cookies crowded the dish, smelling deliciously of butter and sugar, and Ophie's mouth watered as she looked at them.

"How many can I have?" she whispered. Maybe Daffodil Manor wasn't so bad if there were cookies.

"You have as many as you want. One of the few perks of working for fine folks like the Carutherses is getting to spoil yourself just a tiny bit."

Cook fairly beamed as Ophie took a cookie, looking at it for a moment before she took a bite. It was buttery and delicious, tasting even better than it smelled, and it was gone so quickly that Ophie snatched another just in case Cook decided to change her mind.

"Have you worked here a long time?" Ophie asked.

"Most of my life. I started here as a scullery maid

when I was about your age, just before Mr. Caruthers, God rest his soul, met Mrs. Caruthers. Mr. Henry came up from Virginia with the missus, and he and I got married not long after. Our children even worked here at the manor before setting out into the world."

"Are we the only folks who work here now?" Ophie asked. It seemed strange, to only have four people taking care of such a large house. Maybe that was why so many of the rooms were closed off. Ophie's duties had kept her mostly on the same path every day between the kitchen and Mrs. Caruthers's bedroom, but she had gotten turned around once and discovered an entire wing of the house that had not been lived in for a while, empty bedrooms with furniture covered in cloths.

"We have a woman who comes in weekly to take care of the linens and the laundry—Deirdre, you'll meet her at the end of the week. But that's it. Daffodil Manor used to have quite a few domestics, but Mrs. Caruthers cut back a bit after the Great War. Her husband had passed on, and she lost two of her sons to that conflict. Well, one to the war, and one to the bottle after he came home from the fight." Cook clucked her tongue.

"Is that why Mrs. Caruthers is"—Ophie thought for a moment about a word that wouldn't get her in trouble—"so unhappy?"

"Och, no. That woman has always been miserable." Cook reached for a cookie and bit into it, crunching happily. But then she seemed to catch herself, straightening and giving Ophie a stern look. "Mind you, I'm not one to gossip. You remember that, Ophelia. The lives of your betters are not fodder for your amusement."

Ophie took another cookie and bit into it, nodding. Cook seemed kind most of the time, but she was beginning to wonder if the older woman was what Daddy had referred to as Double-Talk Folk. "Ophie, you're gonna meet lots of different people in your life," he once said, after Ophie had told him about some advice she'd gotten from a teacher she'd had who'd come from up north. "Some of them, you'll see, will advise you to act a certain way, while they carry on just however they please. That is, they'll say one thing but do another. These folks are Double-Talk Folk, and, Ophie, you smile and nod when they speak but keep your own truths near."

So she just smiled as the older woman spoke, and tried not to miss her daddy. She ached for those evenings spent around the stove, Daddy carrying on while Mama laughed or groaned at his funny stories. They had seemed dull and forgettable then, but Ophie yearned for one more dinner of beans and fatback with corn bread, Daddy telling stories of the rail yard as they ate.

Ophie stuffed another shortbread into her mouth as she blinked away hot tears. Cook did not notice.

Cook began to talk about the kinds of quality people who had lived in Daffodil Manor over the years, all the many Carutherses plus their cousins and distant relations. That's when Ophie realized something.

"Cook," Ophie said, taking two more shortbread cookies and slipping them into the pocket of her apron when the older woman wasn't paying attention. "Is there a pretty white lady that comes around the manor often? A really nice one?"

Cook paused and frowned at Ophie. "How do you mean?"

"The first day, when I was pouring Mrs. Caruthers her tea, there was a lady who helped me with it." As Ophie spoke, Cook's expression grew concerned.

"It was fine, though, Mrs. Caruthers didn't mind," she quickly finished. "She even calmed down a little when the lady was there."

That was a bit of a stretch, but Mrs. Caruthers hadn't seemed bothered by the woman. Which was saying something because she was annoyed about more things than most folks Ophie had met.

"I'm not sure who it was, Ophelia, but you stay away from any young women if you see them again. Sometimes Mr. Richard likes to bring home . . . a bit of company, but those girls are no business of yours. And they should know better than to go roaming about the house, especially to the missus's room. A good girl knows her place and minds her manners. You might be a bit young to know what that means, but I'm sure you get my drift." Cook pursed her lips and shook her head. "You don't want to risk your position over a friendship you have no business making. That's all I'm saying."

Cook's expression went far away then, almost as if she was looking through Ophie. But then the bell near the sink that connected to the string in Mrs. Caruthers's room set to ringing, and Ophie's break was over.

"Thank you for the cookies," she said. She drank the glass of milk in a few gulps, wiped her mouth with the back of her sleeve, and went to see what the ornery old woman wanted.

Cook said nothing else as she left.

After the conversation with Cook, Ophie did not ask any more questions about the residents of Daffodil Manor. She did not want to seem like a busybody. But as February blustered on into March, she still found herself hoping that the woman in the blue dress might show up again, if only so Ophie would have someone to chat with during one of her long days running around for Mrs. Caruthers. The first week of March, Richard had friends down from Connecticut to visit, and Ophie couldn't help altering her path that first day to pass by the rooms in which they were talking and eating and laughing. But the woman was not among them.

Ophie's duties at Daffodil Manor took on a rhythm that, while not soothing, was at least predictable. She had become good enough at lifting tea and meal trays that she was able to make it up and down the main staircase much quicker than her first day. She still won the ire of Mrs. Caruthers more often than not, usually for the most mundane reasons, but she learned how to be competent enough in her tending to the old woman not to be fired. Which was a very real possibility. The second week of March, nearly a month after Ophie began her tenure at Daffodil Manor, Deirdre, the Irish woman in charge of the household linens, was fired by Mrs. Caruthers.

"She had a terrible attitude," the old woman said with a sniff when Richard asked what had happened to her. Rather than hire another person to see to Mrs. Caruthers's bed linens, it was decided that the task should pass to Ophie. Mama was thrilled at this turn of events, because it meant that Ophie would now be earning a whole three dollars a week. That was only a few dollars less than Mama herself.

"We'll be able to move out of Rose's house by May at this rate," Mama told Ophie a week later, on their ride home. Ophie, of course, was only half listening, mostly doing what she did every day on the trolley: watching ghosts and the people they haunted. The old colored lady, Miss Alice, who rode in the morning, was not there and neither was her sobbing daughter, but an older colored man who smiled and offered everyone peppermints often was. And every time, there was a laughing girl ghost who sat on his lap like she was his sweetheart.

Mostly, Ophie pretended not to see her, just like Aunt Rose had told her. But one day, she couldn't stop staring, and soon, the girl, who was the whitest thing on the trolley, caught her. She floated over, leaning in close to Ophie's face.

"Do you see me?" the dead girl asked, her voice less than a whisper. It was more an impression of sound, like water running over rocks, and Ophie felt the words more than she heard them. Not a single other person in the trolley even glanced in their direction. A chill ran through her, and next to her Mama grabbed the edges of her coat and pulled them closer together.

"You can hear me, too," the dead woman said, and it wasn't a question this time. The sound was closer to water running now, a steady echo that grew louder as she focused her attention on Ophie.

Ophie reached for the small packet of salt and the iron nail in her pocket and nodded, the barest movement. The girl smiled again, impossibly wide. Up close her skin was more blue than white, with long blond hair that looked wet, like she'd just climbed out of a too-cold bath. Her underthings hung heavily on her slim frame, a stained white shift dripping ghostly water onto the floorboards of the trolley. The droplets plinked consistently, and Ophie instinctively picked up her feet just a little to keep her shoes from getting wet.

No one else noticed the puddle blooming underfoot.

The outline of the haint's body was a cool blue—however she'd died, she wasn't angry about it, just deeply sad. But that didn't mean she wasn't dangerous.

"Will you do something for me?" the ghost asked.

Ophie's mouth went dry, but the spirit didn't wait for an answer.

"Tell him that Faith is waiting for him." She floated back over to the old man, touching him tenderly. "Any day now," the woman said, her voice becoming like a river. Ophie and her mother had gone to see one of the Allegheny River's many dams after they'd arrived, a trip to sightsee a bit in their new home. The ghost's voice now sounded like water crashing over the edge of that dam. Around her the puddle grew, trickling under the feet of all the surrounding riders. The trolley even smelled damp, like the woods after rain, fecund and rich.

Ophie shook her head no, but an icy chill gripped her heart. She gasped as the ghost was instantly back at her side, leaning even closer.

"You will help me. Tell him." A boom of sound, loud enough to make Ophie wince. It wasn't a request, and Ophie nodded slightly. As soon as she did, the chill left her body, just a little. Aunt Rose had said that the salt and iron would keep a ghost from possessing her, but she hadn't said anything about their ability to turn a body's blood to ice.

The ghost nodded at Ophie before floating back over to the man. She sat back on his lap, this time caressing his face and talking to him, words that Ophie couldn't hear. She shivered and tried to warm back up, ducking deeper into the folds of her coat.

When the trolley came to their stop, the ghost was gone, and the old man got off in front of them and began to hobble down the block in the opposite direction. Ophie hesitated for only a moment before breaking away from her mother and dashing after him.

"Excuse me, sir?" Ophie said, gently tapping his arm.

"What? Hello, but I'm afraid I don't have any more peppermints, dear." The man squinted at her, and Ophie's heart pounded. She was being foolish and impulsive, two things Mama always warned against. But she couldn't help it. Even though Aunt Rose had said that ghosts weren't to be trusted, she was worried that the ghost wouldn't leave her alone on the trolley anymore. She didn't want to feel that chill again. And besides, what harm could it do, just telling the man what the ghost had told her?

Wouldn't relaying the message be helping? If no one else, then herself?

"I'm sorry to bother you, sir, but I have a message for you." Ophie took a deep breath. She could do this. "Umm, Faith says that she is waiting for you, and it will be any day now."

The man's face crumpled in the span of a heartbeat. "Oh. Oh," he said, grabbing for his heart. His eyes were wide with surprise, and Ophie immediately knew that she had done something terribly wrong in blatantly ignoring Aunt Rose's advice. Regret washed over her as she could feel Mama's gaze boring into her from back where she waited by the trolley stop. There would be questions.

"I'm sorry, I didn't mean—" Ophie began.

"No, no, this is a good thing. Thank you. For letting me know." He sniffed, then reached out and patted Ophie's shoulder heavily. It was only then that Ophie realized his tears were ones of joy.

Ophie nodded as her heart filled with a sense of pride that she hadn't felt in a long time. And then, before the old man could ask any questions, she sprinted back over to where her mama stood waiting.

"What was that about?" Mama demanded as Ophie fell into step next to her.

"He dropped a dime as he was getting off the trolley," Ophie lied. "You always said that dishonesty was punished eventually, so I didn't want to keep it." The words spilled out of Ophie, too fast in an effort to cover the sick feeling of guilt heavy in her stomach. She didn't like lying to her mama, but she couldn't tell her the truth.

How could a body be happy and anxious, all at the same time?

Mama harrumphed but said nothing. And Ophie quietly swore to herself that she would never make eye contact with the ghosts on the trolley again.

But as she walked home, Mama quiet on the way, taken up with her own musings, Ophie wondered if maybe Mama wouldn't be so morose if she knew what had happened that terrible night back in Georgia. The ghost girl on the trolley must have died a long time ago, judging by her clothes, and yet the old man was still happy to get a message from her. Maybe telling Mama the truth could restore her to the person Ophie had once known, warm and loving and fierce.

But . . . what if the truth just pushed her mama further away? Ophie wasn't sure what she would do if Mama once again chided her for being too dreamy and making up fairy stories. She felt alone enough as it was.

Ophie realized that telling her mother the truth about her daddy's last visit scared her more than all the dead in Pittsburgh. And so, once again, she decided to stay silent.

Chapter 6

THE NEXT DAY, GHOSTS WERE THE LEAST OF OPHIE'S problems. She had Mrs. Caruthers and her linens to contend with, and it would be her first time doing it all by herself.

The sheets on the old woman's bed were stripped and replaced every Wednesday morning. The first Wednesday after Deirdre was fired, Cook showed Ophie how to help Mrs. Caruthers into a nearby chair, bundle her up so she didn't get cold, and quickly pull off all the sheets and blankets. After that, she was shown how to put clean sheets on the bed, smooth them just so, and use a hot iron to warm the sheets so that they would not be cold when Mrs. Caruthers was helped back to the bed.

"Don't linger too long with the iron or you'll scorch the sheets. After they're warm, place the missus in the bed, pile clean quilts up on her, and fetch her a warm drink so she doesn't catch a chill." Cook had said this as she completed all those steps in what seemed to Ophie like no time at all. She was not certain how it was that Mrs. Caruthers could catch a chill in a room that was warm enough to cause perspiration, but she simply nodded.

As much as Ophie loathed the responsibility of the bed linens, she kept telling herself it would be worth it to see how proud Mama was of her. Maybe then some of the worry would melt off Mama's face. Perhaps not all of it, but maybe just a little.

But now that she was trying to accomplish the task for the first time by herself, all her fragile hope was shattering. Things were not going well at all.

First, Ophie placed the blanket on the chair just as Cook had, but when she went to help Mrs. Caruthers into the chair the old woman harrumphed. "That wing chair is too lumpy. I want to sit in the rocking chair today."

Ophie looked at the rocking chair, which was the farthest chair away from the fire. The bedroom was crowded with furniture, and the wing chair, heavy and solid, was the most sensible spot for an elderly woman who was unsteady on her feet.

But the old lady was anything but sensible, as Ophie had learned. Before she had been sacked, Deirdre had commented on it one afternoon in the kitchen over day-old bread. "The missus likes being difficult, methinks," she'd said, her accent so thick that Ophie had barely understood her. "She's as stubborn as a goat and just as smart. Aye, I've met a few ornery souls in my day, but none so cross as her." No one else in the room had said anything, and it could not have been any sort of coincidence that less than twenty-four hours later Deirdre was without a job. So instead of arguing with Mrs. Caruthers, Ophie went over to the rocking chair and began to drag it toward the fire.

"Heavens, child, what do you think you are doing?" exclaimed Mrs. Caruthers.

"I was trying to move it closer," Ophie said, voice low.

"Well, pick it up! Don't go dragging it, this isn't a farmyard."

Ophie had no idea what a farm had to do with moving the rocking chair across the floor, but she did as she was told. She grappled with the heavy wooden chair, lifting it a few inches off the floor and heaving it with some difficulty across the room until it was next to the roaring fire.

After the chair was settled and Ophie had taken a deep steadying breath, she placed the quilt from the wing chair on the rocker. She then helped Mrs. Caruthers onto the seat, wrapped the old woman up, and laid another blanket on her lap for good measure.

"Hurry up, now," Mrs. Caruthers said with a shiver. "I'm already chilled."

Ophie nodded and quickly stripped the bed, separating the sheets and blankets out just like Cook had shown her so they could be laundered later. But when it came time to put new sheets on, Ophie found the shelf in the hallway linen closet empty.

Of course. Cook was going to show Ophie how to wash the sheets, but she'd been busy setting up a menu for a dinner party Richard had decided to hold at the last minute. So the sheets were still downstairs somewhere in the laundry, unwashed.

Ophie gnawed on her bottom lip and stared at the empty shelf. There had to be another set of sheets somewhere. Hadn't Cook said as much? Just when Ophie began to despair, she remembered. *If you ever need a set of sheets and there ain't none to be found, just check one of the cedar chests. There's one in the closet of every bedroom. Should be some in there. From now on, it'll be your job to make sure there's always an extra set of bedding, just in case.* The message had been clear. *Just in case the laundry hasn't been done, and the old woman is about to pitch a fit.*

Ophie walked back into Mrs. Caruthers's room and over to the closet. But no sooner had she opened the door than Mrs. Caruthers was on her feet.

"What are you doing?" Mrs. Caruthers asked. "There's nothing for you in that closet." The old woman's voice was flat, nothing like her usually caustic tone.

"I . . . I was going to get some more sheets," Ophie said, one hand on the door handle.

"Not in there. You stay out of there."

Ophie looked into the closet, which was deep and carried a sickly sweet scent. It was cedar, and lilac and decay, something unwelcoming that had been mostly blocked when the door was closed but now seeped out into the warm air of the close space. Something about the scent made her close the door hurriedly, her heart beating hard enough to thump against her ribs.

She did not want to open that closet ever again.

"I'll go . . . I'll fetch some sheets from one of the guest rooms."

Mrs. Caruthers said nothing, just glared at Ophie as she left the room, a quiet stare that chilled Ophie and reminded her that the old woman was dangerous in so many ways. If she said Ophie should stay out of the closet, then Ophie would.

She didn't want to use those smelly old sheets, anyway.

Chapter 7

THE DAY AFTER OPHIE OPENED THE FORBIDDEN
closet in Mrs. Caruthers's room the old woman had
the groundskeeper, Mr. Henry, add a padlock to the
door. Ophie felt a mixture of relief and disappointment as the man worked. What was so important in
that closet that it required a lock? For a moment Ophie
wondered if she had broken some unspoken rule about
being a domestic. Was she supposed to avoid all closets unless specifically told to open them? That seemed
strange. The mystery of the closet poked at Ophie just
until she was distracted once more by Mrs. Caruthers's
endless demands, which was not long at all.

Aside from the brand-new brass lock, nothing in
Daffodil Manor changed. Ophie fetched tea and ran
hither and thither as she was told, and the winter

continued melting into spring.

The longer Ophie was at Daffodil Manor, the more her duties grew. Trays a few times a day became a regular thing, and Ophie ran up and down the grand staircase as Mrs. Caruthers requested this or that. In addition to changing the bedsheets and helping Mrs. Caruthers to the bathroom, Ophie was also asked to fetch a newspaper so that the old woman could check the latest scandals plaguing the Harding administration.

Ophie hated all of it. But the worst duty by far was having to read to Mrs. Caruthers every afternoon.

First, Mrs. Caruthers clearly did not like Ophie, and so having to spend so much time sitting still only a few feet from the old woman was nearly unbearable. Second, Mrs. Caruthers's choice of literature left something to be desired. She liked to listen to histories, the longer the better, and her favorites were written by a man named Ulrich Bonnell Phillips. They were books that discussed slavery and plantations and the time before emancipation in a reverent and honorable way, like it had all been a good thing. Sometimes, as she was cracking the spine of yet another dusty history, Ophie would catch movement out of the corner of her eye, and there would be the ghost boy standing in the doorway. Ophie had seen him a handful of times over the last month, but he had never approached her like the ghost on the trolley had, and she never tried talking to him. Though, whenever she saw him, she wondered if he had any opinions on Mr. Phillips and his nostalgia for a time when people owned other people. The histories made Ophie deeply uncomfortable, for her part. She'd heard stories of the Bad Old Days, and the way in which much of what had happened back then was still happening even in 1923. Ophie knew that colored folks had not always been free, and she understood that her work for the Carutherses resonated within the same patterns of history, even if she was paid a modest wage. But if she tried to read something else Mrs. Caruthers would snap at her, and so she read the irksome tomes until the old woman drifted off.

After that, however, was the best time of the day. Because while Mrs. Caruthers slept, Ophie was free to do as she pleased. Not that she had free run of Daffodil Manor. But she could sit by the fire and read what *she* wanted to read, a luxury she had never been able to indulge in before. On her initial expedition to the library—a whole room full of books!—to find the first of Mrs. Caruthers's histories, she'd spotted a number of treasures: stacks of detective magazines, a handful of boys' life adventure stories that must have been Richard's when he was younger, and a pile of

True Romances magazines that bore the name *Clara* scrawled on the inside. And so, she stuck a couple of them between the pages of the histories, and would sneak them out when Mrs. Caruthers was dozing.

While the stories of adventure weren't her favorite, and the detective stories were mostly confusing, the romance stories were exactly the kind of thing Ophie could delight in. Mama would have had a fit if she knew her daughter was reading such things, stories of girls who were *compromised*, whatever that meant, and kissed boys who left them heartbroken. But who would tell on her? Mrs. Caruthers was too busy snoring, and Cook and Mr. Henry had their own lengthy list of duties to see to.

And so it was that a particularly blustery afternoon at the end of March found Ophie sprawled in front of the fire, a *True Romances* magazine spread before her. She was just to the part where the main character, a shopgirl who was being courted by a mysterious man who Ophie was certain was a secret millionaire, was going to finally kiss her beau when a voice said, "Have you gotten to the part where he proposes to her yet?"

"No, they're just about to kiss—" she began, before slamming the magazine shut and looking up, heart pounding.

There, once again, was the beautiful woman from

Ophie's first day at Daffodil Manor, a friendly smile on her lips.

"You—you came back," Ophie said, unable to keep the excitement from her voice. She had assumed she was never going to see the woman again; now here she was, smelling of pine and honeysuckle, sweet and flowery like the best kind of summer day.

"I'm sorry, I didn't mean to startle you," the woman said, sinking down next to Ophie. The way her skirts and scarf billowed around her as she sank onto the threadbare carpet was utterly splendid, and Ophie had to swallow a sigh. She had never met someone so pretty and graceful. Even the pastor's wife from back in Georgia seemed like a drab mallard next to this swan. The woman fairly glowed with a kind of happiness, like she was sunshine. And in a gloomy place like Daffodil Manor, her brightness seemed even more incandescent.

"It's okay," Ophie said, because that was what one was supposed to say when a beautiful woman smiled at them. Ophie swallowed, and pulled her legs and knees closer to her in case her hands were dirty, the way Mrs. Caruthers always seemed to think they were. "I'm Ophie."

"Where are my manners? Of course, we were never properly introduced. I'm Clara."

"Oh! These are yours, then. I saw your name in them." Ophie flipped to the inside cover and showed her.

"They are indeed. What do you think of them?"

"I like them a whole lot," Ophie said, straightening as she thought about the stories. No one had asked Ophie her opinion on anything in a very long time, and it was nice to think that this very polished, very fancy lady cared what she thought.

"What was your favorite story so far?" Clara asked, her eyes shining with interest. She wasn't just being polite; she actually cared.

"The one about the bootlegger and the sheriff's daughter, hands down," Ophie said, unable to keep the grin off her face.

"Yes! That one is so thrilling! When they're hiding in the blackberry brambles, and you think she's going to turn him in but she doesn't!" Clara put her hands over her heart and mocked a swoon. "I could've just died!"

"Yeah," Ophie said. A peculiar feeling came over her. "Um, did you want them back?"

"Not at all, chickadee—it's good to find someone else who likes to read *True Romances*," she said, lowering her voice conspiratorially. "I've been hiding them in the library for fear someone would pitch them! Not everyone is like you—no one else understands why I love them so much."

The idea of her and Clara having something in common made Ophie's face warm, and she shook her head emphatically. "You don't have to worry about anyone finding them. No one goes in there but me," Ophie said, and it was true. Some afternoons she spent time reorganizing the massive room so that she could find things more easily, although it was too cold to stay in there for long. Without a fire in the hearth, the massive, wood-paneled room was as cold as a tomb.

"That's my favorite room in the whole house," Clara said with a sigh. "What a shame."

Ophie was about to suggest that Clara just have Cook or one of the other servants make sure there was a fire burning, for it seemed criminal that such a beautiful woman should have to be cold like she was just any old kind of person. But that's when the sound of movement from the direction of the bed drew Ophie's attention.

Mrs. Caruthers sat up in her bed, covers clutched to her chin, her eyes narrowed with suspicion. "You, girl, are you talking to yourself? Are you daft?"

Ophie scrambled to her feet and shook her head. "No, ma'am, I was talking to Clara."

Mrs. Caruthers released the blankets and dragged

herself out of the bed, her movements jerky and erratic, like they'd been the day Ophie had looked in the closet. "What? Who told you that name?" she growled, stomping toward Ophie, who could only stare back in shock. "How do you know her? Were you poking through my things? Did Richard tell you about her?"

The old woman was yelling so loud she was shaking, and Ophie didn't know what to say. But when the old woman raised her hand with the intention of slapping Ophie across the face, Ophie knew well enough to scurry away. She ran out of the room before she could think, slamming the door behind her, and scampered smack into her mother in the hallway, whose arms were loaded with clean laundry.

"Ophelia! What is going on?" Mama demanded.

"There's something wrong with Mrs. Caruthers!" Ophie gasped for breath, her heart pounding as though she'd just run up and down the main staircase.

The door creaked open, and the old woman appeared, hair wild, eyes wide, spittle coming from her mouth. She shouted gibberish and her hands were curled into gnarled claws. She still looked like she wanted to hurt Ophie.

Mama set Ophie to the side and walked toward Mrs. Caruthers, hands out in the way she sometimes used to settle the chickens back home. "Ophelia, run downstairs and tell Cook to ring the doctor. Ma'am, let me help you back to bed before you catch cold."

Ophie didn't wait for any further instructions. She lit out, running full tilt down the stairs. Her slippered feet slid a little on the cold tile when she burst into the kitchen, where Cook was laughing with Henry over some joke or another.

"Mama said to ring the doctor round, Mrs. Caruthers is having a fit of some kind!" Ophie panted.

Cook and Henry both erupted into motion, Henry heading upstairs toward the bedrooms, Cook to the black telephone mounted on the wall near the back door.

Ophie, however, was frozen, trying to understand what had just happened. Had she somehow caused Mrs. Caruthers's strange behavior? What had gone wrong? One moment Ophie had been talking to Clara, the next Mrs. Caruthers was yelling, eyes wide as though she had just—

"I'm sorry, I'm still new at this."

The lovely woman stood in the doorway to the kitchen wringing her pale hands.

Ophie thought back to what had happened upstairs. Mrs. Caruthers yelling at Ophie like Clara hadn't been in the room. Clara disappearing the moment the old woman had stirred.

"What . . . happened up there?" Ophie asked Clara slowly.

"Nothing you could have done anything about, child," Cook called across the kitchen. She still held the telephone receiver to her ear as she waited for the operator to ring the doctor, and spoke as if she only saw Ophie. "Why don't you go take a walk out in the garden? There will be no tea for the missus right now, she's going to need something stronger than that, I'm afraid."

Ophie turned back to Clara and blinked slowly. The first time she had met Clara she was deeply focused on not destroying a priceless tea set, which is perhaps why she didn't notice that Clara's dress rippled as though it blew in an unseen wind. And the long, dramatic red scarf, she wore . . . When Ophie looked closely, she could see that it was not a scarf at all but rather a trail of blood that undulated and flowed like an infinite river.

And the glow she had, it wasn't simply her beauty, or the deep hue of her dress. It was a blue shimmer that surrounded her.

Clara was a ghost.

The young woman gave Ophie one last sad, wistful smile, and then vanished from sight completely, leaving Ophie with nothing but questions.

But beneath them all was a feeling she would not lose for a long while after—a deep and profound sadness that the best thing about Daffodil Manor was a dead woman.

The Trolley Car

THE GHOSTS BEGAN TO TAKE REAL NOTICE OF OPHIE after the incident on the trolley. Wherever the living gathered, so did the dead, and nowhere more thickly than the Pittsburgh crosstown trolleys. Some of them followed those they had once loved, clinging to their old lives like barnacles to a ship, unable to navigate any other way. The angrier, more powerful ghosts used the trolley to find new hosts: tired, unsuspecting bodies to possess for a little while, warmth to steal from cheeks and other exposed skin, and ill tempers to stoke.

Not all the haints came for Ophie, of course. Most were happy enough with what they understood of their liminal existence and did not seek help from seers. But a good number of ghosts wondered if Ophie could end their suffering. They wanted nothing more than to be seen, after all. By someone who could truly see them, not just shiver as they glided past. Most people could sense the dead in the corner of their eyes, a shadow that startled and alarmed, but Ophie was not like that. No, the girl could see them for who they were and what they wanted, so some began to ride along with her on the trolley. They didn't talk to her, they didn't press around her and beg her for favors, they didn't even reveal themselves to her. Not all of them, anyway. Not yet.

They wanted to see just what the girl was made of first. Would she be strong enough to help them, to ease their pain, to aid them in finding their eternal rest? Or would she banish them with salt and iron?

Soon, they would know.

Chapter 8

AFTER MRS. CARUTHERS'S FIT, THE DOCTOR ordered her to be kept on bed rest, and even gave Cook a tincture of opium to be added to her tea. The incident alarmed and upset the household, and as Ophie carried the trays up and down the stairs she could sense a change in the air. At first she thought it was concern for Mrs. Caruthers, but the day after the incident, she overheard Mama and Cook talking in the kitchen and knew it for what it was.

Fear.

"You know if the old woman dies, we'll all be dismissed," Cook murmured to Mama, not one to follow her own advice about not minding the business of her employers. "Richard never wanted to stay here, you know. He had plans to move out west with a sweetheart. It's only his mother's ill health that's kept him bound to this drafty old house. She goes, we'll be tasked with shutting up the house, and he will leave for certain. And I don't have to tell you how hard it'll be to find new positions."

"That old woman is too mean to die," Mama said. "Did you see the way she went after my poor Ophelia? The child might be sulky, but she isn't one to provoke."

"Well, lucky for your girl the doctor's left enough laudanum to keep the missus down for a while. Did you and your girl find a place of your own yet?"

At that Mama sighed. "No, everyone and their brother has moved to the city. And what I can find is no place to raise a daughter. I won't leave Rose's house just to move into a neighborhood where I'll have to worry about bootleggers and numbers runners."

Cook clucked her tongue. "I'm sure you could ask Richard about staying here if you're in a bind. He'll reduce your weekly pay, but at least you'll be away from those cousins."

"Maybe, if things get any worse. I'll keep saving for now, hoping that maybe we can find something once the weather warms. As long as Rose is there to keep them in line, we'll be fine."

At the change in conversation, Ophie finally entered the kitchen. She felt strange. She didn't want to hope for Mrs. Caruthers to die, but without the old woman maybe Mama would get a different job—one that didn't make her look so sad and anxious—and maybe Ophie could go back to school.

It was a long shot, but hope was better than despair, and Ophie clung to that glimmer of a better future with clenched fists.

"How's the missus doing?" Cook asked as Ophie took the dirty breakfast dishes over to the sink.

"She's asleep. She ate, and then right out."

"The doctor said rest would be the best for her," said a much deeper voice.

Ophie startled, and she turned around to see Richard standing in the doorway to the kitchen. An odd sight, since he was rarely home during the day, and she had not once ever seen a white man enter the kitchen. It was Cook's domain, and she presided over it like a queen.

But she didn't seem very royal in that moment. Her shoulders drooped, and she seemed to fold into herself, nothing like the woman who usually strutted around the kitchen. Richard didn't seem to notice, but Mama did, judging from the way her eyes widened for a moment before she looked down at the silver she was polishing.

"Oh, of course, Mr. Richard," Cook said, her smile too wide, too bright. "Ophelia just came down from your mama's room, and I was just wondering if she was wanting for anything before I got to putting together the luncheon."

"Don't worry about that, Cook, I'll be eating downtown, and I'm sure Mother will spend the rest of the day sleeping."

"Oh, all right, then, Mr. Richard."

Ophie hated the tremor that had entered Cook's voice, the way her eyes darted around the kitchen as Richard walked across the tiles in his fine shoes, the heels clacking with each step. It hadn't occurred to Ophie that Cook might feel the same kind of simmering terror about making a mistake that plagued Ophie, but why else would a woman like Cook act this way?

"I'm actually here to talk to Ophelia," Richard said with his toothpaste smile, his eyes gleaming. For a moment Ophelia thought of the story of Little Red Riding Hood and how Red had looked at the wolf right before he'd gobbled her up.

"Yessir?" Ophie said, bobbing a curtsy and glancing down at the ground. *Never look them in the eyes; always be respectful; remain humble; remember that they are good, fine people; don't make folks angry; never run around by yourself; be careful, be careful, be careful.* All the lessons Ophie had learned over the years of her life, spoken and unspoken, came flooding back, and her stomach burned with a new kind of worry: that of losing something that mattered to her mother. If Richard fired her, Mama would be cross, but more than that she would turn that look of disappointment and sadness upon Ophie, and feeling the weight of her mother's unhappiness upon her skinny shoulders always made Ophie's belly roil.

"Oh, so formal!" Richard laughed. "Please, Ophelia, stand. The curtsies are all for my mother; I'm not so old-fashioned. Although," Richard said, tapping his chin as he thought, "we should probably have this conversation in the study."

"Yessir," Ophie said again, though she wasn't sure she wanted to be part of any conversation with Richard, no matter where it occurred.

Richard made to head out of the kitchen, and when Mama followed, the man gave her a smile. "Oh, I don't need you, Etta. You can return to your duties."

Ophie paused to see what her mama would do. She hoped for a moment that maybe she'd tell Richard that she was not about to let him take her daughter anywhere on their own. But she wasn't much surprised when Mama nodded and did as she was told.

It was a quick trip through the house to the study. They walked through the dining room, past the library, and to a room Ophie had never been into in the far back corner of the house. This part of Daffodil Manor was freezing cold, and Ophie had often heard her mother complain that the rooms seemed to keep a chill even with a fire roaring in the hearth. So it wasn't much of a surprise when Ophie entered the study behind Richard and found the room to be icy.

What was a bit more shocking was the ghost of a man seated behind the desk, deeply engrossed in some business only he could know.

Ophie paused in the doorway. Although she had seen the sad colored boy a number of times, and Clara twice, this ghost was new. He must not travel through the house like the other two, she thought.

The ghost glanced up at Ophie and frowned. He was white, with an impressive gray mustache that wrapped around his face to make a curious sort of beard. He wore a monocle, which Ophie had only ever seen once before; the ticket clerk in Atlanta had worn one when she and her mama booked passage north. But while that man's clothes had been normal, the man at the desk seemed to be dressed in some kind of old-fashioned brown suit.

"I am extremely busy. Explain this interruption," the ghost said, speaking directly to Ophie. She opened her mouth to answer the haint, but then Richard sat right on the ghost, shivering as he did so.

"This blasted room is always so cold," he said, his smile disappearing into a scowl.

"Do you want me to start a fire?" Ophie asked. The

ghost had disappeared when Richard sat in the chair, and now that she was no longer distracted she was better able to focus on the matter at hand: Richard and his mysterious conversation.

"No, that's not necessary," he said, waving away the suggestion. "This won't take long. Ophelia, I want to ask you what happened with my mother. You were the only one in the room with her yesterday."

Ophie's heart picked up an erratic rhythm, and her palms began to sweat. She swallowed thickly. She couldn't tell Richard the truth, that she'd been talking to Clara, a *ghost*, and then had told his mother that she was talking to a dead woman. That would be enough to get her kicked out of Daffodil Manor for lying, even if it was the truth.

For the most part, Ophie hated lying. She didn't like it when people did it to her, and she'd learned early on that it was better to come clean and take her punishment than lie and get punished twice. Because the thing about lies was that they always gave way to the truth, sooner or later. But since seeing the dead, Ophie had been lying a lot more often, and it was starting to get so that the truth was so unbelievable that fibbing seemed more honest in a way. Any time Ophie thought about that fact too hard her brain started to hurt from the twisting logic of it all, but in that moment, standing in front of Richard, she knew telling a lie was the only possible choice.

"Ophelia?" Richard said, and Ophie realized that she'd been tangled up in her thoughts too long.

"Yessir, I was the only one there with the missus all day, until the doctor came. Oh, and my mama came in to help when the missus began to have her fit," Ophie said, trying to avoid the question.

"Yes, I got that from your mother and Cook. My question is what caused the fit in the first place." Richard gave Ophie a patient smile, but she could see that he would lose his patience soon if she didn't answer him.

"I found a magazine, tucked in with the books the missus likes to read," Ophie said, speaking slowly so that she could see how each word landed. "It was called *True Romances*, and someone had written *Clara* on the inside. I asked who Clara was, and the missus said some things that didn't make any sense before having her fit."

Richard's eyes widened slightly, and then he fell back against his chair, all the menace and tension draining away from him, and in that moment, Ophie was relieved. It was like the time she'd been in her hidey-hole back in Georgia and saw a snake sunning itself only to watch it uncurl. For several heartbeats she'd been terrified it would head toward her, but in the end it had gone off the opposite way into the woods. She knew that even if Richard smiled all the time and spoke to the staff kindly, he could wreak just as much havoc on their small lives as his mother could, if Ophie were to upset him.

"Ophelia, thank you for your honesty," Richard said, taking a deep breath and letting it out.

"Begging your pardon, sir, but was Clara your sister? Or your cousin?" Ophie asked. Even as she knew that she should just leave well enough alone, get out of the conversation and avoid Clara and the rest of the Daffodil Manor ghosts from then on like Aunt Rose had advised . . . well, she couldn't help but feel the prickle of curiosity. There was a story here, and she wanted to know what it was. Besides, there was no way Richard could know that she knew Clara was dead, and so her question was innocent enough.

"No, Clara was not kin," he said softly. "She was someone I cared for very, very much."

"What happened to her?" Ophie asked, captivated by the naked anguish on Richard's face.

"She's gone," he said, sitting up in his chair, his spine going ramrod straight. "And we will not be speaking of her anymore. Just know that this is a sore subject with my mother, who loved her deeply and was sorely hurt by her departure, so I'd appreciate it if you'd refrain from mentioning her again."

Ophie registered the change in Richard's demeanor immediately, and she bobbed a curtsy even though Richard had said it was unnecessary. Ophie, unsurprisingly, trusted her mama's advice more than his.

"Is that all, sir?" Ophie asked as she straightened.

"Yes, Ophelia, that is all. And again, I thank you for your honesty. I know that it does not always come easy for you."

Ophie nodded and left, and returned to the kitchen to wash the dishes from Mrs. Caruthers's tray. But as she walked through the house she thought again and again of Richard's words, and his assertion that he knew honesty did not come easy for her. Had he meant Ophie in particular, who he'd spoken to only twice, or colored folks in general?

As Ophie arrived back in the empty kitchen, she started to think that perhaps she had misunderstood the intricacies of life for the hired help of Daffodil Manor. There were the regular set of whispered rules that governed the lives of colored people when they were around white folks, but there was also another set of rules between the domestics, as Cook liked to call them, and the people they worked for. The question was, where did one end and the other begin?

She couldn't shake the feeling that untangling the truth around what had happened to Clara was important. She had been thinking about what she knew of the beautiful woman, and given that her ghost still looked young and had that eerie scarf of blood trailing from her neck, Ophie had begun to suspect that Clara had been killed. Perhaps it was murder, perhaps it was an accident, but either way, there was a story there, and it linked directly the two people who had the most power over Ophie's life: Mrs. Caruthers and Richard Caruthers.

Daddy, rest his soul, had always said, "Forewarned is forearmed." Ophie had not really understood the saying before, but now she did. Hadn't the warning from Daddy's spirit saved her and Mama from a terrible fate the night he was killed? Perhaps if he had known what those men in town were capable of, he never would have done something so dangerous as vote. And if someone in Daffodil Manor had had something to do with Clara's death, Ophie felt certain she and her mama would be better off knowing that truth.

What she would do with it once she discovered it, well, that she did not quite know.

Chapter 9

MRS. CARUTHERS DID NOT DIE. HOURS TURNED TO days, and the days to a whole week, and the woman lived on. In fact, not only did she not get worse, but she did get better, in more ways than one. The effects of the laudanum felt to Ophie like something almost magical: the old woman became not just agreeable, but friendly, her demeanor and her words soft whenever Ophie had to fetch her anything. She even praised her once, murmuring sleepily, "You are such a helpful girl, Ophelia." It was both surprising and annoying. Ophie didn't want to feel sorry for Mrs. Caruthers, but sometimes she did. It was hard to hate a fragile old lady, even one so vile.

And as things returned to a semblance of normalcy, Ophie began to wonder more and more about the life and death of the mysterious Clara. If she wasn't one of the Carutherses, as Richard had said, who was she? A friend, or a guest? She couldn't ask Richard or Mrs. Caruthers about the dead girl; she had half considered asking Cook about Clara, because the older woman had been with the Carutherses for over four decades and might know who she was, but she didn't want to be scolded again about snooping in the business of others. Ophie couldn't help feeling, however, that it was desperately unfair, someone so kind and lovely being killed and everyone refusing to talk about her, forgetting her, even. How could they put someone they'd cared for aside so easily? Plus, it was a big deal when people got murdered, if that's what had happened to Clara—at least, it was a big deal in the detective magazines Ophie had started reading. They weren't her favorite, but if Ophie was going to take up her own investigation it was best to be prepared, so she relied on the professionals.

Every detective story started with the private eye or police detective taking a case, and Ophie already had that: What had happened to Clara? How was she killed, and did it happen in Daffodil Manor? Ophie felt like it probably had, or that whatever unfinished business Clara had was in the house, because even though haints could travel as they pleased, she had decided to set up in the old manor. There had to be a reason for it. Ophie could not imagine such a vibrant spirit wanting to remain in such a dreary old house otherwise.

If she couldn't ask any living person at the manor about Clara, there was another option for Ophie, of course. *The ghosts.* And one ghost in particular would surely know what had happened to Clara: Clara herself. All she had to do was find her again.

This was how Ophie came to know how well and truly haunted Daffodil Manor really was.

The day after her conversation with Richard, Ophie began her investigation in earnest. Outside, a spring storm raged, and Cook had set out candles for when the electricity inevitably went—the lights were already flickering in an eerie and unsettling manner. Mama looked at the storm and scowled. "Here's hoping this clears up before it's time to head back to Rose's," she murmured. Even though Cook had offered many more times for Ophie and Mama to stay in one of the rooms in the empty servants' quarters, Mama continued to refuse. Ophie was glad; she didn't want to stay in the chilly old house any longer than necessary, either.

As Ophie began her search for Clara—the ghost had to be *somewhere*, even dead people couldn't just be *nowhere*—she found the occasion to venture into the unused portion of the manor she'd spied before but never explored. With Mrs. Caruthers sedated for much of the day, Ophie was free from spending so much time stepping and fetching for her. This was her chance.

Most of the house was shut up, the furniture draped with heavy white cloths to keep the worst of the dust off, the skittering sound of mice echoing hollowly whenever Ophie opened a door. There was an entire wing in disuse, and marvelous bedrooms that were nearly of a size with all of Aunt Rose's downstairs. There was even a massive and chilly attic, though it gave Ophie such a sense of foreboding that she abandoned it completely. Clara's presence felt warm and joyous. If there was a spirit occupying the attic, it was cold and angry, and the incident with the haint on the trolley was still fresh in Ophie's mind.

No, she would avoid the attic altogether. For now.

But that left nearly twenty other rooms for Ophie to explore, and the more she looked, the more ghosts she found. In an unused upstairs bedroom, she found a man in an army uniform crying and drinking from a bottle that never emptied. He must have been one of Mrs. Caruthers's lost sons Cook had mentioned. Ophie watched him sob brokenly for a moment before feeling guilty about intruding and closing the door with a soft click.

In the hallway, near a bank of windows, a pretty maid washed the glass squares before falling forward into nothing. After a few heartbeats she reappeared, as though she was determined to stay until each and every last windowpane sparkled.

In the library, Ophie discovered a finely dressed white man speaking with an unseen partner about the rights of the African. His garb placed him from at least the previous century, and as he argued with whomever it was only he could see, he began to flicker, and before long, he was completely gone. But that didn't mean Ophie was alone: a little girl with pale blond braids and a pinafore sat curled up in a wing chair, reading a book. When Ophie approached her, the girl's eyes went impossibly wide, and she too disappeared.

In the study, Ophie once again found the man sitting at the desk, still murmuring about accounts and shipping fees. This time when he saw Ophie, he waved her away. "I've no time for your games now, Isabel," he said. "And your mother doesn't want you climbing that tree, so mind your nanny." Ophie closed the door without a word, wondering who Isabel was. There was a story there . . . but not the one she was looking for.

In the dining room, a grandly dressed woman sat at the head of the table and laughed until she began to wheeze. Her outline was a pale blue, so Ophie decided to approach her and see if she knew where to find Clara. It seemed that ghosts should know one another, like roommates sharing a house. And this woman was the first spirit that was dressed up, wearing a fancy hat filled with feathers and sparkles and a dress that looked similar to Clara's, a brilliant shade of peacock blue.

"Excuse me—" Ophie said, but she got no further than that. The woman looked at her and then grabbed for her throat, as if she was choking to death. She stood and stumbled a few steps before she collapsed onto the floor, making horrible retching noises, convulsing violently before falling still. Ophie gasped and recoiled, but a few heartbeats later, the ghost disappeared and immediately reappeared right where she'd been, laughing and chatting in the seat at the head of the table.

Ophie was so rattled after witnessing this that she decided to give up her search for the rest of the day. Seeing the Daffodil Manor ghosts had given Ophie more questions about haints than anything else. She had to talk to Aunt Rose. She'd pick up her investigation again after that.

Ophie completed the rest of her afternoon tasks, which were few, and sat with Mrs. Caruthers until it was time to leave. She slept heavily, and when she did wake, it was only to have a dreamy chat with Ophie that the elderly woman would likely not recall later. It was strange to see this version of Mrs. Caruthers. If Ophie had met this old woman her first day at Daffodil

Manor, she would have had a much less stressful day.

That's when a roil of thunder shook the house, and Mrs. Caruthers startled awake. "What? Clara, what was that?" she murmured. Ophie stood and walked over to the bed.

"Ma'am?" she asked, her heart pounding.

"Where's Clara? Fetch Clara and tell her to bring my tea, just the way I like it. She's been gone too long, and I won't tolerate any more tardiness from any maid, not even her," Mrs. Caruthers said. Her eyes were only partially open, so that Ophie could not truly tell if she were asleep or awake. But Ophie was far more interested in what Mrs. Caruthers had just said.

Clara had been a maid, just like Ophie? It didn't seem possible. How could someone who worked at Daffodil Manor be so glamorous, so beautiful? Was that why Mrs. Caruthers didn't like having a colored maid, because she wanted the white maid she'd had once upon a time?

"Mrs. Caruthers?" Ophie asked again, afraid she'd fall back asleep before saying anything else. She didn't want to risk waking the old woman fully and inciting her anger, but Ophie desperately needed to know more about Clara, and this might be her only opportunity.

"Oh, Clara," the old woman said, despair dripping off of every word. "I should have warned you about him. You should have known better. My dear, sweet Clara."

"Ophelia, is everything fine here?"

Ophie turned to see Cook in the doorway. Since Mrs. Caruthers's fit, Ophie had taken to leaving it open; the old woman couldn't complain of an imaginary draft when she was sleeping most of the time. Cook's gaze went from Ophie to Mrs. Caruthers, her dark brow knotted with concern.

"She was asking for someone named Clara," Ophie said, deciding to take a chance. Cook couldn't scold her for snooping when she herself could see that Ophie wasn't prying. "Do you know who she's talking about?"

"Clara? Why is she all of a sudden remembering her?" Cook wondered, walking into the room, making a clucking sound with her tongue. "Clara lived here—worked here, in fact. She arrived here after the flu epidemic and the war had taken the missus's other sons and broken her heart. Clara's mother had worked for Mrs. Caruthers's sister down in Virginia long ago, so the missus was happy to give her a position. Sweet girl. But then, she just disappeared. Right after the Virginia cousins came to visit, if I remember correctly. More than a year ago it was now. Ran off with some boy, most like. Too pretty by half, that one was." Cook's expression went sad, as though she were seeing through time back to those days, before she shook herself back to the present. "Enough gossip. I can take watching over the missus from here. Your mama is waiting downstairs for you, better get a move on before it starts raining again."

Ophie nodded and made her way downstairs, her mind crowded with the pieces of a puzzle that was turning out to be much bigger than she had thought.

Chapter 10

OPHIE WAS MORE EAGER THAN EVER TO TALK TO Aunt Rose about the ghosts of Daffodil Manor. After the revelations about Clara, Ophie needed guidance from someone who knew the dead better than she did. But Ophie was hard-pressed to get her aunt's attention that evening. After months of living with the old woman, the cousins had seemed to decide that Aunt Rose was suddenly worth their time. Ophie suspected this was not a coincidence. After all, if it was something that they thought brought Ophie joy, then they wanted to have it as well.

Every time Ophie tried to get a moment alone with her great-aunt there the cousins were, telling a funny story about school, or asking to help with dinner, or just being a general nuisance. Soon enough, it was time for bed and Ophie's questions were still a hot coal, burning quietly in her brain.

As her mother snored softly beside her, Ophie tried to put her worries and wonders aside. The ghosts of Daffodil Manor weren't going anywhere, and neither was she as long as Mrs. Caruthers was taking her medicine. But it didn't matter. She couldn't sleep. Every time she closed her eyes, she saw ghosts. And not just Clara, but the gruff old man with the funny mustache, and the sad-eyed boy with the bleeding back, too. She couldn't help but wonder why all of them were still there, roaming around the big house, lonely and lost. Aunt Rose had said that the reason she and Ophie and all the other women in their family saw the dead was because they were the only ones who could help them with passing on. That ghosts could linger, draining spaces of their life if they weren't taken care of. And so, if taking care of Daffodil Manor was Ophie's job, maybe it was up to her to help the ghosts there to pass on? Not that Ophie was one to chase after more chores, but this seemed different than carrying trays and making sure Mrs. Caruthers's room was as warm as August. Talking to the dead felt *important*. It was something no one besides Aunt Rose and Ophie could do. Didn't that mean they should help as many haints as they could?

Clearly not all ghosts were angry and vengeful, and Ophie couldn't imagine it was their fault that they lingered. And she just kept imagining what would have happened that night back in Georgia if she hadn't seen her daddy, if she hadn't heeded his warning. What other good could come of talking to the dead? Especially if she was careful, and always kept her salt and nail handy. . . .

Ophie tossed and turned and finally gave up on trying to sleep. She had to talk to Aunt Rose. Mama was snoring fitfully in the bed now, and so Ophie slowly pushed the covers aside, put on her slippers, and tiptoed out into the hall. Downstairs, the radio played and the sound of footsteps crossing the room and then retracing their path echoed up the stairwell. Helen was up again, waiting for her husband.

A light flickered under Aunt Rose's door, and Ophie knocked lightly. There was a soft "come in," so Ophie opened the door.

This was the first time Ophie had ever been in here. The family left this one room for Aunt Rose alone; even the cousins, in all their audacity, would not cross the threshold uninvited. But Ophie had been invited, and the first thing she noticed was that, like the rest of the house, Aunt Rose's room reflected the elderly woman's personality. Lace doilies covered everything, and the furniture was handmade in a style that favored curving lines and dark woods. Her great-aunt had her hair wrapped up for the night, a silk scarf with roses covering her head, and she sat in bed with a short nub of pencil, puzzling out one of the word games in the newspaper.

As Ophie stood just inside the doorway, a fit of unease seized her. It felt especially strange to intrude on her great-aunt in such a vulnerable moment, just a smallish lump under a mountain of blankets, only an old kerosene lantern to keep her company. Even with her cane, Aunt Rose always seemed fierce and unbowed, and seeing her like this, small and frail, reminded Ophie that her aunt was a very old woman, maybe even older than Mrs. Caruthers.

"Ophelia! You should be asleep, girl. What's got you lurking about this time of night? Did you have a nightmare?"

Ophie took a deep breath. "No, ma'am. I wanted to ask you a question. About haints. But I haven't been able to talk to you because of the cousins." Ophie snapped her mouth shut before she could say anything else. Mama always said if a body couldn't say anything nice it was best just to keep quiet.

"Ahh, yes, those girls have been very interested in spending time with me of late." Aunt's Rose's lips twisted in a smile, and she tapped the space on the bed beside her. "Come jump under the quilt, child, before you catch cold."

Ophie hustled across the threadbare rug that did nothing to keep the chill out of the wood and climbed in next to Aunt Rose. Once she was tucked into the warm bed, Aunt Rose patted her on the leg. "So, what seems to be vexing you?"

"Why do some places have lots of ghosts, and others don't have any?" Ophie began. She'd thought long and hard about the best way to bring up the matter of Clara, because it wasn't like she could just come out and tell Aunt Rose she wanted to learn more about her, even help her. The old woman would probably just tell her to ignore and avoid all the ghosts she had seen. Her great-aunt had already warned her away from interacting with the spirits, after all, and the incident on the trolley had been a harsh lesson besides. Ghosts were dangerous, Ophie understood that. But like it or not, there were many ghosts in Daffodil Manor, and she couldn't just avoid them forever. And there was so much that Ophie didn't know that any information would be valuable.

"Well," Aunt Rose said, taking a deep breath and letting it out on a sigh, "some places, it's because that's where folks died, and most ghosts, especially if they died in a bad kind of way, can't seem to get themselves unstuck. People are like that, you know, living or dead. A bad thing happens, and they get bogged down in it, unable to move on."

Aunt Rose paused as she mulled over her next words, and Ophie's heart seized painfully, guiltily.

"Is that bad, to remember?" Ophie asked, voice low, sudden tears clogging her throat and making her voice froggy. Because Ophie wanted to remember, she wanted to spend quiet moments thinking about the good times when Daddy was alive. She wanted to keep living in those warm, happy moments.

"No, honey, it isn't. But folks have got to move on as well, or else they can just get trapped in a moment, unable to do what they must. To live."

Ophie thought about Mama, refusing to even talk about what happened in Georgia, telling everyone that her husband was gone when they asked. Not dead, not murdered by some local boys who thought he'd gotten too uppity—just "gone," as if one day he'd up and disappeared. It made Ophie feel some kind of way whenever her mama said it, like they weren't even allowed to remember Daddy, like he'd been erased from their world. Hadn't she just stopped living when he'd died? It seemed that way to Ophie, like all Mama's good memories had burned down with the house.

But Ophie didn't think Aunt Rose was talking about Mama. Ignoring a terrible pain just seemed like a different way of getting stuck.

Aunt Rose cleared her throat and continued. "I think some places just have more emotions attached to them, and they draw haints to them, like ants going for the sugar bowl. Ghosts are attracted to feelings—sadness and happiness and all the others betwixt and between. They can't feel like you and I can, so sometimes they cling to the emotions of all the living folks around them, so they can remember." Aunt Rose took a deep breath, and her gaze went looking off into the distance at something Ophie could not see. "I went to a carnival once, when I was not much older then you, and there were so many haints twisted in and amongst the living that I told my friends I was ill and ran home."

Ophie nodded. That made sense, and explained why there were so many ghosts in Daffodil Manor. The house was big and had been there for a very long time, so lots of people had probably died there. Plus, she'd never met anyone as mean as Mrs. Caruthers, so it made sense that all those unhappy ghosts would stick close to her. The old woman had to be angry about something to want to make everyone around her unhappy as well. Back in Georgia, the pastor's wife once talked about sin as a heavy burden that folks carried around: "When you carry that sin around, when you let it weigh you down, you want to make sure that everyone around you is suffering as well. You lash out, you say hurtful things that you later regret. So give that sin away, let Jesus take it and hold that burden so that you can carry on as a light in this world."

Ophie wondered what Mrs. Caruthers was carrying around that weighed so heavily on her soul. Ophie thought of the boy with the welts on his back. How had he come to be at Daffodil Manor? Did he have something to do with Mrs. Caruthers? Or, perhaps it wasn't a sin at all, but something else. Maybe she had lost someone dear to her—Clara?—and instead of putting it aside like Mama, she carried that hurt and anger around with her like a sin. *That* might cause so many spirits to want to be close to the old woman.

"Can a *person* be haunted?" Ophie asked.

"Oh, folks most definitely can be haunted. That's why I told you to carry around salt and an iron nail. You don't want haints sticking to you. If they do, you'd get a chill and take ill, because the haint would slowly begin to sap your strength."

That *definitely* sounded like Mrs. Caruthers. Ophie chewed her lip, trying to think of a way to ask her next question, the one that was closest to what she really wanted to ask about. She turned the possibility of it over and around in her head and finally decided there was no other way to say it than to just ask.

"Are there good ghosts, Aunt Rose? Are there haints and spirits that aren't bad? Like how there are good and bad people?"

Aunt Rose didn't answer at first. She considered Ophie for a moment, then said, "Child, what are you mixed up in?"

Ophie blinked. "Nothing, Aunt Rose, I swear it. I just meant . . . like your husband? The ghost in the backyard? He was a good person, right?"

Ophie realized then that she'd made a mistake. The elderly woman's expression was hard in a way Ophie had never seen, not even the time she'd yelled at the cousins for tracking mud through the house. Her brows drew together and her lips thinned into a nearly invisible line.

"You have to understand that ghosts are *not* people," she said, quiet and intense. "They are a shadow of who they were in life. Some might say the worst part. They are all hunger and want and need, and a creature made of nothing but selfish parts can't be good. They aren't bad, exactly, any more than, say, a mosquito is. Haints can't help what they are. They crave something, and that longing keeps them from moving on. And like a starving man, they will do whatever they can to get whatever it is they need. That isn't good or bad, it just is."

Aunt Rose sat up a little straighter in bed and took Ophie's hand. "Look at me, Ophelia." Ophie did as her aunt said, meeting the elderly woman's eyes in the dimly lit room, the kerosene lantern making the shadows behind her jump and dance so that the moment felt infinitely more ominous than it was. "The dead don't care about you, because they can't. They can only care about themselves. Do not ever trust a haint. I warned you to stay away from ghosts, but now I can see that was foolish of me. This city has far too many people and far too much death for you to completely avoid the spirits. So let me tell you this instead: Ignore the dead, Ophelia. Do not talk to them, do not let them catch you staring. Because if they figure out you can help them they will do whatever it takes to get what they want, even if it means hurting you. And that salt and iron might keep you safe for a while, but if a haint is determined, even those protections won't stop them. You hear me, girl?"

Ophie nodded. Her heart pounded so loudly that she could hear it in her ears. Aunt Rose wanted her to be afraid, and Ophie was a little bit scared. But she also knew that Aunt Rose hadn't talked about her husband, even though Ophie had asked. Maybe something had happened with him, something that made her sad and distrusting of haints. And Aunt Rose didn't know Clara. She was the only person in Daffodil Manor who had tried to help Ophie. Cook was too busy, and Mama had her own tasks; Mrs. Caruthers was too mean, and her sly, handsome son was never around. It was Clara who had helped Ophie learn how to keep Mrs. Caruthers happy enough to keep her on, who had been kind to her when she caught her with the magazine, who had even apologized when Ophie discovered what she was. How could she be bad, even if she was dead?

However, Ophie was not about to back-talk Aunt Rose, because she knew better. So instead, she just nodded and gave her great-aunt a chaste kiss on the cheek. "Thank you, Aunt Rose," she said, climbing out of the warm bed, the chill of the room biting at her bare legs.

"Good night, Ophelia. I promise, there will come a time when your Aunt Sarah and I will teach you more about handling haints. For now, please, for the love of all, leave those ghosts be."

Ophie said nothing as she let herself out of the room. She had no intention of leaving anything be.

Daffodil Manor

THE DEAD WERE RESTLESS.

Usually, the ghosts of the house remained in their own, separate spaces. They did not appear often, and when they did, they went about their own business, trapped in a cycle of behavior only they understood.

But Ophie's presence had stirred up a kind of nervous energy amongst the departed, and as they woke from their half sleep some of them began to do something they had not done in a very, very long time.

They began to ask questions.

Mr. Caruthers no longer tried to balance his bank sheets; instead he stared out the study window and murmured about climbing a tree. How long had he been working? Days? Years? "I should've gone out with the children more," the ghost muttered to himself.

In the library, a little girl stared at the doorway, waiting for her papa. She was supposed to sit and read until he came to fetch her, but she was beginning to think perhaps she had waited too long and she should venture out on her own.

Across the room from her, a man forgot what he was arguing about, why he was even arguing. How long had he been trapped, yelling with unseen friends about the state of the nation and preserving the Union? Perhaps it was time to let the matter drop.

In the dining room, the endless dinner party finally stopped, and the ghost at the end of the table stood up and stared into the fireplace as if seeing her surroundings for the first time in half a century.

And the maid in the attic stretched her phantom limbs and began to plot.

Chapter 11

THE NEXT MORNING, OPHIE WOKE GROGGY AND out of sorts. She hadn't had enough sleep, and when she stumbled outside after her mother, it was to find that the sun was already up. The light was warm, promising more temperate weather in the near future, but even the sight of robins scrabbling for worms couldn't brighten Ophie's mood. She rode the trolley with her mother sullenly, her eyes hooded as she watched the crying girl ghost next to the chatty old colored woman. Ophie was half tempted to tell the girl that her mother thought she was on a grand adventure and was having too much fun to send word. But what good would that do?

Besides, Ophie was preoccupied with her own thoughts. After Mrs. Caruthers's dose of laudanum the day before, there hadn't been much left in the bottle; soon enough, Ophie's days would be cluttered once more with stepping and fetching for the old woman. She hadn't had any luck finding Clara, but she'd found a bunch of other ghosts, and she reckoned that one of them might know where Clara was.

Aunt Rose had said that ghosts stuck around because they wanted something; maybe if Ophie helped them get what they needed, they could help her find Clara. *I don't have to trust them in order to help them*, she thought, *and I have my salt and nail*. And so, once Mrs. Caruthers had her lunch, Ophie returned the tray to the kitchen and then made her way quietly to the study, where the very busy ghost resided.

The room was still icy cold despite the bright spring sunshine that streamed in through the window. Dust motes danced in the light, the brightness setting off the dark, heavy wooden desk that dominated the room. Books cluttered the shelves, but they were so covered in dust that when Ophie tried to pull one down to check the title, she had a sneezing fit. The very fancy oriental rug covering the wooden floor and the slate flagstones of the hearth only served to make the room seem even more imposing. Ophie could understand why Richard found this room dull. It had obviously been decorated by someone with very little joy in their life.

Like the ghost who sat behind the desk, grumbling to himself.

Ophie was once again struck by the man's size, his suit jacket straining against his massive belly. He still wore his hair in that funny style, his mustache seeming to curl up into his sideburns. Every now and again he would lift his monocle to his eye and grumble about something. Today his complaints were about the cost of imports; last time she'd seen him his bluster had been about the business cost of the war in Europe. Either way, the man seemed to have been dead for a long time.

"Excuse me," Ophie said, her voice small and weak. She cleared her throat, stood up straight, and tried again. "Excuse me, sir, do you have a moment?"

It was a silly question. The man was dead. He had all the time in the world. But maybe he didn't think that way, because he looked up from his invisible paperwork and his gaze settled on Ophie. "You again."

Ophie blinked. He remembered her. It surprised her, because the man had seemed to be stuck in a sort of time loop, living the same moment over and over. But then, Clara had apologized for being new at being a ghost. That had to mean she had some concept of time, of what was happening around her.

Ophie realized that the man was waiting for her to

answer him, and so she nodded. "Yes. I work here."

"Well, that is spectacular. Now, I am afraid I must get back to my work. These southern accounts are bleeding me dry. This business is nothing like when my father ran it. . . ." He trailed off as he made a notation on an invisible document.

Ophie shifted her weight from one foot to the other. She had thought that she could offer the man something in exchange for information, but it seemed that all he cared about was his work in front of him, which Ophie couldn't even see. She took a deep breath. "Yes, sir, one more thing. I was wondering if maybe you could help me out. See, I'm looking for someone—"

"My dear, I'm afraid I cannot help you. I am very, very busy, child. You should go ask that diva causing a scene in the dining room, she seems the sort for gossip."

Before Ophie could try another tactic, the ghost disappeared completely, ending the conversation. It seemed a bit rude, but there was little Ophie could do about it. The man was gone.

She left the study and headed toward the library. She didn't care for the ghost in the dining room, and she thought maybe she could try a different one first. But the haints there were skittish and faded away before Ophie could even ask them anything. The little girl in the wing chair was gone before she could even get a word out; the man who argued with another unseen man turned toward her and dissipated the moment he saw her, dashing Ophie's hopes and leaving her frustrated enough to stomp her foot. She was going to have to talk to the fancy lady ghost after all.

Ophie trudged toward the dining room. She heard the ghost before she even entered. She was howling with laughter, an ugly kind of humor, the sort that comes from making fun of another person. Ophie knew that sound well: it was the way her cousins laughed when they'd landed a particularly sharp barb.

"I swear," the woman exclaimed as Ophie slipped inside of the dining room, "Agnes Riley would not know a well-cut seam if it hit her upside the head. Did you see that monstrosity she wore to the Callahan ball? Simply horrid!"

"Pardon me, ma'am, have you seen someone named Clara?" Ophie asked all at once, not bothering to introduce herself. This was the ghost who always died violently before reappearing at her place at the table, and Ophie worried that she did not have time for much conversation before the woman choked. A not-so-tiny part of Ophie was hoping that she could get an answer to her question and get out of the dining room before the whole production started.

But the woman simply adjusted her fancy hat and ignored Ophie, as though Ophie were the ghost and not the other way around.

"Excuse me—"

"Child, I am in the middle of a story," the woman shrieked, rounding on Ophie with comically wide eyes. Ophie took half a step back before squaring her shoulders. The salt and iron were heavy in her apron pocket, but she didn't reach for them. This haint couldn't hurt her. Besides, this ghost did not seem like a very nice person at all, and Ophie was getting awfully tired of dealing with rude people.

"You aren't telling a story, you're gossiping, which is mean and ugly besides. I'm looking for Clara. Do you know her?"

"I do not keep track of lowly maids! Do you know who I am?" the ghost howled. She stood up at that, her dinner party quite forgotten.

"You aren't anybody anymore," Ophie said, frustration and annoyance igniting her temper.

She had never spoken to a white person this way before; Mama would have a fit if she could hear her. But who was the ghost going to tell?

"You're dead! Just like almost everyone else in this house. No one cares about you because they can't even see you."

That's when the woman's mouth began to work, and she clutched for her throat, and Ophie, who really did not want to witness the whole scene again, spun on her heel and stomped out of the dining room.

Ophie clomped over to the wide staircase that led to the second floor and plopped down on the bottom step. Angry tears pricked her eyes, and she dashed them away with the back of her hand. Aunt Rose had been right. Nothing good had come of talking to these stupid Daffodil Manor ghosts. They were selfish and awful, and they deserved to be stuck in limbo. All Ophie had wanted was to help them and find Clara, who was nothing like they were. And here she was, with no idea where Clara was, not having helped anyone. Maybe some haints just didn't get to move on. Maybe the people who were too terrible for Heaven got stuck on earth with all the living folks, everyone just making each other unhappy forever and ever.

For the first time in a while, Ophie let herself linger in the memory of the night her daddy died. Whenever the memory would arise she would usually squeeze her eyes shut and think of something else, anything else. Singing hymns, reciting jump rope songs, anything to keep her mind off the fear and awfulness of that night. Happy memories were okay, but that last terrible night? She'd convinced herself that there was no reason to let her thoughts linger there.

But as Ophie thought about it and replayed the sight of her daddy standing at the end of her bed and how he later faded into sparkles, she started to feel a little bit better. Because at least he wasn't stuck somewhere in Georgia, walking around playing at being alive.

"She's in the attic, you know."

Ophie scrubbed away her tears and looked up to find the little boy with the injured back standing before her. His appearance unsettled Ophie, but it wasn't because he wore no shirt or shoes or even that he was grievously injured. It was because he was the only colored ghost in the manor, and he was also the saddest. There were a lot of terrible ways to die, and even if Ophie didn't know what all of them were, she had a feeling this boy knew at least one.

"What happened to you?" Ophie asked.

The boy shrugged. "I tried to run away. They found me. Now I can never leave."

"Why can't you, you know, move on?" Ophie asked. "Is there something you want? Can I help you?" Ophie realized that she desperately wanted to help the boy in that moment, to offer him something to remove the sorrow from his eyes.

The boy shrugged. "Ain't nothing I want. Not that you can give me, anyway. Can you keep Henry safe?"

Ophie bit her lip, a sharp pain lodging under her ribs and stealing her breath. Mr. Henry? He was an old man, and this boy was just a kid like Ophie. How could he keep Mr. Henry safe? How could she? Aunt Rose had said all ghosts want something, but what was Ophie to do with the ones who wanted something impossible?

The boy confused Ophie and gave her a peculiar sensation, as though she had more in common with him than anyone else in all of Daffodil Manor, even Clara. He was dead, and yet so close to life that Ophie could talk as if he were there with her. In another life, she could have been him—a ghost trapped in a terrible place. She knew why those men in Georgia had killed her daddy, even if everyone pretended she was still a baby and couldn't understand. She knew that even in Pittsburgh, it was dangerous to go into the Polish or Irish neighborhoods because bad things happened to colored people, especially girls. All the unspoken rules that Ophie and her kin abided by in order to stay safe, this sad boy was a stark reminder that every single one existed because colored folks had once been property, and that some people still saw them as nothing more than that.

"I'm Ophie," she said at last. She might not be able to give him what he wanted, but she could be his friend.

Did the dead need company? It seemed like the answer to that question was yes.

"I'm Colin," the boy said, before darting a glance up the stairs. "Be careful, Ophie. This house is even more dangerous than it looks."

With that, Colin evaporated into the air. This time, it didn't seem nearly as rude as when the other ghosts had.

Ophie took a deep breath, straightened her skirts, and then headed up in the direction Colin had indicated. Except she wasn't going up to Mrs. Caruthers's room.

She was going to the one place she wanted to go even less than that.

Chapter 12

THE ATTIC COMPRISED THE ENTIRE THIRD FLOOR, the floor above where the family lived in Daffodil Manor. The doorway to the stairs was on the second floor at the end of a long hallway in the vacant western wing, the door itself narrower than the rest and the knob rusted from disuse. During her initial search for Clara, Ophie had yanked open the door, expecting it to lead to yet another room filled with covered furniture. Instead, a skinny stairwell wended up into the gloom and the scent of dust and mold, heavier there than anywhere else in the house, had seeped out from the darkness. That day she had felt a deep sense of foreboding, an indescribable wrongness that had nothing to do with the way the walls pressed in against the steps upward into the dark room above. Nor was it tied to the small sounds of scurrying rodents that echoed down to where she had stood at the bottom of the stairs. It had everything to do with the certainty that something bad had happened in that attic. At the time, she'd still had so much of the house to search that it had been but a small matter to close the door and slip away to another part.

But today, the attic was the only place she hadn't checked in which she'd felt a ghostly presence. So, to the attic Ophie went.

Before walking to the hidden staircase, Ophie stopped to check on Mrs. Caruthers. Even though spring sunshine peeked around the closed curtains, there was still a fire in the fireplace. Ophie tiptoed into the room and peered at Mrs. Caruthers, who snored as she slept. The doctor's tincture was still doing its job. Ophie added another log to the fire, waited to make sure it caught, and then took a deep breath and made her way down the hall.

The door to the attic was just as Ophie remembered it, narrow and ancient, covered in dusty white paint. Ophie twisted the crystal knob. It squeaked mournfully, but the door opened and the same rush of musty, cool air greeted Ophie. She took a deep breath and climbed the steps.

There was no electricity in this part of the house, but light filtered in from outside through a bank of windows, cutting bright lines through the gloom. Ophie's eyes quickly adjusted, and she took in the contents of the attic.

It was packed with all kinds of treasure.

Ever since she'd come to Daffodil Manor, Ophie had been silently cataloging the differences between rich white folks like the Carutherses and poor colored folks like her and her mama, and this was perhaps the biggest difference yet. It was an entire room filled with unwanted things, generations of castoffs and set-asides. The attic was huge, and the more Ophie explored, the brighter the small fire of jealousy in her heart grew. There were wardrobes stuffed to bursting with fashions years out of date and dressers full of children's clothes. There were entire boxes of the detective magazines Ophie had found stashed throughout the library, dusty but otherwise pristine. She even found an illustrated copy of *Grimm's Fairy Tales* with brightly colored pictures of pale princes and princesses that she put aside to take downstairs for later. There was an old wooden rocking horse, the paint faded and covered in a thin layer of grime, and a jack-in-the-box that played a discordant harmony when Ophie turned the handle before sending a mournful clown up and out of the box, bouncing wildly.

But no matter where Ophie looked in the attic, she did not see Clara, or any other ghosts for that matter.

If Clara was here, she was hiding. And Ophie had the feeling that a ghost who didn't want to be found, wouldn't. Haints seemed to have their own minds and agendas, despite what Aunt Rose might think.

The dead were just as frustrating as the living.

"Clara, I'm not afraid of you," Ophie finally said after a long moment, standing in the middle of a patch of sunshine that filtered in through a dirt-encrusted window. "I'm . . . I'm sorry that I didn't know you were a ghost. But I really liked talking to you, and you were really helpful. I never would have been able to keep from making Mrs. Caruthers angry that first day without your help. And I know something bad happened to you. So, even if you decide to stay gone, I just want you to know that maybe I could help you. Like you helped me."

Ophie sniffled, tears pricking her eyes. It wasn't until she'd said it out loud that she realized the first person who had truly listened to her since running away from Georgia, who had even made her feel special and fun, had been a ghost. It was too much in a year filled with hard things. Ophie wasn't a bad person, she listened to her elders and helped out and did as she was told, and yet it felt like she was being punished. Here she was in a strange city living with relatives she'd never met, most of whom weren't very nice, and working in a strange and scary old house when all she wanted to do was go to school. She had nothing, and people like mean old Mrs. Caruthers had everything. It was desperately unfair.

Tears slid down Ophie's deep brown cheeks, and she buried her face in her hands, all the feelings she'd tried to keep at bay overwhelming her. It wasn't right. Her mama had gone cold and her daddy was dead and she saw ghosts everywhere she went, and even those ghosts had no time for her unless they wanted to yell at her or boss her around. All Ophie wanted was a friend, someone to share her troubles with.

"Oh, don't cry, chickadee. Please. I cannot bear it."

Ophie wiped at her face to see Clara standing a few feet away. She seemed dimmer than she had the last time Ophie had seen her. And she was dressed differently. Before when Ophie had seen her she'd been dressed like a fine lady about to go out on the town, her bob curled and styled, bright red lipstick covering her lips. But today she was plain. She wore no makeup, and while Ophie had thought she was around her mama's age, she could see now that Clara wasn't all that much older than she was, maybe nineteen or twenty. Her hair was pinned back, and she wore a plain gray dress similar to what Mama wore to work. But the scarf-like trail of blood, deep and red, still wrapped around her neck, undulating in an unseen wind, and she could see now the wound in her throat from which it ran.

"What happened?" Ophie asked. A tendril of unease curled through her, but she swallowed and pushed it down.

"I don't know," Clara whispered, running her fingers absently through the scarf. "I never know what is happening. Not anymore."

Ophie nodded. "Do you know who . . . hurt you?"

Clara looked down at the blood flowing freely from her neck and shook her head. "I can't remember. If I even knew to begin with."

Ophie shifted her weight from foot to foot. Talking about her death was probably hard for Clara, so an easier topic might be better for the moment. "You were a maid here in Daffodil Manor." It didn't come out as a question, but Clara's sad expression melted away into happiness.

"Yes! Oh, I remember that. Mean old Mrs. Caruthers. She knew my ma from way back, and when I sent up seeking a position she hired me on. Of course I didn't quite know what I was getting into. At the time I was just happy to be out of Virginia."

"What's Virginia like?" Ophie asked. Her mind was abuzz with questions, her head a hive full of curiosity. Here she was talking with a ghost as normal as talking to anyone else, except this ghost seemed to be enjoying the conversation as much as Ophie did. It was the first time in a very long time that Ophie didn't feel like an annoyance, a burden meant to be borne.

"Virginia is hot in the summer, cold in the winter, and miserable all year long," Clara laughed. "I do not miss it at all. I daresay I never stayed anywhere so fine as Daffodil Manor when I lived down there." Clara paced a little, her form flickering as she moved. For a moment Ophie was afraid the ghost would disappear just as suddenly as the other Daffodil Manor haints had a habit of doing, but when Clara rounded on Ophie she looked the tiniest bit more solid.

"What about you, Ophie? You aren't from here, not with that molasses coating your words," Clara said with a grin. No one had ever called Ophie's accent sweet, and she decided she liked just about everything about Clara, but the way she talked was her favorite by far.

"I'm from Georgia. But we had to leave because something bad happened," Ophie said. Sudden tears pricked her eyes as they always did when she thought about the terribleness of that last night, but Clara was there, laying a chilly hand on Ophie's shoulder.

"Oh, I can only imagine. Virginia was full of bad things as well. Say no more, Ophie. We shall only focus on bright happy things from here on out. After all, Mrs. Caruthers is enough of a trial for anyone," Clara said with a high bell-like laugh, and Ophie's heart took flight.

Ophie nodded and gave Clara a small smile in return. Clara was right. No more sadness. Besides, it was awfully hard to be glum when Clara was around, ghost or not.

Clara flickered again and sighed. "I'm sorry, but I don't know how much longer I can hang in here. I'm so tired now, it takes a lot out of me to appear, even more to be down there, in the house."

Ophie nodded. "It's okay. Can I—should I come back and visit you tomorrow? I could come up here to the attic so you won't get so tired. We could talk more about that story I was reading in the *True Romances* magazine, the one with the sheriff's daughter and the bootlegger."

Clara nodded and began to dissipate into nothing. "I would like that," she said, fading into the dusty attic air. Ophie was once again alone.

But, somehow, she was a little less lonely than she'd been when she climbed the stairs.

Chapter 13

OPHIE WENT TO THE ATTIC TO VISIT CLARA THE very next day while Mrs. Caruthers took her nap. She carried a bucket with a washrag and some hot water, ready to make an excuse in case anyone asked what she was about.

No one did.

Ophie climbed the stairs to the attic proper, huffing and puffing by the end. She was used to carrying weight up and down stairs by this point, but the attic stairs were much steeper than those of the grand staircase. There was still something off-putting about the attic, but if that's where Clara was, then that's where Ophie would go.

Her plan at this point wasn't much of a plan. She hoped that if she could talk to Clara, then the young woman would be able to remember more about her life and, hopefully, what—or who—had killed her. Clara had clearly died violently, which meant that either Cook didn't know that Clara was dead, or she hadn't been telling Ophie the truth when she said that Clara had run off. Richard, too, had simply said she was "gone." Did neither of them know that she was killed in Daffodil Manor? That her spirit lingered, unable to leave, never spoken of? Ophie was still worried about her and her mother spending every day in this house with all its dark secrets, but finding out what happened to Clara, maybe helping her to move on . . . it also felt like the *right thing* to do.

Daddy had often said that when presented with two choices, a hard thing and an easy thing, the right thing was usually the more difficult one. "The good Lord is always testing us, Ophie, in big ways and small. You do the thing you know to be right, always, no matter what." Mama had clucked her tongue at Daddy, but she hadn't disagreed. Now Ophie had decided that the easy thing to do would be to ignore Clara and continue on with the routine of Daffodil Manor, carrying trays and cleaning up after an angry old woman and never, ever wondering what had happened to all these sad, lonely ghosts, including her friend. The harder thing would be to put aside what Aunt Rose had told her, what Cook had told her, even what Mama would probably say if she knew about the haints and Clara's sad end, and find out the truth. Didn't Clara deserve the kind of justice so many folks never got? Someone had to find out how she had died, even share her story. Maybe that was the way to help her move on, too.

So, that was exactly what Ophie was going to do. When she thought about it that way, that talking to Clara was about justice and fairness, the bucket she heaved up the narrow staircase to the dusty, disused attic didn't seem quite so heavy.

As she did, she thought about what little plan she had. Since there were no lights up in the attic and she had the water and rags anyway, she figured she'd clean the windows. She also had a packet of Cook's short-bread cookies in her apron pocket, taken from Mrs. Caruthers's tray. Aunt Rose had said back on that first chilly night that haints love treats, so Ophie would leave some out for Clara. Maybe they would help her get the ghost's attention. And then, once Clara came out, Ophie would question her the way detectives were supposed to, gathering facts until the truth of the matter was clear.

She was not certain what she would do after that. Tell Richard and Mrs. Caruthers? Richard had said that he and his mother cared deeply for Clara. They'd want to know how she died, especially if she had been killed in their own house. That was . . . unless they had something to do with what had happened to her. The thought niggled at Ophie as she set down her bucket and began to wipe at the windows, the water sloshing a bit as she worked. Ophie couldn't imagine old Mrs. Caruthers killing anyone, especially Clara. She remembered the old woman's words when she had been half awake and mistaking Ophie for her previous caretaker: *My dear, sweet Clara.* Ophie had a feeling she knew why Mrs. Caruthers preferred Clara to the other help, with her smooth hair and pale skin. As for Richard, he was a fine, upstanding person, as Mama and Cook were always saying. Fine, upstanding people, despite a number of faults that Ophie could see, did not commit murder.

Ophie finished with the first window and was moving toward the next when she felt a chill draft. She dropped her rag in her bucket and turned to find Clara watching her. The ghost still wore a maid's uniform, and her head tilted as she studied Ophie.

"Chickadee, what on earth are you doing?"

"Washing the windows," Ophie said. "It's dark up here, and I thought you might like some sunshine."

"Well, that is the nicest thing anyone has done for me in a spell," Clara said. She walked over to a nearby dresser and boosted herself onto it, sitting atop and crossing her legs. It was such a normal thing to do, not at all like the ghosts Ophie usually saw, who just floated everywhere. Was that because she hadn't been dead very long?

"Here, I brought you these as well. Haints—that is, you, I mean. . . . You like sweets, right?"

Ophie pulled the handkerchief with the cookies out of her apron pocket and spread them out on the dresser, careful not to touch Clara. Not that she thought the ghost would mind, but it seemed rude to put her hand through someone else.

Clara's eyes lit up. "I do! When I was alive I used to go to this sweet shop all the time, not far from here. They have the best ice cream. Ah, chickadee, I wish I could take you." Clara ran her hand over the cookies, eyes closed and a smile on her face. She seemed to get a little less transparent as she touched the cookies, and Ophie nodded and went back to washing her windows.

"Ophie, you are such a hard worker." Clara sighed after watching her for a few minutes.

"I only did it so I could spend more time up here with you," Ophie said, her face heating after the words were out. "I, ah, wanted to . . . I know we were going to talk about that story, but I've been thinking. I think I might be able to help you find out what happened to you."

"What happened to me?" Clara asked, pausing in

the midst of touching the baked goods next to her. "Well, someone killed me."

"Yes," Ophie said, and hesitated. She'd assumed as much, but to hear Clara say it directly gave her a little shock. "My Aunt Rose says that the reason spirits don't pass on to the afterlife is because they've got unfinished business. I think yours is finding out who killed you, and why."

"What good would that do?" Clara asked, lips turning downward into a pout. "I'm already dead." Her form flickered, the way Daffodil Manor's electric lights did during a storm, and Ophie decided to change the subject.

"Do you remember what your life was like? Before, I mean? Not back in Virginia, but here at Daffodil Manor."

Clara brightened. "Oh, yes! The attic used to be my room, if you can believe that. Of course, it was not in such a state when I was here," she said with a high laugh. "I used to care for Mrs. Caruthers, like you do now. She could be sour as a lemon, but you say the right thing and she can turn as sweet as a bowl of cherries. And Richard." Clara sighed and leaned back. "So dreamy. He looks just like Rudolph Valentino, don't you think?"

Ophie did not know who that was, but she could

tell a story from a *True Romances* magazine when she heard it. She might be twelve, but she wasn't stupid. "Was Richard your beau?"

"Oh!" Clara exclaimed, her form becoming more solid. Her hands flew to her face as she hid a smile. "So bold, chickadee. A lady never kisses and tells."

Ophie decided to take that as a yes.

"What about Cook and Mr. Henry? Did you spend much time with them?"

Clara's expression sobered. "I'm afraid not, Ophie. It wasn't because they weren't nice people, it's just that . . ." The ghost trailed off and seemed to look at something in the distance. "You ever have a secret so big that you were afraid to be friends with folks, to let them get close? Because if they found out about that secret it could be bad for everyone?"

Sudden dread rushed through Ophie. Was Clara talking about her relationship with Richard or something completely different? For a moment Ophie found herself chilled with a bone-deep fear, and she realized it wasn't for Clara but for herself.

What would happen if people were to find out she could see the dead? What would they do, how would they react? She'd been pushed by the cousins and dismissed by Mama, but what else could happen if people knew?

Could she end up like Daddy?

"Yes," Ophie said, her fear coloring her voice. "I know what it's like to have a secret."

Clara came off the dresser, disappearing and then reappearing right in front of Ophie, her ghostly face twisted with pain. Ophie's heart thundered in her chest, and she squeezed the washrag so hard that water dripped onto her house slippers.

"Sometimes, even now, I get so afraid of what could happen if folks knew the truth about me that I just fall to pieces," Clara whispered, her voice rattling like fall leaves skittering across the ground. "I'm glad you know what that's like, too."

And with that, she disappeared completely.

Ophie took a deep breath and let it out. She waited until her heart had calmed before she dropped the washrag back into the bucket, her breathing ragged. Clara had never been unpredictable before, but that was something different. Something awful.

What kind of secret could be so big, so terrible that it scared a dead girl?

Ophie picked up the washrag and got back to cleaning the windows. She had promised Clara sunshine, and she was one to keep a promise, even if the ghost was not around to appreciate it.

As she washed, Ophie let her mind wander. It had seemed like she was just getting somewhere, only for

Clara to disappear. *That's ghosts for you*, she thought. She shivered, and scrubbed a little harder. The sun had retreated behind some clouds, casting the space into deep shadow and returning the chill Ophie first felt there. But the task she'd set herself was only half done, so Ophie finished washing the remaining windows as quickly as possible.

Soon, the bucket's water was a dingy gray and the washrag was heavy with grime. As Ophie picked them up and turned to go, a dresser drawer opened slightly, like it had been pulled by an unseen hand. Ophie set down the bucket and slowly approached the dresser.

Inside were letters, written in cramped handwriting. They looked new compared to the rest of the attic's contents. Ophie pulled one out but got through only a few lines before her face flushed, and she folded the paper hastily and put it back. It was a love letter. Reading it made Ophie feel like she was catching people in the middle of something improper. Besides, she didn't need to finish reading the letter to know that Richard and Clara had definitely been in love. No one wrote a sappy letter like that unless they were. It seemed like romance had been Clara's secret after all.

The question was, how did that get Clara killed?

Chapter 14

OPHIE SPENT THE REST OF THE WEEK WITH CLARA in the attic. The ghost couldn't come downstairs, even the daily cookie offerings weren't enough to coax her out of the attic. When Ophie pressed her on it she only flickered in that way Ophie had come to learn meant it was not something the spirit wanted to discuss. Ophie got the sense that Clara did not like being seen as weak or asking for help, which reminded Ophie too much of Mama. But at least Clara did appear to talk whenever Ophie went upstairs.

The cookies did help. After the doctor had dropped off a second bottle of medicine meant to keep Mrs. Caruthers calm for at least another week, Ophie made a habit of pocketing the cookies left on the tray, return-ing it to the kitchen before taking the purloined sweets up to the attic for Clara. The ghost would appear and stroke the cookies. She couldn't eat them, but she seemed to appreciate touching them, as though the sugar and flour gave her strength, the same way they would a living person.

"Mrs. Caruthers sure is hungry in the afternoons," Cook said the third day Ophie brought an empty tray into the kitchen.

"Oh?" Ophie said. She stared down at the empty plate. It hadn't occurred to her that Cook might be keeping track of how much uneaten food was brought down.

"Don't you worry none, Ophelia," Cook said, smiling slyly and handing her a couple snickerdoodles still warm from the oven. "I had young'uns· once. I know how hungry you get at this age. But you ain't got to sneak, you hear? You just ask and I'll fix you up right. I've always got a little something extra."

Ophie nodded, feeling deeply embarrassed. The cookies she left for Clara never lasted long enough for Ophie to have one—whenever she found them the next day they were always sad, moldy black lumps of nothing.

But Ophie's shame at being discovered only lasted as long as it took for her to unwrap the snickerdoodles and devour them as she climbed the stairs to the attic.

She had enough sweets to lure Clara out; there was no shame in eating a few herself.

Ophie sat in a chair, one that she had moved so that it sat in the sunlight that filtered in from the windows. Clara didn't appear immediately, and so she waited patiently, crunching through the cookies, and thought about the one question that had come to plague her thoughts:

Who had hurt Clara?

Ophie had already come to realize that everyone else in the house was a suspect. If Clara's spirit was trapped at Daffodil Manor, it made sense that she had been killed there, possibly by someone who lived there. So that meant it could have been Richard, Mrs. Caruthers, Cook, or Mr. Henry. But Richard spoke so fondly of Clara, and said that his mother felt the same way; and Ophie couldn't imagine Cook or Mr. Henry hurting anyone, even if perhaps they did.

Unless . . . maybe it was someone else who had worked at Daffodil Manor? Maybe someone who worked there the same time Clara did?

If so, there was one person who would know. Someone who didn't like to gossip, even if they secretly did.

Cook and Mr. Henry had lived with and worked for the Carutherses since they were young. Cook had mentioned that Mr. Henry had come with Mrs. Caruthers when she came north from Virginia as a young woman to marry her husband. Cook had worked in the scullery for the previous Mrs. Caruthers. They were both very proud of the fact, of how well they knew the family. If anyone could provide a history of Daffodil Manor and its many staff who had come and gone, it was Cook.

Ophie stood, steely in her resolve. There was always a point at which a detective began to question his suspects, and she figured talking to Cook was a kind of detecting. After all, it had been Cook who had told Ophie the most about Clara, even if she didn't know that Clara had been killed. It had worked once; maybe talking to the older woman would work again.

Plus, there were more cookies in the kitchen.

The kitchen was overly warm when Ophie entered, the oven turning the space into a sweatbox. It was a welcome change from the chilliness of the attic, although Ophie was beginning to wonder if it was the weather or the many ghosts of Daffodil Manor that made the rooms so cold.

At the prep table Cook wiped at her brow as she pinched dough into dinner rolls. She looked up as Ophie entered.

"Well, hello there, Ophelia. Is the missus ready for her supper?"

"She's still asleep," Ophie said.

"And you had a hankering for some more snicker-doodles, I reckon," Cook said, giving her a wink.

Ophie smiled. "Maybe."

"Well, then, you can help me with this, and then I'll see what I can do about that. I swear, Mr. Richard loves having company, but if I could get more than a few hours' notice it would be a miracle. Thank goodness I had a chicken in the icebox."

Ophie washed her hands in the nearby sink and returned to the center island to help Cook with the rolls. As she pinched and rolled the dough she turned over her questions in her mind, searching for a way to bring up Clara.

"Maybe you should ask to hire more help?" Ophie suggested, voice low.

Cook laughed. "Oh, I have, trust me. When it's just her and Richard, it's easy enough to manage most of the time—that is, until spring rolls around and Richard begins to have his dinner parties. But the missus doesn't like having too many strangers in the house. She doesn't trust easy, that one. I can't remember the last girl she took to as easily as she seems to have taken to you."

"Clara, maybe?" Ophie asked. She liked the way her hand sank into the dough as she pinched off a small bit, the rhythm of it soothing. It calmed her nervousness and made it easier to pry.

"Why are you so taken with that poor girl?" Cook asked, and gave Ophie a probing look.

Ophie swallowed and then shrugged. Being cool and unruffled was the hallmark of a good detective, so Ophie was the same, even as her heart pounded. "Mrs. Caruthers talks about her sometimes in her sleep. Maybe she would be open to the idea of hiring more work if they were like Clara. She seems to have really liked her."

"Hmph," Cook said in response, which seemed like it would be all the answer Ophie would get. "But to your question, when Clara was on staff as Mrs. Caruthers's caretaker, there wasn't anyone else working here save me and Henry. In fact, since Clara lit out in the night, I don't think anyone we've hired has lasted longer than a couple weeks—until your mother arrived, that is. Anyway, don't you worry about us handling the work around here. You just worry about Mrs. Caruthers, that's plenty for you. She's an old woman, and while she's always been ornery, I've noticed she's gotten quite a bit meaner since her health took an ill turn about a year ago. Right about the time Clara left. I'm pretty sure that girl running off might've finished breaking that old woman's heart." Cook paused and looked

Ophie meaningfully in the eye. "Don't you go sharing that with anyone, you hear?"

"Share what?" Ophie said, and Cook laughed, loud and boisterous.

"Oh," said a voice from the door, and the laughter died as Cook and Ophie turned to see a very plain white woman standing in the doorway.

"Yes, miss, can I help you?" Cook said as the white woman walked into the room.

"I'm sorry, I'm Edwina, a friend of Richard's," she said with a kind smile that still put Ophie on edge.

The woman's brown hair was cut in a short bob and looked mussed, as though she had just woken up, even though it was late afternoon.

"I know you're probably preparing dinner, but Richard sent me down to see if you could send up a luncheon tray. We are simply famished," she said with a nervous laugh.

Ophie realized the woman was wearing a dressing robe, not an actual dress, and she thought once more of Clara and her refusal to come downstairs.

Was this why? Did Clara know that Richard was having friends over, friends who walked around the house half-dressed after sleeping in most of the day?

"I'll have a tray sent up right quick," Cook said, her voice thick with disapproval. The woman smiled, opened her mouth to say something, and then thought better of it, floating out of the kitchen as quickly as she had appeared. If Cook hadn't spoken to the woman directly Ophie might have half thought the strange white woman was a ghost.

"Here." Cook wiped off her hands and fetched another snickerdoodle from a cookie jar. Ophie took it with a grin. "Don't go mentioning this to your mama, she's got enough on her plate as it is, and she does not need to spend the rest of the week cross. After you eat that you run up and sit with Mrs. Caruthers until she wakes. She should be stirring shortly, and you don't want to not be there."

"Yes'm," Ophie said. Despite the uncomfortable interruption in the kitchen Ophie was feeling mighty pleased with herself as she climbed the grand staircase. Her investigation was progressing! She had only got ten a tiny bit more information—that no one else was working there when Clara did—but it was enough to know she was on the right track. She felt like kicking up her heels in celebration.

That was, until she stepped onto the landing and remembered being right meant someone in the house was potentially a murderer.

The Attic

EVERYONE HAD FORGOTTEN ABOUT HER.

That's how it felt more days than not to the attic. Here she was, unloved and neglected, dusty from disuse and filled with memories everyone would rather avoid. Didn't she provide an excellent hiding spot for games of hide-and-seek? Weren't her rafters strong and straight, holding aloft the roof and keeping everyone below safe and dry?

No one cared.

So the attic was delighted when the little girl from down below, the one who made the house sigh and the dead stir, began to spend her afternoons sitting in the sunshine that came in through the dormer windows.

The attic stretched contentedly as her windows were scrubbed and cobwebs were dusted away. She creaked and settled under the girl's footfalls, and felt a little less lonely. It was nice to have company once more. This was not the first girl to spend her time reading and dreaming in the attic, after all.

The attic just hoped the new girl's story would end differently than that of the last one.

Chapter 15

BY EASTER MRS. CARUTHERS WAS NO LONGER SO dependent on the doctor's tinctures and she began to spend more and more time awake. She was much changed from the woman Ophie had first met, her tone still sharp but her overall demeanor a bit more reserved, as though she were embarrassed that Ophie had seen her in such a vulnerable position for the past couple of weeks. Her afternoon naps grew shorter, which meant that Ophie was forced to wait on the old woman. She itched to get back up to the attic.

When she'd first started caring for Mrs. Caruthers, Cook had told Ophie that she had to sit by her side even when she was asleep, so that there was always someone to keep an eye on the old woman. But the freedom of the past few days had pushed this rule far from Ophie's mind. She had gotten used to having her afternoons to explore the house and visit with Clara; it had become the only bit of independence she had in her life. At home in the evenings at Aunt Rose's house there were always chores to be done and cousins around every corner, and the rest of Ophie's day was taken up with seeing to Mrs. Caruthers's needs. Ophie had experienced a taste of freedom, and now she was loath to give it up.

She managed to keep herself from bolting to the attic when Mrs. Caruthers laid down for her much shorter afternoon nap for two days in a row, but on the third she decided to risk a short trip up to the attic. Mrs. Caruthers had been awake all morning, longer than any days previous, and the old woman was clearly feeling better because she was growing crankier by the hour. Ophie had tried to open the curtains to let in the glorious spring morning sunshine and had gotten an earful, and that was only the beginning. By lunchtime, Ophie just wanted one simple moment of peace.

So when the old woman finally nodded off, Ophie tiptoed out of the room and made a mad dash for the attic door at the end of the hallway.

The April sunlight had already warmed the attic to a delightful toastiness. Though the lingering dust always made Ophie sneeze, there was something nice about having her own little hidey-hole at Daffodil Manor. For a moment she thought back to her secret hideout in the woods, the one her daddy had helped her build. But remembering that place also made her think about her last night in Georgia, the smell of smoke as their house burned and the sad-eyed ghost of her father. So she clamped down hard on the memory and pushed it into the attic of her own mind.

Ophie sighed as she leaned back in the rocking chair. In her apron was tucked a small piece of chocolate Cook had given her, and Ophie pulled it out to savor it slowly as she took a moment for herself.

"Hey there, chickadee."

Clara appeared before Ophie, looking brighter than she had in a very long time. She was back in her fancy dress, and the blood trailing from the wound on her throat looked more like the vibrant, fashionable scarf Ophie had originally mistaken it for. Clara was also more solid than she had been in weeks.

"You look like your old self again," Ophie exclaimed.

Clara nodded. Her smile was radiant and pulled an answering grin from Ophie's own lips. "I feel more like a real person, better than I have in days. And, Ophie . . . I remember!"

"Remember what?" Ophie asked.

"I remember how I died!"

Ophie was glad to have a bit more information to help Clara pass on, since she was convinced solving the murder was the thing keeping Clara in Daffodil Manor, but something about Clara's ghostly exuberance set Ophie a bit on edge. She couldn't help but remember the waterlogged specter on the trolley car who wouldn't leave her alone unless she promised to deliver her message.

"It happened up here," Clara continued. "Right here in the attic. I was getting ready for a party, a magnificent party, and someone attacked me." Clara's smile faded, and for the briefest moment her outline flickered violet.

Ophie stood, her hands instinctively going to the bundle of salt and the iron nail she kept with her. But just as quickly as Clara had gone purple she was back to her usual self, no outline at all, looking more like a real person than a spirit. It unsettled Ophie, but she was also curious.

"Who was it?" Ophie asked, voice low.

Clara's shoulders sagged, the manic excitement draining from her just a tad. "I don't know. It's like someone or something doesn't want me to remember that bit. I think and I focus, and, well . . ." As Clara trailed off she flickered a little, her expression twisting suddenly into one of rage and her outline going purple before she was back to her usual half smile.

Ophie took a half step toward the staircase, wariness seeping into her bones. Clara had never seemed like a particularly dangerous haint, but Ophie knew that the violet spirits were nothing to mess with. She'd seen the way they screamed at the living, their fits of impotent rage on the sidewalks and in the train stations. Once, she had seen a haint raise such a bluster on the sidewalk that a living man stumbled as it spun through him, falling hard into the street and nearly getting flattened by a streetcar. There was something terrifying about their anger and how quick they were to turn it on the living.

It made Ophie think of the angry white men who hunted down colored folks just because they could. Ophie had heard stories of the Ku Klux Klan, men who came in the night and hurt people who forgot their place. Even in Pittsburgh there were stories, whispered between the adults when they thought Ophie and the cousins weren't paying attention, of the horrors they visited upon colored folks, casual cruelties that served only to remind Negroes of their limits, which were numerous.

Clara's sudden flashes of purple reminded Ophie of the rules Aunt Rose had laid down about dealing with haints, rules that felt very much like the ones set forth by Cook and Mama about working in Daffodil Manor, about life in general. It was a warning, and she would be a fool to ignore it.

And yet, there was Clara, beaming at her, the prettiest person living or dead Ophie had ever met. If the ghost was mad, didn't she have a right to be? Her life had been cut short, and no one even knew she'd been killed. Both Richard and Cook had said that Clara ran off, which meant that everyone had forgotten her, her end an unacknowledged tragedy.

It wasn't fair that someone so nice and kind and bright should be murdered, but how would it feel to know that there was a killer out there and you couldn't do anything about it?

It certainly made Ophie angry. So maybe, just maybe, the furious ghost standing before her had a valid reason. Being angry didn't always mean a person was bad, especially when they had ample reason. And that had to be the case with Clara. Surely this woman who had helped her out, who had laughed with her and shared Ophie's excitement over stories, surely she couldn't be awful?

"So that should help you. Right, chickadee?" Clara said suddenly, her form brightening, coming into crisp focus.

"With what?" Ophie asked.

"With your investigation, silly! Didn't you say you were going to solve my murder? It'll be just like an Agatha Christie! Oh, but you won't be able to confront my killer, because that would be dangerous. But maybe I could do it? I wonder if there's a way for me to get strong enough to appear to someone? The cookies really have been helping, but I think a stiff drink might be even better. Say, do you think you could get your hands on some gin? Spirits for the spirit!"

Before Ophie could answer Clara the creak of a stair echoed throughout the attic.

"Ophelia! What are you about?"

Clara vanished, and not a moment before Mama emerged from the stairway, her dark brows drawn together and her mouth turned down. Her expression lay somewhere between anger and disappointment but settled into a familiar look of annoyance as Ophie began to stammer out an excuse.

"I—I, um, thought I heard something up here, and I didn't want Mrs. Caruthers to worry," she said, too fast. And from the look on Mrs. Harrison's face, she was not fooling her.

"What's this, you've been having a party up here?"

Ophie's heart pounded, and her face flushed guiltily. She turned around and looked at her hidey-hole, the out-of-place chair, the obviously too-clean windows, the cookies laid out like a picnic. Her crimes had seemed minimal, but now Ophie could not help but see her afternoon respites through her mother's eyes, and shame ran through her, hot and itchy.

"Ophelia, this is not playtime," Mama said, voice low. "You are supposed to be working."

"I am," Ophie said, but a powerful urge to cry choked off her words and sent her gaze to the tips of her toes.

"No, you ain't. You up here faffing about." Ophie shrank into herself. She knew Mama was mad when she let the familiar cadences of Georgia slip into her voice.

Mama walked over and grabbed Ophie by the wrist, dragging her back toward the stairs. Ophie was half afraid her mama would hit her, but that wasn't her mother's way. The silent treatment would be Ophie's punishment, but for now Mama seemed more intent on getting them out of the attic than anything else.

"Mrs. Caruthers has been hollering for you since she woke from her nap, but you didn't hear her, did you? Foolish child. We are so close—" Mama's words broke off as they descended the steps, but once they were back in the hallway proper she pulled Ophie close. Mama's gaze fairly burned into Ophie as she spoke.

"Ophelia, time is not on our side. We can't go on

living in your aunt's bedroom forever, and every day more colored people come into the city, taking up what housing there is. We have to be willing to work hard to get ahead if we want to make a go of it in this town. And I know we've taught you better than to run off when things get hard. Your daddy—" Mama caught herself, and she took a deep breath. "This job is the best we are going to do, and if you aren't going to take it seriously, then we are going to end up on the streets, begging for scraps. Because if a fine family like the Carutherses gives us a bad recommendation that is what's next. You hear me?"

Ophie nodded, a few shameful hot tears sliding down her cheeks as despair roiled in her belly. Ever since Daddy had died she had tried to be strong and helpful, but she wasn't, not like Mama. She was selfish and always made the wrong decisions. She had to be responsible, but the first chance she'd gotten she'd run off to the attic to eat cookies and talk to a pretty ghost.

But it wasn't fair. She was just a girl, and she shouldn't have to worry about things like rent and rec- ommendations from rich people and keeping a good name for herself. She should be reading fairy tales and taking her nickels to the sweet shop for a bag of penny candy.

But no one ever cared what Ophie thought, and so she was stuck with how things were. She wanted to be helpful to Mama, to give her the dream of her own place, but she also just wanted to be a kid, like back in Georgia. Maybe, Ophie realized, her best days had withered and died with Daddy just like Mama's had. Maybe Georgia was the best things would ever be, and the future would be nothing but struggle and the memory of those better days. The thought made her shoulders droop.

"Don't disappoint me again," Mama said, ignoring the tears tracking down Ophie's cheeks. "Now get in there and be sweet as molasses to Mrs. Caruthers, and pray she doesn't dismiss you for your negligence." And then Mama turned on her heel and headed back to her cleaning duties.

Ophie made her way back to Mrs. Caruthers's room, scrubbing at her cheeks as the old woman howled for her afternoon tea, the racket enough to wake the dead.

That's when Ophie felt a presence behind her. "It isn't fair, chickadee," came a voice. "Your ma should know how hard this is for you. That old battle-ax is ornery and spiteful to boot. Maybe waiting for her tea will teach her a lesson."

Ophie forced a smile as Clara made herself visible and laid a chilly hand of reassurance on her shoulder.

"I wish I could help you," the ghost continued. "Be your real friend, not just a restless spirit. Take you to the movies and buy you ice cream."

"Me, too," Ophie whispered. She hadn't even considered such a thing could be possible, seeing a movie with a friend, and now that someone had said it, it made her heart ache. She turned toward the staircase to head down to the kitchen to get Mrs. Caruthers's tray.

Colin stood at the bottom of the staircase, staring at her balefully, his sad countenance seemingly a manifestation of Ophie's own wretched feelings.

"Sorry you got in trouble," he said, jumping slightly as Mrs. Caruthers yelled for Amelia, the old woman still confused about Ophie's name. "But it's better you hurry up now before she gets the whip."

As he disappeared Ophie wondered how she was supposed to help Clara when she couldn't even find a way to help herself.

Chapter 16

OPHIE'S MOTHER WAS CROSS WITH HER FOR THE rest of the day, making the silence on the trolley ride home more fraught than usual. Ophie knew she had made a mistake, but even so, she did not feel as sorry as she knew she should. It was hard to explain the way she felt around the ghost, but Clara seemed to be the one person in Ophie's life who spent time with her by choice, and that was in short supply. So even though she'd disappointed her mama and vexed Mrs. Caruthers—who might have held Ophie's fate in her hands but truthfully was always in a mood of some sort—Ophie had no regrets about abandoning her duties.

And she couldn't stop now. Ophie couldn't help but feel like she was so close to finding out what happened to Clara, and if finding out who had killed her would also help her to move on, well, then Ophie would not abandon her. And Ophie had already come up with a plan. If Clara was sure she had been killed in the attic, then there might have been clues left behind. Detectives were always finding clues in the stories, so Ophie would just have to find a way to get to the attic and do a little investigating.

How she would do that after getting in trouble, though . . . that part she was still working on.

Dinner was a somber affair, with Ophie and her mother eating warmed Heinz baked beans from a can. Aunt Rose was out at Bible study, and the cousins were nowhere to be found.

"Here's hoping they ran off to join the circus," Mama said to Ophie, the first words she'd uttered since her reprimand earlier in the afternoon. "It would at least make our time here a little more comfortable until we can find lodgings of our own."

Ophie said nothing, just scooped beans into her mouth until they were gone.

That night, lying next to her mama, Ophie dreamed. She was in a field with other colored folks and they were all working side by side to plant empty rows while a man on a horse yelled at them to move faster, to work harder. In the distance, the sky was dark, furious clouds stampeding across the sky, and the wind tore at the threadbare dress Ophie wore.

A fat rain droplet landed on her head as the thunderstorm broke free, and that was when she woke. Ophie lay blinking in the dark for a moment, the dream more real and complete than any she'd ever had. Before she could question what she was doing, she got out of bed and walked over to the window. There, standing in the garden, was Aunt Rose's husband.

It was strange to see the ghost standing there in the garden. Ophie had not seen him for weeks, and she had been sure to keep an eye out. She couldn't help but be curious about the man who loved Aunt Rose so much that he refused to pass on. And now here the spirit was, once more, just when Ophie was talking to the dead regularly. Ophie's curiosity had not waned, but her fear of the dead had, and so she decided it was time to have a conversation with the dead man haunting the garden.

Ophie crept out of the bedroom and down the stairs, stopping only to grab the iron nail and salt out of the pocket of her work apron. The house was cold but not freezing thanks to the unusually warm days Pittsburgh had been having, and when she opened the back door the ghost was still there, puttering around the rosebushes that had begun to bud.

Ophie paused on the safety of the porch for a moment, Aunt Rose's warnings coming back to her. But if she had heeded Aunt Rose's ominous predictions about the dangers of the dead, then Ophie would not have befriended Clara. Besides, the old man shuffling through the garden did not look the least bit dangerous.

"Was that you?" Ophie asked, stepping off the porch and onto the path that ran down the middle of the yard.

"My apologies, little one," the ghost said. His voice was creaky, like the sound an old rocking chair made on a porch. "I was reaching for my Rose, but she was resting too deeply."

"You lived on a plantation."

"I did. It was not so long ago when our people were enslaved, though it seems most would like to forget that. But even death is not strong enough to erase the memories of a white man owning me."

Ophie had grown up in Georgia and had heard the stories. Once upon a time white folks had owned colored folks and forced them to work until their fingers bled. Her teacher had even said that was why it was important to be respectful to white people now, even if they didn't rightly deserve it. Not only was it the Christian thing to do to turn the other cheek, but there were still many more whites than Negroes, and if white folks got it into their heads to be angry about something a colored person did, well, bad things could happen. And bad things often did.

It was, of course, a lesson Ophie had learned first-hand.

But here was a ghost who had once been property, a man who had died peacefully in his sleep and instead of passing on had decided to wait for his wife. Ophie was interested, and since she was less afraid of the haints than she'd been when she'd first discovered her powers, it seemed like a good time to give in to curiosity.

"Can you tell me what it's like to, um, be a spirit?" Ophie asked.

The apparition chuckled, the sound like wind through the leaves, faint and wispy. "When I first died, I couldn't feel anything. It's like I forgot how to be a person for a little while. But my first instinct, when I came into myself, was to go to places I remembered. The restaurant Rose and I liked to go to on Fridays. A grand old oak tree that always made me glad. I even walked my old mail route one day, touching postboxes even though I had nothing to deliver. And finally here, with my roses. After a while of just traveling from place to place, I started to remember what it was like to live, even if I wasn't alive anymore."

Ophie nodded in understanding. She felt the same way about the memory of her daddy. When they had first gotten to Pittsburgh, thinking about Georgia and her life there had made her chest squeeze tight as she fought the tears that would inevitably come. So she just didn't think about it. Because that was easier.

But now, she wondered if she had been wrong. There was still the dull ache of loss when she thought about Daddy, truly considered that she would never see him again. But maybe that was okay. Losing him still hurt, but not as much as before. And the good memories made her feel nice for a little while, even if they did turn to ashes when she remembered he was gone. Was that how it was supposed to work?

"Why are you still here?" Ophie asked, thinking now about Clara. "Aunt Rose says ghosts stick around because they have unfinished business."

The ghost nodded. Ophie couldn't quite think of him as Aunt Rose's husband; she'd never met the man when he was living, and his spirit seemed to be a person all its own. "Rose was always smart about the spirits, and she's right. Before I died I promised that I would wait for her. Because I loved her with all my heart and I never wanted to spend a day apart from her. And so, here I am, taking care of her roses until she's ready to come with me."

"But . . ." Ophie hesitated, because she didn't want to say anything the ghost didn't want to hear. *But he's a ghost*, she thought. *Could anything I say upset him all that much?* "Aunt Rose told me that she won't talk to you. That ghosts are dangerous. Even you."

The dead man sighed. "My Rose has always been set in her ways. Once she's got an idea into that pretty head of hers not even wild horses could pull it free. She's told me a number of stories about how the dead can chill a body so they fall ill or hound someone to their early death, and she seems to think that means all ghosts are to be feared. And perhaps she's right, maybe there is something in me that's missing, something different than when I was living. But I know one thing for certain: I still love Rose, and when her time comes I will be right here waiting for her."

The ghost smiled, and a chill breeze danced across Ophie's skin, raising goose bumps on her arms. He looked up at the sky. "It won't be long, now."

Far off, a rooster crowed, signaling that the day would soon begin. Ophie glanced in its direction, and when she turned back, the ghost had faded, gone back to wherever the dead went when they didn't inhabit the world of the living.

Ophie stood alone there in the garden for a very long time, thinking about the dead and their reasons for staying. Clara had been murdered. Someone had hated her enough to hurt her, to end her life. But the same thing had happened to Ophie's daddy, and she'd watched him move on, she'd felt it in that moment he'd sparkled away into nothing.

So why was Clara still around and Ophie's daddy passed on? The rules for the dead seemed as flexible as chewing gum in August.

Ophie walked back to the house, kicking a plate tucked under a nearby rosebush. Cookies, set out by someone. Black, moldy lumps that looked just like the ones Ophie had left for Clara. Which meant that they'd been out there long enough for the ghost to do whatever it was that they did to sweets.

Aunt Rose was the only person besides Ophie who would know to leave out treats for the dead. Perhaps the elderly woman was a Double-Talk Folk, after all, telling Ophie to avoid the dead while she left sweets for her husband.

But then Ophie stopped, gaze going to the path before her, the dawn's light revealing what she had missed on her trip into the garden. Fresh rose cuttings littered the walkway, the remnants of the ghost's night-time gardening. The sight made Ophie's palms slick with sweat, and she swallowed drily as she turned to look back to where the ghost had stood.

Perhaps the dead were not as powerless as Ophie had imagined.

The Rose Garden

THE GARDEN BEHIND THE BUNGALOW WOKE IN FIT-ful spurts. And the ghost watched it all.

The roses woke first, their buds growing fat in anticipation of warmer days, new thorns sprouting on branches and the glossy leaves unfurling. Then the azaleas began to bloom, a garish display of pink, the rainy days leaving the flowers littering the ground. The apple tree in the far back of the yard, planted with a promise on the day the ghost had been married, bloomed late, the tender blossoms peeking out reluctantly before shedding onto the grass below in a shower of white, not unlike his bride's homemade lace veil on their wedding day.

The ghost stayed in the garden because every single one of the plants had been seeded with love. They were his anchor to the world of the living. Apples were his wife's favorite fruit, the pink of the azaleas her favorite color, and the roses her namesake.

But even so, he was beginning to forget.

He remembered the day they'd been told they were free, and their bold decision to move north, away from the memories of the fields and the overseer. He had vague notions of struggling to learn his letters while he worked in the coal mine, every day a battle to survive the dangerous work. He could recall the day he'd been able to leave the mine for good and get a job at the post office because he knew how to read, rare among colored men of the time; and his route through the colored neighborhoods of the city, full of refugees like him and his Rose.

But beyond those, the only other memories he still had were of Rose. Her laugh, her smile, her smell. He existed only for her. And each day that existence became a little harder. He wasn't supposed to be there; he could feel the pull to go somewhere else, somewhere he belonged, now that he was what he was.

But for now, he would wait. Because he had made a promise.

The rose garden sighed with him and readied itself for the onslaught of summer, hot and sticky, bright and merciless. As the ghost waited, running wispy fingers over the blooms every now and again to remind himself of his vigil, the sweets left out by his wife strengthening him, the garden waited as well, and the breeze through the boughs of the apple tree whispered with the ghost's long-dead voice.

Soon.

Chapter 17

OPHIE SPENT THE NEXT DAY IN MRS. CARUTHERS'S room, only leaving long enough to head down to the kitchen and fetch this or that. But staying busy was nice, because it gave Ophie time to think.

Aunt Rose had said that ghosts were stuck, in a way. In talking to Aunt Rose's husband, Ophie was reminded that it wasn't places that ghosts haunted, but people. Aunt Rose had said as much, but Ophie had not quite understood what it meant for a person to be haunted.

Now, she saw the patterns emerging with crystal clarity. The ghosts followed the people they knew, which meant that maybe by helping the dead communicate to the people they haunted, Ophie could help some of the ghosts she saw every day.

Indeed, it did seem as though the longer she lived in the city the more spirits she saw. The pretty crying Negro girl still sat next to old Miss Alice every morning, and there were dozens of other ghosts who came and went throughout the ride. This gave Ophie a light feeling, because there was a pattern to the movements of the dead, and by understanding the rhythms, the ebbs and flows, Ophie could be that much better at helping the dead pass on. But that left her with a bigger question.

If ghosts haunted people, not places, what did that do to the living they were attached to?

Ophie had no idea. But she did believe that helping the dead pass on might just be a matter of making them realize that the people they well and truly wanted were gone, giving the errant spirits a direction of pursuit.

But what if what the ghosts wanted were the people they missed most to be dead like them? What if Clara really was waiting for Richard to pass on the way Aunt Rose's husband was waiting for her? Ophie shied away from that line of thought. One thing at a time, like Daddy had always said. If discovering her murderer didn't let Clara pass on, well, Ophie would just deal with that matter when it arose.

That didn't mean she couldn't try out her theory about how to help the dead pass on with the rest of the dead in Daffodil Manor. There were plenty of spirits she could help in the big old house.

But Ophie had no way of doing so when she was stuck running around all day, fetching fresh tea and sitting by Mrs. Caruthers in case she needed another log thrown on the fire. The inability to test out her theory irked Ophie something fierce. She could be figuring out how to help the dead move on, and here she was helping a mean old woman to the lavatory instead.

"Amelia," Mrs. Caruthers creaked, her voice like the hinges on the attic door. Even after months of working for the elderly woman, she still called Ophie everything but her given name most of the time. "Go down to the library and fetch me a book. The title is *A Children's Garden of Verses*. Surely you can manage that?"

Ophie nodded, trying to hide her excitement at being given a small bit of freedom. "Yes'm," she said, bobbing a curtsy and leaving the room. The hallway was at least twenty degrees cooler than the room. Even though it was now warm enough that Ophie and her mother didn't need to wear coats when they traveled to and from the house, Mrs. Caruthers still complained about being cold all the time. Ophie had hauled more firewood in the past month than she had all winter, and still the old woman complained of being chilled.

Ophie ran down the stairs quickly, and when she

reached the bottom, she was surprised to see the old ghost from the study standing in the middle of the foyer. He looked around uncertainly, as though he were just as surprised to find himself outside his study as Ophie was.

"Hello," Ophie said, approaching the haint cautiously. She felt for the iron and salt that she always kept in her apron pocket, the bundle a reassuring weight in her hand. "Did you, uh, need something?"

The man looked at her. "Edward Caruthers. My father built this house, you know." His voice was strangely accented, and his bushy gray eyebrows pulled together as he studied the room. "I grew up here, but I do not think I have ever seen these furnishings before."

"When was the last time you left your work in the study?" Ophie asked.

The ghost stared at her for a moment. "I . . . I am not sure."

Ophie pointed outside where the sun shone. "Have you thought about taking a walk? There's a bird nest in the big oak out back, and if you're really quiet you can hear the babies chirping. It's finally starting to get warm."

"Actually," the man said, puffing out his chest just a bit, "I am looking for my daughter, Isabel. Have you seen her?"

Ophie gnawed on her lip as she thought. She didn't

know what old Mrs. Caruthers's name was, but she didn't think it was Isabel. But thinking on it, Ophie realized that she had never heard anyone refer to the old woman by her first name. Richard called her Mother, and the household staff all called her Mrs. Caruthers or ma'am. Perhaps the ghost was looking for her?

Ophie shook her head. No, Cook had said that Mrs. Caruthers came up from Virginia to marry Richard's father. So maybe someone else, someone who had lived in the house their entire life? A few of the books Ophie had rescued from the attic, the fairy-tale book and another book about frontier life, had a note scrawled on the inside to an Isabel, but surely it could not be the same girl?

Could ghosts haunt one another? If so, that was quite the twist to Ophie's theory.

"Can you tell me what your daughter looks like?" Ophie finally asked when the ghost did not seem inclined to leave without an answer.

The ghost frowned. "No, actually, I cannot. But if there's a pile of books to be found she's usually not far off. The girl really should be minding her tutors instead of always running off to read."

Ophie brightened. "I know exactly where your daughter is. Um, if you'll follow me?"

Ophie did not wait for the old ghost to follow her. She set out for the library, and as soon as she opened the door an apparition came running toward her.

"Daddy!" the little girl in the wing chair said. "I was waiting for you!" She ran toward the businessman but dissipated into sparkles before she reached him, and the older spirit didn't seem to realize she had even been there. Ophie blinked as the little girl passed on. Had she spent all this time in the library just waiting for the older man?

And if he was looking for the girl, Isabel, why hadn't he passed on?

The spirit looked around again, still confused, and he nodded. "Yes. This seems like some place she would be."

"I'm sorry she doesn't seem to be here anymore," Ophie said. What to say to the man to help him see that there was no longer anything for him in the world of the living?

"Ah, but she was. And you raised an excellent suggestion earlier. I should take a walk outside."

Ophie nodded, hoping there was something to be gained by getting the spirit out of the house. "You have been working very hard for such a long time. I think a break is well earned."

The man smiled slightly, his facial hair curving in response. "I suppose since Isabel isn't here she's out there climbing that tree again. That child is going to break her fool neck one of these days. I should go check on her. The accounts can wait."

The ghost walked straight toward the windows, passing through the wall. He walked outside and lifted his face to the sun, and Ophie watched in surprise as he began to sparkle and fade just as the little girl had. It was just like Ophie's daddy had done, what now felt like a lifetime ago.

Bringing the two ghosts together had helped them pass on, but not at all like Ophie had thought.

"He's gone."

Ophie turned around to see Colin watching her from the doorway. His shoulders still drooped, and he still wore no shoes nor shirt, but he seemed a little less sad.

"You helped him and Isabel pass on," the boy said, his whispery voice full of wonder.

"Did I?" Ophie asked, her victory feeling a bit hollow. She'd thought it would be more exciting to help the ghosts. "Seems more like they figured out there was no sense in keeping on here."

"Without seeing her father she couldn't move on. She told me she was waiting for someone, but she didn't know who. And he never left his office, never had fun in life, so your suggestion that he take a walk outside helped him get unstuck."

"I just told him to go outside and enjoy the day,"

Ophie said, feeling a little defensive. Was this what it meant to help a spirit pass on? She'd thought it would be harder.

"How do you know so much?" she asked Colin.

He shrugged. "I pay attention. And, Ophie, you helped. You listened. That was exactly what they needed," the boy said before turning and walking away. "It's all anyone needs."

As Colin disappeared, Ophie's frustration dissipated into a strange sense of satisfaction. For so long she had been wrong, wrong, wrong, making countless mistakes and never quite living up to her mama's expectations. And now, now here she was finally doing something right. The thing she was born to do.

When Ophie turned back toward the library to find the book Mrs. Caruthers wanted it was sitting on an end table in plain sight. And she was quite certain it had not been there a few moments before. Gratefully, she took the book and returned to the old woman's room, her mind whirring with plans for what to do next.

That night, back at Aunt Rose's house, Ophie kept replaying the events of the day. The dinner dishes had been cleared, and the cousins had all gone out to see a picture show. Ophie told herself she wasn't jealous, and she mostly wasn't. The cousins might be spoiled, but Ophie had ghosts.

That had to be better than going to a theater. At least, that was what Ophie told herself to soothe her envy.

It was warm enough to sit outside, and while Mama went right up to bed as usual, Ophie sat outside under the safety of the blue porch, half hoping Aunt Rose's husband would make a reappearance. He did not, but Aunt Rose hobbled out of the house to sit in the creaky old rocking chair set aside for her.

"Do you mind if I join you?" she asked Ophie, which seemed silly because it was the old woman's house.

Ophie shook her head, and for a few moments they sat in peaceful silence. Ophie's thoughts were thick with questions about Aunt Rose's husband, about the cookies tucked under the rosebush, about so many other things to do with ghosts. She opened her mouth and closed it several times, but kept losing her nerve.

"Well, whatever it is you want to ask, child, go right ahead," Aunt Rose finally said, her voice gentle.

"How did you know I wanted to ask a question?" Ophie asked.

Aunt Rose laughed, the sound rusty. "Because I've felt you giving me curious looks all evening. So I figure there must be something pressing you."

Ophie nodded and pointed out to the garden. "I

saw your husband out here last night. And the cookies. And the rose clippings," she said, talking faster as Aunt Rose's indulgent smile melted into a disapproving frown. "I just want to know why you avoid him when you still love him, when you still want him to be strong."

Ophie bit her lip once she got the question out, waiting for the censure she was certain would follow. But none was forthcoming. Instead, Aunt Rose sighed heavily.

"Ophelia, let me tell you a story. Like you, I grew up way down south. My mama was like us, she could see haints, and she did what she could in the town where she lived to make sure the dead cleared out. She didn't live on a great big plantation like some folks, but in a house with only one other colored girl. My mama learned quickly that ghosts hanging about made things bad for the living, so she did what she could to keep her life calm, which is sometimes all that a body can do when their life is not truly their own.

"When my mama was still young, too young to be married, the master's wife died. As soon as the mistress of the house passed, her husband took ill. He had chills all the time and would complain about drafts constantly. My mama told me that she walked into the room one day and saw the mistress sitting right there next to the master's bed, knitting and looking fit as a fiddle. But the woman was dead. That was when my mama realized the dead woman was stealing her husband's breath, using it to make her stronger."

Ophie blinked and thought of Mrs. Caruthers. Was one of the ghosts in the house stealing her breath? Was that why she always complained of the chill, even when it was hotter than August in her small room?

Ophie put the question aside for later and turned back to Aunt Rose. "What did she do?"

"Nothing," Aunt Rose chuckled. "My mama said she hated that man so much that she didn't do anything to chase off that haint. He was a terrible man who cheated his friends and beat my mama, so she let that ghost do what it wanted. The master of the household died a few months later. Everyone said it was due to a broken heart, but my mama knew better."

Aunt Rose stopped rocking and leaned toward Ophie. "I tell you this now so you can understand why I don't get too close to the ghost that my husband became. I know that spirit is only an echo of who he once was, that something of who he was remains. But there is also a good chance that he would steal my breath if given half the chance. Not because he means to, but because it is just what ghosts do. So, if you won't avoid the dead, Ophelia, be cautious around them. Keep your salt and iron with you, and know that they are what they are."

Ophie nodded and stood with a yawn. Her eyes felt heavy, and she was ready for bed. "I understand, Aunt Rose," she said before bidding her aunt good night. Because she did.

But she also understood that sometimes the world was just a little bit more complicated and grown folks liked to operate in absolutes. Right, wrong. Dangerous, safe. Sometimes a body had to go through a little danger to get to the safety.

Helping Clara get justice was the right thing to do, and just like Aunt Rose's mama, Ophie intended to do the right thing, even if it was hard.

Chapter 18

THE DAY AFTER ISABEL AND HER FATHER PASSED ON, Ophie's afternoon was interrupted by a visit from Richard. He blew into his mother's room like a summer storm, appearing without any warning.

"Mother, guess who just rang me?" he asked.

The older woman had startled from her doze and tried to pull herself up in bed. Ophie went to her side to help rearrange the pillows but had to duck aside when Mrs. Caruthers slapped her hands away. "Let Richard do that," the older woman snarled.

Her son laughed at his mother's ill temper. "Here, Ophelia, I'll take care of it."

Ophie moved away from the bed and toward the fireplace. She pretended to tend to the guttering flames while Richard spoke to his mother, but it was impossible not to listen in.

"Agatha and her brood have decided to come north for the summer. And of course she's going to bring her mother and aunt. So you will get to spend June surrounded by Virginians!"

Ophie glanced at Mrs. Caruthers, and for the first time since she had come to Daffodil Manor back in February, she saw the old woman smile. It was an unsettling sight. But just as quickly, it was gone.

"Agatha and the family, they haven't been here since . . ." She trailed off, and Ophie froze, trying to hear what she was going to say next.

"I know, Mother," Richard said before she could finish. "And I thought it was about time we have them back, don't you?"

Were they talking about Clara without actually saying her name? Cook had mentioned that Clara ran off shortly after the family from Virginia visited.

"How did you convince them to make the trip, dear boy? You know my sister hates to travel. And after the awkwardness of the last trip a few of the cousins swore they would never return."

Mrs. Caruthers had a sister? Ophie tried to imagine another woman just as mean and ornery as her and couldn't.

But mostly, she wondered why it was that the

family from Virginia hadn't wanted to return to Daf-fodil Manor. Could it be because one of them was a murderer?

Ophie stopped pretending not to listen to Mrs. Caruthers and Richard's conversation, and just openly eavesdropped. They seemed to have forgotten she was even there, anyway.

"Honesty, Mother. I told them that you are ill and that seeing them might be just the sort of medicine that you need, and that no doctor could prescribe." Richard took his mother's hand and cradled it in his much larger ones. "We'll have to open up the entirety of the house, of course. . . ."

"Well, of course we will," Mrs. Caruthers said with a sniff. "We cannot let the Virginia cousins think we're impoverished!"

"Which means we'll need to hire extra household help," Richard finished. "I just want to make sure you won't put up too much of a fuss."

Mrs. Caruthers's bright disposition faded as quickly as it had arrived. "You know I loathe the idea of a house full of domestics."

"Yes, but how else are we going to open up and maintain all these extra rooms? We'll need the space, we can't go stacking family up three to a room like a tenement."

Mrs. Caruthers said nothing, which was apparently all the answer Richard required. He released his mother's hands and pressed a kiss to her cheek. "I'll speak to Cook about bringing on some additional help. Please say you'll try to tolerate the new servants, Mother. No dismissing anyone without talking to me, okay?"

Mrs. Caruthers harrumphed and crossed her arms, but Richard just gave her a smile before taking his leave. After he'd gone, Mrs. Caruthers rounded on Ophie. "Amelia, go down and fetch Henry immediately. Tell that man not to tarry." Her words were sharp, but her voice quavered.

Ophie knew better than to argue. She ran to find Mr. Henry, all the while trying to puzzle out why Mrs. Caruthers was so unsettled by the idea of more people in the house.

What secrets were the Ca111111111111111111utherses hiding?

But more important, who of the Virginia cousins could have wanted to hurt Clara?

Ophie had been hoping the opportunity to check the attic for clues would present itself, but the next week turned out to be the busiest she'd spent in the manor so far. Richard had decided that the arrival of his family from Virginia justified having a grand gala for his birthday the last week of May, when the first relatives were scheduled to arrive, so everything in the mansion turned toward the monumental task of preparing the manor for company.

Richard hired two extra people, even though Mrs. Caruthers grumbled nonstop about the additional cost. The extra help was necessary to make sure the house was ready in time. With family coming from Virginia, as well as friends coming from other places for the birthday party, all the rooms would need to be opened up, aired out, cleaned, and decorated.

But there was also a party to plan, which meant the grand ballroom had to be refreshed and prepared as well, not to mention an extra cleaning for the other rooms of the first floor. This meant the regular household staff had to work twice as hard, and nearly twice as long. Ophie and her mother were kept there so late in the day that they took to eating supper at Daffodil Manor, making it home when it was nearly time for bed.

Richard had kindly offered to let them sleep in the servants' quarters off the kitchen, but Mama still refused, which was a relief to Ophie. She had plenty of reasons not to trust the Carutherses, and had only found more since they learned of the family coming to visit. She could hardly get through a day without Mrs. Caruthers talking about their family plantation back in Virginia.

"Those were the days," she would murmur, telling Ophie stories that sounded like nightmares even to her young ears. After one tale about a stolen chicken and a boy being whipped "until the white meat showed," Ophie had left the old woman's room to find the ghost of Colin edged in a terrifying violet aura before he disappeared completely.

Mama had another reason not to want to stay at the manor. "We leave those cousins of yours to their own devices and they'll rob us blind," Mama said to Ophie. She thought maybe Mama was being too cautious, but sure enough, that night, they came back late to find their things misplaced, as if someone had gone searching through the room they shared. After that, Mama asked Aunt Rose to hold their little pile of money, and Rose agreed, locking it up in a dresser drawer in her room.

But even with their money secured, they still traveled back and forth to Daffodil Manor instead of staying on like Cook and Mr. Henry did. The new folks who were hired stayed at the mansion as well: an older colored woman named Gladys, who grumbled about the work when she thought no one was listening; and a younger colored girl named Penelope, who was rather dour, and snuck drinks from a flask tucked into her garter when she thought no one was looking. Ophie liked them both, but when they spoke of having nightmares of blood and anger since they came to work at the old house, she thought maybe Mama had the right of it not to stay in Daffodil Manor overnight. From the evening with Aunt Rose's husband and the subsequent conversation with Aunt Rose, Ophie knew the dead could do things to the living, especially when they were asleep. She was plagued enough by haints in her waking hours; she didn't want them stalking her dreams as well.

So there was plenty of good reason to keep on at Aunt Rose's house.

Ophie didn't much mind the extra work in the house; as Mrs. Caruthers's caretaker, her days stayed fairly the same. What she did mind was the fact that all the extra activity seemed to have pushed the ghosts into hiding, most especially Clara. Ever since the conversation with the ghost in Aunt Rose's garden, Ophie had been eager to talk to Clara. Because she'd had a lot of time to think about who could have possibly murdered her.

Ophie's first list of suspects—Cook, Mr. Henry, Mrs. Caruthers, and Richard—now seemed silly. She didn't think that Cook or Mr. Henry had done it; they were too nice and loyal to Mrs. Caruthers and Richard, who had no reason to want Clara dead. Richard had been in love with Clara, from what Ophie had read in those love letters. And Mrs. Caruthers said nothing but nice things about Clara, which might be vexing but also made Ophie think she wouldn't have wanted Clara killed.

But someone else, a visitor who could have hurt Clara, maybe even kidnapped her, made perfect sense. Women were always being kidnapped by cads in both *True Romances* and the detective stories. Maybe someone had done the same to Clara. Only, no one had come to save her.

Ophie considered just how to go about questioning Clara about the Virginia family members—maybe mentioning them would jog Clara's memory—as she and her mama rode the trolley back to Aunt Rose's house a week after Richard's announcement. Although the sun was still up, it was quite late, and most of the people on the trolley were making their way to the theater or a picture show. They ignored Ophie and her mother, which was fine by Ophie. She was trying to figure out a time during the day when it would be safe to sneak up to the attic and ask, while Mama dozed beside her.

The trolley screeched at the stop right before Aunt Rose's, the squealing of the brakes jostling Mama out of her sleep for a moment. Ophie glanced over at her as she yawned widely and settled her eyes on someone standing over Ophie's shoulder.

"Rose, what are you doing out at this hour?"

Mama laid her head back on Ophie's shoulder and fell back asleep, but Ophie whipped her head around, and sure enough, standing behind her was Aunt Rose. The expression on her deeply lined brown face was distraught, something Ophie had never seen before.

"I'm sorry, Ophelia," Aunt Rose said, taking a halting step forward. "I am afraid you are going to be on your own now."

Ophie started to ask Aunt Rose what she meant, but then she saw it: the hazy blue outline around the elderly woman's body.

Ophie's heart felt like it had frozen in her chest. She had so many questions, but the one that came out first was "How come Mama can see you?"

"That is your last lesson, Ophelia. Sometimes, when a body is asleep, it's easier for the dead to communicate with them, to speak to them in the form of messages and dreams. Pay attention to your dreams, child. Be well, my dear."

Ophie reached out for her, trying to get a grip on the fabric of the old woman's dress. If Aunt Rose was dead, who was left to explain things to her? She would be completely on her own.

The trolley started back up again; the next stop was

theirs. Aunt Rose was already gone, fading away. Not into the sparkles of a spirit passing on, but of a haint going on about its own business. Ophie jumped to her feet, and next to her Mama startled fully awake.

"Ophelia, what is going on?"

"Something bad," she said. "Something bad."

As soon as the trolley stopped, Ophie sprinted to the door, running down the trolley steps and hopping the curb to sprint toward Aunt Rose's house. Mama called after her, but Ophie kept on.

She had to know.

As she approached Aunt Rose's house, she saw that the front door was hanging open and there was a horse and wagon parked out on the street. Instead of running to the door, she went around to the back alley, which connected to the rear yard, her hands fumbling as they unlatched the back gate. Ophie skidded to a stop on the edge of the rose garden, chest heaving, breath coming hard. There, standing in her Sunday best, was Aunt Rose—only she looked much younger. Her husband, no longer a stooped old man but a handsome young gentleman, walked toward her wearing a dapper suit and holding a single pale pink rose. Tears tracked down Ophie's cheeks as Aunt Rose took the flower, both of the spirits bursting into glittering shards as they moved on.

"Ophelia, what is going on?"

Ophie dashed away her tears and turned to her mama, who was giving her a look somewhere between confused and irritated.

"Nothing, I just . . . I thought I saw a raccoon." Ophie sniffed. The lie came easy this time, something that should have worried Ophie more than it did. "We should go in and pay our respects."

Mama frowned. "What exactly do you mean by that?"

Instead of explaining, Ophie just took her mother's hand and pulled her through the garden and into the house so she could discover the truth for herself.

Aunt Rose's House

∽∞∾

THE SMALL HOUSE DID NOT LIKE CHANGE. BUT THAT was not entirely the house's fault. The same sparse furnishings, all built by hand just like the house, had occupied the space for decades. The house liked the warm predictability of the lives lived inside him. But in the past year, he'd had more than his share of upheaval. First, there had been the ones who tracked mud across his floors and slammed his doors, so that the whole of him vibrated uncomfortably. Then there had been the newcomers, who only whispered in hushed tones, as though they were afraid to attract the attention of the world. Now, with the passing of the woman who lived there longest and loved him best, the house was feeling a peculiar sense of loss.

Who was going to care for him the way she and her husband had? Certainly not the late-night lurker and his crying wife, and definitely not the stomping dirt trackers. Perhaps the whisperers could polish his banisters and wax his floors? They seemed like the kind of people the house could care for and who would care for him in return.

But that hope was dashed when the whispering pair packed up their things in the middle of the night and made their way out as dawn was pinkening the horizon, their few possessions tucked up into a bindle as they left without a backward glance.

The house settled into itself with a sad sigh and waited for the long and inevitable ruin to come.

Chapter 19

MAMA WASTED NO TIME IN PACKING UP THEIR things once the undertaker had left with Aunt Rose's body. They didn't have much: a couple of dresses and some underthings for each of them and a single pair of shoes, as well as an ivory comb Mrs. Harrison had found at a secondhand store and a few hair ribbons. They'd arrived in Pittsburgh empty-handed and they didn't buy much beyond the necessities in their time in the city, all their money going toward the possibility of having their own place.

And now even that was gone. As soon as they had entered the house and learned that Aunt Rose had passed away while dozing in her favorite chair, most likely a heart attack, Mama had climbed the stairs to Aunt Rose's bedroom, Ophie on her heels. She could tell something was amiss, and they soon discovered the reason.

The drawer that had held the majority of Ophie's and her mama's earnings over the past few months hung open, the money gone.

"Are you looking for something?" The cousins' mother appeared at the door, her arms crossed, her eyes narrowed, a smug smile on her face.

"Where is our money, Helen?" Mama asked, voice soft and full of menace.

Helen waved the question away. "Was that yours? The undertaker wouldn't take poor Rose without having half the cost upfront, and I knew that Rose kept some petty cash here for the household."

Mama must have known there was nothing they could do—that the money they'd given Aunt Rose for safekeeping was gone now, whether it was into the undertaker's hand or, more likely, Helen's pocket. "Jesus will give you yours" was all she said before pushing past Helen and leaving Aunt Rose's room.

And that was the end of the house fund.

After the confrontation, Mama had pulled Ophie into their room and locked the door. "Pack your things up in the quilt, Ophelia, and then lie down and get some rest. We're going to start living at Daffodil Manor tomorrow."

Ophie packed her things quickly and sat down on the bed. "Is it really all gone?" she asked. The words seemed to stick in her throat, because Ophie did not want to know that the reason she had left school and spent every day bearing the wrath of miserable old Mrs. Caruthers had suddenly been stolen by the cousins and their awful mother. Just considering it gave Ophie a terrible, mean feeling in her chest. She wanted to leave the bedroom and claw out Helen's too-light eyes, wanted to box the cousins' ears like she never had before.

"No, we have a little money left. But not enough. Not enough," Mama murmured. "Go to sleep, Ophelia. We still have work tomorrow." Her tone made it clear that there would be no further conversation on the matter.

Ophie slept fitfully, and when her mother nudged her, early enough so that they had to light the kerosene lamp to find their way to the front door, she moved as if through a dream. She was going to be living at Daffodil Manor, all her days and nights spent in the big house. She dreaded what that meant but concentrated on one thing: she would finally have the opportunity to investigate Clara's death and discover the secret of her end.

They waited a long time for the trolley, which ran less often that early in the morning. When they climbed aboard there were only a handful of people, most of them clearly heading home from a night of carousing as opposed to going off to work. Ophie realized with a start that this would be the last time that she would travel this route—that from now on her journey from home to work would be one of steps, not miles. It was a sad thought. She realized she wasn't sad about Aunt Rose—the pain of losing her was balanced by the knowledge that the old woman was with her beloved husband in a much better place. But the loss of a routine that had given her life structure the past few months found tears pooling in the edges of her vision as she watched the city go by outside the window.

Her thoughts were interrupted by the trolley jerking to sudden stop and a scream from outside. The people around her were immediately on their feet, craning their necks to see out the car windows. But Ophie didn't need to see outside to know what had happened. She shivered as a harried-looking white man boarded the trolley right through the closed door, his suit torn and bloody, his hat missing entirely. He was gripping a handful of pamphlets, and his gray suit and pale skin made the blood dripping from his head all the more vivid. The man was very much dead, a fact made clear by the way the few people on the trolley rushed through him in their efforts to peer at the scene unfolding in front of the car.

"What seems to be going on?" the man asked no one in particular. He seemed dazed and unsettled. Ophie had never seen someone so very newly dead before. It was quite a sight, and she found herself answering him before she could help herself.

"I think, um, you just got hit by the trolley car, sir. You're—" She bit her lip, but then realized there was no point in not telling him the truth. It wasn't as if he wouldn't realize it for himself in a moment, and wouldn't it be nicer to hear someone tell it straight? "You're . . . dead."

"Ophelia, who are you talking to?"

In her fascination with the dead man Ophie had completely forgotten about her mother sitting next to her on the trolley. For a moment Ophie and her mother just stared at one another, before Ophie ducked her head. "I think I was dreaming," she said. "I dozed off."

"I'm dead?" the man said, voice faraway. "This won't do. This isn't even my trolley. How am I supposed to pass out these pamphlets? What a mess."

Ophie eyed the papers he was holding, which were emblazoned with the words *Join the Communist Party.* "Well, I bet more people than ever will read them now,"

Ophie murmured absently, gesturing to the driver and passengers leaving the trolley, all of whom were fixated on the poor man's body and the papers strewn about the street. The man turned toward them and nodded.

"By George, I think you're right. I did it." He was already dissipating into a fine mist of sparkles. As the man disappeared, Ophie's breathing eased and the warmth returned to her fingertips. She was getting so used to being around the dead that she hadn't noticed the chill until it was gone.

"Ophelia, you need to pull it together," Mama said, still scowling down at her daughter.

"Are you okay?" Ophie asked, changing the subject. Worry was always part of her mama's scowl, but now it etched deep lines in her brow.

"I'm fine, child," Mama said, leaning back and closing her eyes. "Just hush up now so I can get a little sleep until we get moving."

Ophie said nothing, and the other passengers stumbled and lurched back to their seats after getting their eyeful of the tragedy on the street.

Eventually, the dead man and his pamphlets were cleared from the tracks, a horse-drawn wagon coming to take his body away just as it had Aunt Rose's. No one demanded any cash, they just took the dead man away. There was no way Helen and the cousins hadn't stolen their money outright. Though Ophie was exhausted from her sleepless night, she found she still had enough energy to fume over the unfairness of it all.

The trolley continued on its way, but every time Ophie glanced through her eyelashes at her mother she could sense the older woman was awake and looking at her, worried. For the first time, she wished her mother would go back to ignoring her. She had made a promise, back in Georgia, that she wouldn't bring up the fact that she could see spirits ever again. But it was getting harder and harder to pretend, to keep this part of herself locked away from her mama. The dead were everywhere.

And now they would be living in a house full of ghosts.

Cook cried in happiness to see Ophie and her mama when they knocked at the back door—it was as if she had been preparing for them to arrive ready to take up residence at Daffodil Manor for weeks. She was already up and bustling about, and as they came in she pressed a cup of coffee into Mama's hands.

"You stay here and drink that, you look like you've been through it. I'll show Ophie to the room I set aside for you. Gladys just quit, though—something about the dusty old unused rooms being haunted. Funny, because I never took her to be superstitious. Anyway, if you find the rooms too small you can always switch."

"I'm sure it will be fine," Mama said, voice heavy.

"I get my own room?" Ophie said, almost unable to believe it.

Cook smiled. "You surely do. I am glad you both are here. I figured you'd eventually come around."

"It wasn't exactly a choice," Mama said, but Cook ignored her and continued chattering on at Ophie as they walked down the narrow hallway to the servants' quarters out behind the house.

"I kept telling your mama that it made more sense for you to stay here, what with the terrible family of yours and all the work that still need be done. We're only halfway through airing out the rooms, and do not get me started on the linens. There is enough work for three more housemaids, but with you staying here we'll have a better chance of getting everything done before the party next week."

"We're here because my aunt died," Ophie said, interrupting the tide of Cook's speech. "Not because my mama changed her mind."

Cook paused in unlocking the door to a room. "Oh, child, I am so sorry to hear that. Your mama said the two of you had grown close."

"She's in a better place now," Ophie said, holding her head high as she walked past Cook into the room. The sudden prickle of tears behind her eyes surprised her. She wasn't sad Aunt Rose was gone, was she? She saw her meet up with her husband. She had moved on, just like Daddy and so many other spirits. So why was Ophie about to cry again?

"That might be," Cook said, her expression knowing. "But the missing them doesn't get any easier just 'cause you know they've gone to Heaven. Don't be afraid to grieve, child. Once you get settled come on back to the kitchen and I'll fix you up some breakfast before we get to work."

Cook left to lead Mama to where she'd be staying, and Ophie turned her attention to the room. While she was hungry, she was more interested in taking in her new surroundings. The room contained two narrow beds, and a thick layer of dust covered everything as per usual in Daffodil Manor. But there was something off about the room, a scent that was part gardenia and part sunshine.

"This was her room."

Ophie turned. Colin stood in the doorway.

"Whose?"

"Your friend's. I don't want to say her name because . . . names have power."

Ophie figured he meant Clara, and she sat down on the bed. "I thought she stayed in the attic."

"That was later. After . . ." He trailed off.

"It's probably nice being up there in the sunshine," Ophie said. The sullen ghost boy didn't say anything.

Colin hovered outside the room awkwardly, and Ophie yawned, her jaw fairly cracking with the strength of it. "Why won't you come in?"

He pointed at the threshold. "I can't cross that."

Ophie looked where he indicated. Someone had put down a thick barrier of salt just inside the door. Ophie didn't know who would have known to do that, but she went to the door and brushed the salt aside with her hand. "There, now you can."

"You shouldn't have done that," Colin said, his lips turning downward at the corners. "It's dangerous."

"Why?"

"Because the ghosts here have unfinished business with the living," Colin said. "Something bad is going to happen, soon. You're going to end up in the middle of it. You should be more careful."

"What do you know about Clara?" Ophie asked him, tired of cryptic answers and secrets. "Do you know what happened to her? Do you know how she died? Did you see?"

Colin hesitated only for a moment before shaking

his head. Before he could say anything else, however, there came a sound from behind him, like someone pounding on a door. With a frightened glance over his shoulder, he faded away, leaving Ophie with nothing but questions.

Chapter 20

AFTER A BREAKFAST OF FATBACK AND GRITS WITH lots of butter—Cook foisting a second helping onto Ophie despite her protests—Ophie was sent to take Mrs. Caruthers her morning tray. For the most part, Ophie's day progressed as usual, but by the late afternoon, when she would normally be reading aloud to the old woman, she had been conscripted to help the rest of the household staff clean various rooms, since Gladys was gone. There was no time to hire a replacement, not before the extended family would arrive.

At first Ophie had thought this would give her a chance to sneak away to the attic to look for clues. If that was where Clara had died, then there might be something there for her to find. What, she was not quite sure. It was a long shot, but she didn't have anything else to go by. But Ophie was teamed up with Penelope, the other new girl, so they could clean and make ready the rooms more quickly. The list for Richard's party was ever expanding, and no sooner had they finished readying one room than another needed to be prepared for yet another guest. The work was difficult, and it gave Ophie watery eyes and a runny nose every time she beat the dust out of an old mattress or shook the cobwebs off an ancient set of drapes.

While dusting and wiping and fluffing and sneezing, Ophie wondered what it would be like to have people spend weeks getting a room ready for her. She decided that like everything else about being rich, it must be nice.

One of the things about the mansion that was most decidedly not nice was Penelope. Ophie had sort of hoped living at Daffodil Manor would give her a chance to get to know the older girl better, maybe even be friends, but Penelope seemed to see Ophie less as a coworker and more as an annoyance.

"Are you actually reading these?" she asked the one time she'd caught Ophie in the library reading one of Clara's old *True Romances* magazines. It had been a rare break for Ophie, a return to the old patterns of her day, and she regretted it as soon as she saw the expression on Penelope's face.

"I was just—"

"You were faffing about, avoiding work," Penelope had said, jerking the magazine out of Ophie's hands. "This is stupid," she said after flipping a few pages, and Ophie wondered if Penelope knew how to read. Daddy had taught Ophie to read even though she complained about how hard it was, because he didn't want her to be like so many folks who never got a chance to learn.

"I can read it to you," Ophie offered, and as soon as the words were out of her mouth she realized it was the wrong thing to say. Penelope's expression darkened, and she tore the magazine in half.

"What you can do is help me turn this room over. Come on, before I tell Cook you're reading smut," Penelope said, her tone calm even as she continued to rip the magazine pages. After that, Ophie went out of her way to avoid Penelope. Which was, of course, nearly impossible once they were assigned the same tasks in the afternoon, day after day.

On the third day of Ophie working double duty, Penelope arrived in Mrs. Caruthers's room to fetch Ophie a little earlier than she had before. Whereas Mrs. Caruthers had previously been drifting off on her afternoon nap, this time Mrs. Caruthers was still awake; and when she saw Penelope standing in the doorway, all awkward angles and night-dark skin, she scowled.

"Is this where you've been disappearing to, Amelia? Gallivanting around with this jigaboo instead of seeing to my needs?"

Penelope started at the racial slur, and Ophie, who was unfortunately used to such exclamations from Mrs. Caruthers, just ducked her head. "I was assigned to help clean out the rooms for the new guests in the afternoons, since they're going to be here next week, ma'am," Ophie tried to explain.

Mrs. Caruthers ignored Ophie and stared daggers at Penelope. "I've got my own tasks for Amelia; your laziness is not an excuse for taxing my girl."

Penelope looked from Mrs. Caruthers back to Ophie, confused. "I thought your name was Ophelia," she said.

"It is," Ophie said in a low voice, glancing over her shoulder at Mrs. Caruthers. The surly old woman harrumphed and crossed her arms, not saying anything else, and Ophie pushed Penelope out into the hallway, closing the door behind her.

"I'd better stay with her. The missus gets upset easily," Ophie said. The truth was she would rather stay in the too-hot room and read than strip the dusty beds and sweep out moth-infested closets.

Penelope huffed. "Sounds to me like you trying to get out of work. It ain't like any of this is easy. It takes two people. And with Gladys gone, you're the only one who can help. How am I supposed to get an entire room done by myself?"

Ophie shrugged. "I don't know. I'm sorry."

Ophie went to open the door and Penelope blocked her, grabbing for Ophie's hand on the knob. "She talk to you like that all the time?"

"She's not a nice person," Ophie said. Richard might love his mother, but Ophie had yet to find a single redeeming trait about her. The only times she was remotely tolerable was when she was asleep or on medication. But Ophie wouldn't dare say that out loud.

"She's white," Penelope said, glaring at the door. "The sooner you learn that nice white folks are few and far between, the easier your life will be, kiddo. At least, they're not nice to girls like you and me."

Ophie didn't say anything, just nodded in acknowledgment of Penelope's words.

Penelope sighed heavily. "All right. I'll tell Cook. I ain't about to have her pitching a fit because I didn't get everything done. But you owe me one."

Ophie nodded again and went back into Mrs. Caruthers's room. When she entered, the old woman was snoring loudly, mouth agape and a slight trail of drool beginning to trickle from the side. With a leap of her heart, Ophie realized this was her chance to get up to the attic and snoop around.

"Oh, chickadee, why haven't you been up to see me lately?"

Clara stood next to the fireplace. As usual, something about her presence brightened the room and lightened Ophie's spirits a touch.

"I finally have a chance to go to the attic and investigate where, um, you got hurt," Ophie said. She was normally blunt with the dead, but it felt unseemly to talk about Clara's murder in such a matter-of-fact way. "Do you remember when the cousins came to visit? It would have been right before, ah, you died."

Clara pursed her lips. "Well. My memory of that night is ever so hazy," she said, tapping her lips. "But I do remember dressing up because there was a party. Oh, yes, that must have been because the family was in town! I was wearing a very nice hair comb that fell off in the midst of the attack. Oh, Ophie, I can't—" Her outline flickered, and for a moment Ophie was afraid that she would vanish altogether. But then she solidified and came back into view. "Yes, that might be something to search for. A tortoiseshell hair comb. Next to a gray bureau in the far back corner. That's where I got this fabulous dress," she said, twirling. "I'd completely forgotten about that."

Ophie didn't have a chance to ask anything further, because Clara dissipated, gone as suddenly as she had appeared. Ophie gave one last look to the sleeping Mrs. Caruthers, then quietly stepped out of the room, closing the door softly behind her. She had an opportunity and a plan. She would not waste either.

From one of the newly opened second-floor bedrooms came the sounds of Penelope complaining to herself, and as Ophie hurried by on quiet cat feet, she saw the girl making a bed. Penelope didn't look up as Ophie passed, but the ghost in the army uniform did, raising his bottle in silent toast to Ophie. She didn't respond, her heart pounding in triple time as she made her way to the attic.

"Why do you want to help her so badly?"

Ophie froze, then turned to find Colin standing behind her. Like Clara, he seemed more solid than he had in a very long time, and for a moment Ophie thought about what Aunt Rose had said about ghosts craving the emotions and warmth of the living. Were the ghosts in Daffodil Manor getting stronger because there were more people living there now? Would they continue to build in strength when Richard's guests and family filled the house in a week? What would happen then?

A shiver of premonition ran down Ophie's arms, but she shrugged it away. The ghosts on the trolley cars had never been able to hurt the passengers, and there were far more people riding the trolleys of Pittsburgh than anywhere else. And besides, she had her salt and nail to protect herself, if she needed them.

Colin had not moved, and Ophie considered his question. It poked at her in a way she didn't care for. "Why wouldn't I help Clara? She was murdered. She deserves to know what happened to her."

"What would it change?" he asked with a shrug. "She would still be dead."

"But maybe she could pass on," Ophie said. For the second time, she offered, "I could help you, too, you know."

"No, I got to stay here forever," Colin said, and his outline darkened into a deep blue. "I ain't gonna get to move on."

The squeak of a door opening down the hall startled Ophie and shocked her into motion once more. She hurried to the attic door, flinging it open and running up the steps before anyone could enter the hallway and spy her.

She knew she didn't have much time before someone noticed she was gone, and if Mama found out she was in the attic again . . . Ophie didn't want to see the disappointment on her face. In a heartbeat she made her way to the farthest corner of the attic.

Even with the afternoon sunlight slanting in through the dormer windows, the farthest reaches of the attic were deep in shadow. Ophie knocked her shin into a wooden crate full of Christmas ornaments and stumbled into a hatstand before she managed to gain her bearings. She reached into the pocket of her apron. She had a couple of matches she kept there for when she had to relight Mrs. Caruthers's fireplace, on the rare occasion it went out. She pulled out a match, but as she did something else fell out, landing with a tinkling sound before rolling under a nearby bureau.

Her iron nail.

Ophie's heart skipped rope in her chest. She fell to her knees and reached under the dresser with her hand, the scrollwork of the front bottom edge scraping against her arm painfully. She couldn't see anything but darkness, so she lit the match, carefully using it to peer under the dresser. If she wasn't careful the match would singe her fingertips, or worse, light the entire attic on fire. She had no intention of doing either.

There was no sign of Ophie's nail, but there was something else. The match burned close enough to Ophie's fingertips that she blew it out before lying flat on her stomach and reaching farther under the bureau.

Her fingertips brushed against dust and finally something slightly curved, and after another moment of straining she managed to get her fingertips around it enough to pull it out.

It was a hair comb.

"What you got there, Ophelia?"

Ophie scrambled to her feet, but it was too late. Penelope stood a few feet away, hands on her hips. "I thought you had to look after the missus?"

"I, uh . . ." Ophie searched for some plausible lie to tell Penelope but found none.

"I can see why you snuck away up here," Penelope said.

She didn't sound mad, or like she was going to tell on Ophie. She crossed her fingers and said a silent prayer that the girl would be kind. "Yeah, sometimes I like to come up here for a minute to be by myself. When Mrs. Caruthers is being particularly mean."

"I get it." Penelope gave her a sympathetic look, then spun slowly, taking in everything in the attic. "They must have all kinds of treasures up here, huh? This is the bee's knees. Say!" Penelope exclaimed as her eyes landed on Ophie's hand. "What you got there?"

Ophie wasn't quick enough, and Penelope plucked the tortoiseshell comb from her hand.

"No, that's . . . Well, it belongs to someone who—"

"Gee, this is first-rate," Penelope said, ignoring her. "Tell you what, I'm going to take this, and in exchange I won't rat you out for being up here. I'm thinking Cook won't turn a blind eye to you ducking out on work and nicking the family valuables. Or your mama."

Ophie didn't even get a chance to argue before Penelope dropped the comb in her apron pocket and began heading back toward the stairs. When Ophie didn't move, Penelope called over her shoulder, "You coming, kid? The jig is up, and if Mrs. Caruthers doesn't need you, you're going to help me finish making this bed. It's a bear to do all this work by myself."

Ophie huffed out an annoyed breath, but she was smart enough to know when she was beat. She followed Penelope down the stairs and back into the bedroom she'd been cleaning earlier. The bed was made, most of the surfaces gleamed with a fresh coat of lemon oil, and a bucket and mop were propped up in the corner.

"Since you missed out on beating the mattress, why don't you mop while I take a breather?" Penelope said with a grin. She plopped down in a wing chair, her limbs loose and relaxed, and Ophie envied her for a moment. Penelope didn't seem to worry about anything except for being assigned more work. As she grabbed the mop and bucket from where they'd been left in the corner, Ophie wondered what it must be like to have so few things to worry about.

"Hey, what's this?"

Penelope was rubbing at the tortoiseshell comb, and Ophie leaned the mop against the wall and came over to see what she'd found. A layer of grime, russet flakes and dirt, clung to the back edge of the comb, and Penelope rubbed it in her apron, leaving rusty stains on the white material.

"I think—" Ophie said, swallowing before continuing, "I think that's dried blood."

Penelope gave Ophie an annoyed look. She hated it when people older than her looked at her like she was being dumb. "That's disgusting. But don't go thinking I'm going to give it back to you. This is quality, and besides, it'll look better on me than you."

Ophie didn't say anything, just went back to mopping. Even as the work in the summer heat started to warm her, Ophie could have sworn she felt a chill in the air.

Chapter 21

THE NEXT FEW DAYS OF OPHIE'S LIFE WERE ENTIRELY consumed by work. As the day of Richard's birthday celebration drew near, she was given a list of tasks each morning that found every moment of her day filled. Among them were the usual: take Mrs. Caruthers her breakfast and lunch and dinner trays as well as see to her various needs. But there was also a growing list of additional jobs that had to be done before the family and their guests arrived at the end of the week. It was these tasks that took up far more of Ophie's time. Shining silver, rubbing water spots off fine glasses, and the endless dusting and wiping . . . Everything in Daffodil Manor had to gleam and shine like it hadn't in years.

"It has been so long since we had proper guests—that's why the missus and Mr. Richard are so wound up," Cook said one evening during dinner. "Last time the family came to visit, one of the household staff went missing, and the visit was cut short after it cast a dark cloud over the event. So they've got good reason to be nervous."

The household staff ate together like family, everyone crowded around the big table in the kitchen where Cook kneaded bread and plucked chickens and did all the hard work of preparing food. Their meals were not so fine as the ones enjoyed in the main dining room by Richard and his no-good friends, who snuck around the house so that Mrs. Caruthers wouldn't know there was company and spent most of their time all blotto, as Penelope said. But the food was good and there was plenty of it, which was more than Ophie had enjoyed back at Aunt Rose's. Mealtimes were the only times her mama didn't look worried anymore, either. Though she still rarely said anything.

Ophie and her mama spent all their time together in silence. Ophie did not want to bring up the stolen money or Aunt Rose's death. The one time Ophie had asked about a funeral, Mama's expression had gone hard.

"We are not returning to that nest of vipers. Besides, the Ca007u000therses won't give us the time off, not with everything that needs to be done."

And that was the end of that.

If Mama had gone silent, Penelope had become an absolute chatterbox. The older girl had never had any interest in Ophie, the most they'd talked had been the day she took the tortoiseshell comb for her own. But over the next few days as they worked to give every-thing in Daffodil Manor one more cleaning, shining, polishing, Penelope chatted with Ophie like they were old friends. It seemed to Ophie that the gift of the tortoiseshell comb—or rather, the unprotested theft—had changed Penelope slightly for the better. She told Ophie stories of her childhood and asked her questions and told jokes that she laughed at before Ophie could even process the punch line. If anyone would have seen them they would have thought that the two were fast friends, but Penelope's suddenly easy manner made Ophie nervous.

She wasn't used to so much attention or warmth. And she was afraid that if she started to appreciate it the kindness would disappear.

"Say, chickadee, are you listening or are you giving me the cold shoulder?" Penelope asked one afternoon as they cleaned the windows on the second floor. The bank of windows was opposite the narrow attic door, and every now and again Ophie found herself gazing longingly at the small door as she remembered her days of blessed freedom. But mostly she was thinking about Clara, and where the haint could have gotten to.

Ophie hadn't seen the ghost since the day she'd searched the attic, and as the Virginia cousins got closer to arriving, the more Ophie found her quiet moments taken with puzzling through everything she knew of Clara's end. Clara's death had to be the key to helping her pass on, but Ophie didn't have any suspects except for the relatives who would be arriving on the morrow. The closer she got to the day that the relatives from Virginia would arrive, the more Ophie worried that she would end up face-to-face with a murderer. Or even worse, be no closer to the truth of Clara's end than she'd been when she'd first discovered the ghost.

"Now I know you're ignoring me!"

Ophie startled and turned toward Penelope, whose full lips were puckered in annoyance.

"What?"

"Ophie! I was just telling you this story about the movie I went and saw last week. Chickadee, believe me when I tell you that the leading man was just the cat's meow."

"What did you just call me?" Ophie said, her suspicions suddenly flaring. "Chickadee" was entirely too familiar.

Penelope widened her eyes. "What, 'chickadee'? It's

a term of endearment. Don't they have chickadees in Georgia? Tiny little birds, oh, so adorable. Like you."

Ophie didn't know whether there were chickadees in Georgia, but she did know it was something Clara called her. "Why did you call me that?"

"It's from the movie I was telling you about!" Penelope said with a dramatic sigh. "Ophie! You've got to get the cotton out of your ears. I was telling you how dashing the leading man was and how the leading lady calls him chickadee and he laughs and she gets mad." Penelope grinned at Ophie. "It was funny. Haven't you ever been to a picture show?"

Ophie shook her head and went back to washing the windows. She felt embarrassed and awkward, like she'd accidentally stepped on someone's foot. Here Penelope had been trying to be nice and Ophie had tried to make it something else. Of course it had been because of something Penelope had seen. It wasn't like she could see the dead; it wasn't like she knew Clara. There was no way she could copy a dead woman. It was just silly.

Ophie yawned. She was so tired. She felt like she spent more time working now than ever before and got less sleep. She hadn't had any nightmares like everyone else, but she found it hard to fall asleep in the bed all by herself. She was used to having Mama snoring softly next to her, and she realized that she missed the closeness, even if it was when her mama was asleep.

"We should take you to the movies, Ophelia Harrison," Penelope announced, seemingly out of nowhere.

Ophie blinked. "What?" Had she missed another lengthy lecture on a movie plot and the dreaminess of the leading man?

"I'm just saying, you're what, twelve? If you're old enough to work you're old enough to go with me to the movies. Come on, we can go after dinner."

"My mama wouldn't let me go downtown without her." And there was very little chance Mama would want to take Ophie to a picture show. She thought they were silly and frivolous, and now that they were living at Daffodil Manor they were making even less money each week since their room and board were covered. Ophie could not see Mama parting with a nickel, let alone a whole quarter for a picture show.

Penelope pursed her lips before her expression brightened. "We can sneak out! Just tell your mama you're tired and you're heading to bed early. We'll even get ice cream after. It'll be the perfect night!"

Ophie paused in her wiping and looked at Penelope. The girl had been rubbing at the same single pane of glass for the last few minutes, but that wasn't why Ophie stared at her. "You want me to sneak out to go to the cinema with you?" She wasn't quite sure what to say.

"Yes! You ever been? It's amazing, the way a story unfolds on a screen. Oh, I love it so much."

Ophie wanted to go. She could feel the desire burning in her chest. They could go to the cinema and then a sweet shop. She could have just one evening of fun, one small taste of the indulgence she had heard about the cousins enjoying time and time again.

Ophie let herself imagine it for one shining moment: riding the trolley downtown, her and Penelope laughing and telling secrets and jokes, sitting in a theater—here her imagination got a bit hazy because she didn't really get what a picture show was besides moving pictures and music—getting a bag of penny candy, peppermints, and eating them until her lips turned red.

It was a nice fantasy, but Ophie knew that's all it was.

"I'm not going to lie to my mama. She would catch me out, no problem." Ophie didn't even like lying to her mama about the ghosts; something like sneaking out was out of the question.

A whistling came down the hallway, and Richard rounded the corner, spinning his hat in his hands as he walked. A sly look came over Penelope's face, and she dropped her washrag in the bucket at their feet.

"We're gonna get you to the cinema yet."

Before Ophie could say anything else, Penelope was running down the hallway toward Richard, who turned in surprise when she tugged on his jacket. Penelope stood on her toes to whisper something in his ear, and he laughed. Ophie frowned. When had the new girl become so familiar with Richard? But then he was reaching into his pocket and pulling out a money clip. As Ophie watched in surprise, he handed Penelope two whole dollars.

"Have fun at the cinema, Ophelia!" Richard called as he walked toward the staircase, and Penelope jogged back to their bucket of dirty window water.

"What did you say to him?" Ophie said, her heart thrumming with fear. Now that there was no Aunt Rose and no money, her job was more important than ever. Ophie could feel the fear and desperation that radiated off her mother since they'd moved into Daffodil Manor, the same way it had when they rode the train away from Georgia. If Penelope got her fired, they would have nothing left.

"Don't be such a nervous Nellie. I simply told him that you had never been to a picture show and that with everyone arriving tomorrow you wouldn't have a chance for a good long bit. And isn't that simply a tragedy?" Penelope's eyes shined with a feverish light, and Ophie turned away in discomfort, focusing on the bit of window that she had been cleaning over and over for the past minute or so.

She was excited, too, so much so that her belly hurt. How was she supposed to repay such kindness?

"Anyway," Penelope said, continuing on. "Richard agreed that you deserved a nice night out, and so we are going to the picture show as soon as we finish these windows. And he even gave us two dollars to cover the tickets and get something to eat. So go get changed, chickadee! I'm taking you to the movies."

"My mama is going to say no, even with Mr. Richard paying our way," Ophie said. She didn't want to rain on Penelope's parade, but she also didn't want the girl to be disappointed when no one supported her grand scheme.

"Ah, Ophie, that's no matter! We just tell her that Richard insisted that we go to the movies and have a good time because we've been working so hard. She won't be able to say no. Trust me. You leave everything to me and we're going to have a first-rate time."

Ophie stopped wiping at the window and turned to look at Penelope, really look at the girl. Her smile was open and honest. The idea of doing something fun gladdened Ophie's heart. Some of the sadness that had hung over her like a dark cloud for the past few days dissipated. Penelope seemed so sure that everything would work out just fine. It was hard for Ophie to doubt her.

"Thank you, Penelope. That's . . . that's real nice."

"Pfft, I'm excited, too! I want to see that new Felix the Cat. And if there's a Charlie Chaplin we should try to get into that one as well." Penelope bounced up onto the toes of her feet in excitement. "So let's get these windows finished so we can catch the evening show."

They finished washing up the windows quicker than they ever had before and took the bucket of wash water down to the kitchen to empty out. Penelope told Ophie that if Ophie took the bucket outside to clean it, she would take care of telling Cook and Mama that they were going to change and head downtown to see a picture show.

When Ophie entered—her shoes wet because she'd poured out the water too fast in her excitement to go to a movie—she paused on the threshold at the twin expressions of Cook and Mama. Both women had crossed their arms and looked like they'd just had a sip of too-tart lemonade.

"Ophelia, you have a hand in this?" Mama demanded, giving Penelope a bit of side-eye.

"No, Mama," Ophie said. "I mean, Penelope asked Richard while I was still washing the windows. And he told us to have a nice time." It wasn't a lie, and Ophie just hoped it bolstered whatever pleas Penelope had made.

"Mrs. Harrison, you aren't going to keep her from

going, are you?" Penelope asked, a look of horror coming over her face. "Richard specifically told her that he wanted to hear what she thought of the cinema." Penelope gave her a sly smile.

Ophie couldn't believe it, but it sounded like this would work.

"That sounds just like something that fool boy would say," Cook muttered, before sighing. "Well, what do you think, Etta? I suppose these two should go and have a good time? I'd not like to be explaining to Mr. Richard why it was that his gift went unappreciated."

Mama's pinched expression did not waver, but she turned to Ophie and said, "Make sure you stay with Penelope. She knows the trolleys and will make sure you get to the show and back without a fuss."

"Yes'm," Ophie said, but she was unable to keep the grin off her face.

Penelope ran over to Ophie and grabbed her hand. "Let's change first and then we'll go. I want to fix my hair."

"Speaking of which," Cook said, a tone entering her voice, "where'd you get that tortoiseshell comb?"

Penelope dropped Ophie's hand to reach up to her head, and for a moment it was like she'd forgotten she was even wearing the hair ornament. Her eyes went far away, and a grimace played over her lips. But a fraction of a heartbeat later the expression had faded and she gave Cook a wide grin.

"Cook! Don't you know that a lady never kisses and tells?"

And then Penelope had Ophie's hand in hers and was pulling her through the kitchen to the hallway, and onward to new adventures.

The Trolley Cars and the Cinema

PITTSBURGH WAS MADE OF STEEL AND DREAMS, AND so were her trolley cars. Trolleys went to every corner of the city, zipping up and down hills, their clanging bells a warning for anyone careless enough to wander onto the tracks. Usually folks would dash out of the way in moments, so familiar they were with the trolley and her signal. But sometimes the warning was not heeded, and when that happened the trolley car would add one more ghost to the horde that prowled the Steel City.

And trolleys did not care for the dead any more than they cared for the living. There was a schedule to be kept.

Hundreds of miles of track crisscrossed Pittsburgh, taking people to work and play, back home and out once more. People of all ages and colors used the street-cars to get where they needed to go, yet another way in which the living and the dead were not as different as they might think.

And the one place a body could count on finding both the living and the dead in the evenings was the theater.

The dead loved the movies. Not just because it was a place where the living gathered, but because for a few minutes at a time they could see all the world, not just their little corner of North America. Books required fingers to turn the pages and a heart to feel the emotions of the characters on the page, but the cinema was different. A haint could sit in a theater seat, turning the room frigid even in the middle of summer, and simply watch. Movies gave them a window into nearly everything they so longed for. There was the newsreel that told of amazing inventions and adventures in far-off lands; there were the cartoons and the slapstick comedies, Charlie Chaplin and Buster Keaton. And then there were the proper films, the dramas, sweeping histories and heartbreaking romances. And although the films had no dialogue to accompany them—not just yet—the actors on-screen did all the work of feeling a million different emotions for the dead, giving them a taste of what it meant to be alive once more.

Ghosts congregated thickly in the theaters. For every living body enjoying a show there were four or five haints crowded in close, the people and the ghosts coexisting like they did in few other places, and the moving pictures connecting all of them to a world they would never know again. This was why there was always a number of restless souls in the theater, no matter the film.

And it was there that the spirits would get their first look at the girl who could see the dead walking arm in arm with a dead girl determined to live once more.

Chapter 22

OPHIE DISEMBARKED FROM THE TROLLEY FEELING light for the first time in as long as she could remember. She was going to the cinema. She'd put on her Sunday best, which was really just a nice blue dress with a pair of plain black shoes that didn't pinch her toes, a gift from Cook, who still had some of her children's old things lying about. Ophie felt both fancy and bubbly, like she was made of soda pop. She was still worried about Clara, and what might happen once the relatives from Virginia arrived, but she tried to push it all to the back of her mind. *I can have fun for just one night, can't I?* she thought, and vowed to ignore the ghosts that pressed in all around her out in the city. She was going to have a good time.

There were two cinemas in Pittsburgh. The first one they came to was the Orpheus, but Penelope put her arm around Ophie's shoulder and dragged her away from there before she could even read the names of the films on the marquee.

"That's not for you and me," Penelope said, pointing to all the fancy white folks climbing out of their cars curbside. "We'd have to sit in the balcony where it's smoky and loud, and that's no good for a girl's first picture! Come on, we're going down to Center Avenue. Just you wait until you see the Elmore Theatre. You're going to flip."

Ophie followed Penelope as she walked fast enough that her pace was nearly a run. The air was humid and sticky, but a breeze from one of the three rivers that intersected in Pittsburgh provided some relief. Still, by the time they made it to the theater Ophie was sweaty and a bit out of sorts. She had spent most of her time in Pittsburgh moving between Daffodil Manor, Aunt Rose's house, and the African Methodist Episcopal Church on Sundays, since that was the one that Aunt Rose had favored. So seeing all the storefronts, automobiles, and people in this part of the city was new and fascinating. But Penelope's pace was relentless, as if she was worried this might be the last time she'd get to go to the cinema. She dodged around pedestrians and traffic, pulling Ophie along, never slowing, not even for the trolley that went clanging past.

"Why didn't we just ride the trolley all the way there?" Ophie asked, grabbing Penelope's arm and dragging her back from the crosswalk before she could be smashed by the rumbling streetcar.

Penelope frowned as the trolley went by. "I . . . don't know. I just always walk to this part of town. This is the way I always went." The confusion on Penelope's face dampened some of Ophie's enthusiasm, but then the older girl shook herself and grinned widely. "Anyway, there it is. Look! A theater just for us."

At first Ophie wasn't sure what Penelope meant, but as they got closer she could see that all the people filing into the theater were colored. Not a single white person was around, even though some of the men and women had the lightest of brown skin tones. "Passing light," Mama called it. Negroes who were pale enough to pretend to whiteness if they so desired.

Ophie was so surprised to see a theater just for colored folks that she stopped in the middle of the road and Penelope had to grab her by the hand and pull her up onto the sidewalk. There was only one movie playing, and as they waited in line to buy tickets Ophie couldn't help but bounce a little in excitement. She didn't even care what they saw—if movies were half as good as Penelope described, she was in for a treat.

After they'd bought their tickets, Ophie followed

Penelope through the lobby to the theater itself. The seats were made of polished wood, most of them still empty as people filed in for the showing, and Penelope wasted no time sitting right in the front row nearest to the piano. "This is the best spot, because you can feel the music in your bones," she whispered. Ophie was overwhelmed by all there was to look at: the finely dressed colored folks, the heavy drapes that made the space feel grand and special, the wide white screen waiting for the film. She shivered and looked around to find that more than half of the people milling about were ghosts, the dead crowding in for the evening show the same as the living.

A particularly large white man dressed as a butcher, with a blood-spattered apron and a meat cleaver, stopped in front of them. Ophie pushed back into the seat, her heart pounding. The man was filmy, and staring through him at the screen was like looking through a dense fog. It was somehow more disconcerting than if the haint had been solid.

"Get along," Penelope muttered, her voice low. When the ghost turned toward her, she huffed. "Not here, not if you know what's good for you."

The ghost looked at Penelope and then at Ophie and moved away, leaving their view of the screen clear once more. But Ophie could hardly focus on the screen, even as a colored woman sat down at the piano and played a rousing opening and the lights went down.

Penelope saw the dead man, just the same as she could.

"You can see," Ophie said, her mouth suddenly dry as she stared at Penelope.

"Hmm, what? Oh, of course, that's why you sit in the front. Otherwise someone walks in with an ugly hat and that's what you get for the whole show. Hey, it's starting!"

On the pale screen the story had begun to unfold. Ophie felt a brief thrill at the thought that Penelope might have the same ability she did—a new friend, and one to whom she might be able to talk to about ghosts. Could she see the haints at Daffodil Manor as well? Finding out what had happened to Clara would surely be easier with a partner.

But even as Ophie's body vibrated with excitement, she couldn't shake the feeling that something was off. "Penelope, if you can see them, then—"

"Shh! You're not allowed to talk during the picture, silly!"

Ophie fell quiet as the story of a man falling in love with an Indian princess on a rugged frontier began to unspool. The questions swirling in her mind would have to wait.

After the film, which Ophie liked but was sure she had only really half understood, she and Penelope made their way to a nearby sweet shop for ice cream, the storefront visible from the doors of the theater. Like most businesses in that part of town the sweet shop was run and owned entirely by colored people, and Ophie realized she had never ever seen such a thing before. It filled her with a sense of ease, and as they approached, she spun around, taking in the small part of Pittsburgh where it seemed that being a Negro was no more unusual than wearing a hat. A tension that Ophie always carried with her melted away. It was the constant fear of saying the wrong thing or looking the wrong way at a white person, the inevitable consequences of such a trespass. There was something nice about realizing that there really was nothing wrong with being colored, despite what some folks thought.

The breeze had died down, leaving the night muggy and hot, and Ophie felt the smaller hairs that had pulled free from her braids curling up. Even Penelope's own hot-ironed coif was looking a little frizzy, as she talked nonstop about the movie. "You know, that is the third time I've seen that film, and it's always so great! The director of that film is Oscar Micheaux, and he is one of the finest race men of our times. Do you read the *Courier*?"

Ophie blinked. She'd had trouble following along with Penelope's chattering all day, and so she gave a polite smile and shook her head.

Penelope continued barreling along. "Well! The paper said Mr. Micheaux has a new film coming later this year, and I am desperate to see it on opening night. You will have to come with me, chickadee. I demand it." And then Penelope let out a laugh that was high and bright.

A laugh that Ophie had definitely heard before.

Penelope pulled Ophie into the crowded sweet shop and into line at the counter, nattering on about the movie. Ophie, though, was frozen. She thought about the ghost at the theater; Penelope had most definitely seen him. But had she seen him because she had the same power Ophie did, or could she see him because . . .

Ophie eyed the comb in Penelope's hair.

"Hello?" Penelope was talking to her. "What flavor do you want, Ophie?"

"I . . . I'm not . . ."

"Oh, I'll order for you, slowpoke."

Ophie watched in a daze as Penelope ordered their cones, then led them to a table in the front of the sweet shop.

Ophie turned to look out the window, and it was then that the last of her happiness and joy melted away. It was full dark now, and there were fewer streetlamps in this part of the city than in the more affluent neighborhood where Daffodil Manor was located. The darkness outside created a mirrorlike effect in the glass of the display window. Ophie could see herself holding her cone. But it was not her own reflection that unsettled her.

As she glanced toward Penelope, the face reflected back was not that of the dark-skinned girl. Instead, Clara was there, grinning at Ophie, her bright smile and pale skin shimmering in the glass.

Ophie turned, and there was Penelope, same as before.

Penelope frowned. "Why the stormy look, chickadee? Is there something the matter with your cone?"

"No, nothing at all," Ophie said, the lie sticking in her throat. She gave her vanilla cone a lick, but barely tasted it. "It's exactly what I wanted."

Her heart pounded as she remembered Clara's words in the hallway, about how she wished she was real so that she could be Ophie's friend. Ophie took a deep breath and thought about what Aunt Rose had said that first night she spoke to Ophie—that some of the more powerful haints could take control of a person's body. Is that what Clara had done to Penelope?

Had Ophie accidentally made Clara too strong with all those cookies?

Ophie couldn't puzzle out what she was supposed to do. Before that moment, she wouldn't have thought Clara would ever want to hurt her, or anyone else. But why hadn't she told Ophie? Why did she let her believe that Penelope was the one taking her out for movies and ice cream? As much as Ophie didn't want to believe it, she worried that if Clara was able to take over someone's body against their will, then she probably had some sort of plan about what she wanted to do with it. Maybe it was just that she wanted to spend an evening of movies and ice cream with Ophie.

Or maybe it was something else entirely.

Penelope—or Clara, Ophie supposed she should call her—laughed and reached for Ophie's cone, exchanging it with hers. "Here, take mine so you can try chocolate. Even though you've already eaten more than half of yours. Gosh, you sure are lucky that I'm such a stand-up gal." She grinned as she took a bite of the vanilla cone while Ophie gave her a wan smile.

Clara exclaimed, and Ophie turned to see that she was looking at a nearby woman's hat. Clara stood and walked over to the woman. Ophie took a deep breath and let it out. She still saw Penelope in front of her, but in the reflection of the plate-glass window, it was Clara who walked up to the woman, Clara who grinned and complimented a stranger's fine sense of style.

Clara had been hurt as badly as anyone Ophie knew. It wasn't fair. Clara deserved to know who had hurt her, and why. It was what anyone would want, what everyone deserved. And Clara deserved it, too. But Clara was a ghost. Ghosts couldn't help but be drawn to the living. And from what Ophie had seen, from what Aunt Rose had always said, ghosts didn't always have a choice about what they wanted—or how they went about getting it.

This was why it was so important to help them. Seeing what Clara was capable of, Ophie finally understood what Aunt Rose was trying to teach her about haints during that first lesson, so many weeks ago. Ghosts, it seemed, were like painful truths—you could ignore them, try to keep them secret, but sooner or later, they were going to come out, for better or worse.

What sort of painful truth was hiding in Clara?

Ophie decided that for the moment she couldn't do anything about Clara. And until she had a better idea of what Clara wanted she would act normal so that the ghost would not suspect that Ophie was on to her. She ate the chocolate cone quickly, anxious to get back to Daffodil Manor and think on this new development in the safety of her room. It seemed like the most benign of tragedies that she didn't like the chocolate ice cream nearly as much as she had the vanilla. A small sadness in light of everything else.

There were so many questions swirling around in Ophie's mind, but it was the loudest one that caused Ophie's shoulders to droop and dread to weigh heavily in her belly.

Just what would a murdered girl do when she had a body to do as she pleased?

Chapter 23

OPHIE SLEPT TERRIBLY, HER DREAMS PLAGUED BY ghosts walking around Pittsburgh wearing the skins of other people. At one point in her dream her daddy had appeared, only he was possessing Richard Caruthers, giving Ophie a dollar so that she could go see a movie and get an ice cream cone. When Ophie had begged him to stay, he'd taken the arm of a pretty white lady and walked away, his hat at a jaunty angle.

Ophie woke crying, her cheeks still damp. In the darkness of the room she listened to her even breathing and knew right then and there that it didn't matter what Clara's reasons were for possessing Penelope. Whether she was trying to find out what happened to her, or even if she just wanted to be able to spend time with Ophie, like they were true friends . . . *No*, Ophie thought. Clara's life had been taken unfairly, but it wasn't fair of her to take Penelope's in return. Clara was in pain, and Ophie promised herself she'd help her; but first, she had to find a way to get the ghost out of Penelope's body.

It wasn't often that Ophie woke before her mother, and she used the rare opportunity to tiptoe into Mama's room and fill the ewer of water in the corner so that it was one less chore Mama had to attend to before she started her day. As much as Ophie was worried about Clara riding around in Penelope's skin, she was also worried about her mama as well. Losing their savings and moving into Daffodil Manor had done something to the older woman's spirit, causing her skin to go sallow and her eyes to lose the snap of temper that belied Mama's true feelings even when she was being gracious to folks who didn't deserve it. Ophie wanted to help. But how did one go about mending a broken dream? It hadn't just been the idea of their own place that had spurred Mama—it had also been the promise of a better life, the chance to own her own hair salon. Now, with the loss of their savings, those dreams felt as far away as ever. It would be months before they could simply save up enough to even think about moving out of the manor. And what if the Caruthers decided they didn't need as much live-in help before their financials were sorted? Ophie saw how quickly and easily the Carutherses hired and fired help, and it once again lit a fire of anger in her that her and her mama's fortunes were so out of their control. She had a profound moment of helplessness before she hefted the ceramic pitcher and went to fetch water so her mama could wash her face.

If Ophie couldn't fix the big things happening, she could focus on the small tasks that she could accomplish, and right now that was filling a pitcher with water so that her mama didn't have to.

The closest spigot was out the back of the servants' quarters toward the garden, so that's the way Ophie went, feeling her way along in the near dark. A little gray light filtered in from the window in the back door, and she used it to guide her out of the hallway of the small house. Once outside, Ophie filled the pitcher and returned to Mama's room. Then she used some of the water to wash her own face, changed from her nightgown to the maid's dress she wore for her usual chores, and finally made her way to the kitchen.

Cook only grunted when she saw Ophie, which was not unusual. The woman was not, as Mama said, a lark, but more a night owl. She only rose early in the morning because Mrs. Caruthers liked to have her first cup of tea with the dawn, and now that Ophie lived in

Daffodil Manor that task fell to her. Once Cook had prepared the tea set, Ophie hefted the tray and took it up to the old woman's room.

Ophie froze at the top of the stairs. By now the sun had full come up, and sunshine streamed in from the windows at the far end of the hall. The electric hallway lights were also still on, so it was easy to make out the figure standing in front of Mrs. Caruthers's bedroom.

Penelope.

Was Clara still possessing her? The girl didn't move, didn't knock. She just stood next to the door, nose an inch away from wood, hand on the knob, as though she had fallen asleep in the midst of opening the door.

"You're up early," Ophie said, trying for a friendly tone and failing miserably. She swallowed hard. The salt and iron nail, a replacement for the one she'd lost in the attic, were both in her apron pocket. But that did not mean that fear did not uncurl in her middle. She saw that the tortoiseshell comb was still in Penelope's hair, and for the first time Ophie began to wonder about it. There was no doubt that the comb had belonged to Clara, and the ghost had sent Ophie to retrieve it the last time she'd seen her. Was it possible Clara had intended for Ophie to wear the comb? Could it be Ophie Clara would be riding around in if Penelope hadn't stolen it? Thinking about it made

Ophie's hands shake, and it was the chiming of the unstable porcelain that finally got Penelope's attention.

"Oh, I didn't see you there. I must have gotten lost in the clouds," Penelope said. She laughed, stiff and creaky. The girl shook her head and gave Ophie a smile. "This isn't Richard's room?"

"No, it's Mrs. Caruthers's," Ophie said.

Clara was still in there, she was sure of it. There was no reason Penelope would be bothering Richard at such an early hour; everyone knew he never woke much before eight. Penelope, in fact, had no business near Richard's room, no matter what the hour. But Clara . . . she might.

"How are you feeling?" Ophie ventured.

Clara laughed. "Just woolgathering!" she said, not really answering Ophie's question. "I suppose I should go and break my fast before Cook gives away my portion to that scallywag son of hers, Leo!"

Ophie blinked. Cook's children had grown up in the house but had left and gone off to other places a couple of years ago, California and Boston and the like. Ophie had even gotten a pair of shoes left behind by one of Cook's grown daughters. What was happening? Had the ghost lost touch with the world around her? And if so, what would happen next?

Clara walked away, unsteady and confused, and

Ophie paused on the threshold to Mrs. Caruthers's room for a moment before she entered. Her mind was a whirl of questions and panicked thoughts, and she had to take a deep breath and push them to the side before she could twist open the knob and go in.

Mrs. Caruthers still snored, and Ophie placed the tray on the small table before going to open the curtains for the older woman. When Ophie turned back toward the bedroom door she finally understood why it was that Clara/Penelope had paused outside the room in such a strange manner.

Someone had placed a thick band of salt across the threshold just inside the bedroom door.

Ophie had no time to investigate who might have placed the band of salt in Mrs. Caruthers's bedroom. Because shortly after breakfast, the relatives from Virginia began to arrive.

Ophie had imagined that the "cousins" would be children like her own cousins, just maybe white and a little bit nicer, judging by how excited Richard was to see them. But the cousins were not young—in fact they were all very, very old. Ophie quickly got lost in the names of them all, so she began to give them names of her own making in her mind. There was the Blue-Haired One and the Fancy-Hat One and the

Laughs-Too-Loud One and on and on until Ophie realized that she probably didn't even need to have names for them all.

She just had to stay out of the way.

Penelope—Clara—and Mama were responsible for settling each of the cousins into their various rooms, while Ophie's task remained the same: care for Mrs. Caruthers. The old woman's room had been opened up to allow in a fresh breeze, and the cousins stopped by to pay their respects throughout the morning as they arrived. Mrs. Caruthers was uncharacteristically gracious and bright, sending Ophie off to fetch things with much more polite words than usual, and praising her each time she returned with a new tray for yet another cousin who had stopped by to catch up.

"Ophelia is simply a lifesaver," Mrs. Caruthers said at one point, nearly making Ophie drop the tray of dirty teacups and empty cookie plates in surprise. "She may be young, but she is a fine, fine girl."

It was a strange day indeed, and when Mrs. Caruthers decided to take a nap before dinner Ophie took that moment to escape to the safety of the kitchen. Cook was nowhere to be found, but Mr. Henry leaned against the counter drinking a tall glass of tea. He saw Ophie enter and poured her a glass as well, complete with ice.

"Here you go. You earned it," he said.

The tea was tooth-achingly sweet, and Ophie sucked it down gratefully after a day spent running tea trays up and down the grand staircase.

"Thank you," she said with a grateful smile, and he held up his glass to her. Then they fell silent. Ophie didn't know Mr. Henry all that well. They spent their days in different parts of the manor, and Cook and Penelope did most of the talking at dinner. But he had always been kind to her, and it was nice to be able to sit comfortably in silence with him now. As she sat and sipped, Ophie considered who in the household could have put the salt inside Mrs. Caruthers's room.

That's when Colin appeared in the kitchen.

"Ask him," the boy said, pointing to Mr. Henry.

The old man shivered visibly and gave Ophie a small smile. "I guess someone just ran over my grave," he said.

"Ask him about the salt, Ophie," Colin said once more, before evaporating into nothing.

Ophie gnawed on her lower lip, before taking a deep breath and letting it out. Even though Ophie was skeptical about trusting any ghosts at the moment, Colin had never steered her wrong, that she could tell, anyway.

"Mr. Henry, I noticed there was some salt just

inside of Mrs. Caruthers's door."

The old colored man paused in taking a drink of his sweet tea and set the glass aside. "Now, what do you know about salt lines, Miss Ophelia Harrison?"

Ophie stood as tall as possible. "I know the salt lines keep haints out, and for protection you've got to carry a bit of salt on you along with some iron so that the dead can't go riding your flesh, which is a thing powerful spirits can do."

The old man grinned at her and pulled out a heavy key that he wore on a string around his neck. "My mama gave me this before I left Virginia, a long, long time ago. And I suppose you already figured that I've got some salt."

Ophie nodded. "Who are you afraid of, Mr. Henry?"

The old man's eyes narrowed. "Child, what are you nattering on about?"

"Is it . . . Clara?"

Mr. Henry dropped the key back down his shirt and sighed, scrubbing a hand over his face. "That's a sad story if ever there was one. Everyone says that she just ran off the last time these relatives were in town, but I have my suspicions that . . . well, that ain't a bit of business you want to go poking after, Miss Ophelia. Leave it alone."

"I can't," Ophie said, crossing her arms. "And if you know about haints, then you know as well as I do that secrets never stay buried, especially when the dead have unfinished business." Ophie didn't know why, but she was feeling mighty bold. She was tired of adults telling her what to do. For once, she was going to boss right back. Even if she would maybe regret it later.

Mr. Henry opened his mouth to respond, but before he could say anything Penelope burst into the kitchen, eyes feverish and excited.

"Get the champagne Richard hid in the root cellar, Mr. Henry. He said he has an important announcement to make. And everyone gets champagne!"

Mr. Henry set aside his glass and pulled a rag out of his back pocket, wiping away the sweat that sprang up on his brow. "I've seen this play out before, and I got a bad feeling."

"What happened last time?" Ophie said, her mind and heart racing.

Mr. Henry's friendly expression shuttered, his eyes going hooded. "Nothing good, dear child. Nothing good."

Ophie gripped her sweet tea as Mama and Cook entered the kitchen and began placing champagne flutes onto silver trays. Cook's expression matched Mr. Henry's, grim and resigned, and Ophie knew right then that she, too, was thinking about Clara.

It seemed more and more that it could have been

one of the cousins from Virginia who had killed Clara. Ophie fit the puzzle pieces together once more in her mind. Clara remembered dressing up for a grand get-together when she was attacked. Then there were Richard's words when he told his mother that their relatives were coming—the way he'd trailed off when he said they hadn't been to Daffodil Manor since . . . since when? Since something happened to Clara?

But why would any of the Caruthers' relatives want to do harm to someone like Clara? Mrs. Caruthers's favorite servant, someone who everyone, apparently, adored? And if one of them did kill Clara, did that mean there was a danger to Ophie, or her mama, or anyone else?

Ophie didn't have any guesses, yet. But she knew if someone was going to find out, it would have to be her.

Daffodil Manor

◦◦◦

THE HOUSE AND THE ATTIC ARGUED. IT WAS INEVI-
table. At least once or twice a year the house had to
turn in on itself as parts of it became agitated, and the
attic was usually the loudest of them all. She would
complain about her dusty rafters, her neglected heir-
looms, the leaky roof, anything and everything.

But this was the first time she had complained about
her missing ghost.

"She's here. You stole her," the attic said, communi-
cating through creaky timbers and the chittering sounds
of rodents nesting in forgotten boxes of clothing.

"I have my own ghosts. I don't need yours," the
house sent back in noisy floorboards and squeaky door
hinges. Their argument had been carrying on for days,
until the house was too preoccupied with the influx of

new people into its rooms to pay attention.

But that was when it sensed it.

It was a house's job to know everything about the people within him, to track movements and bear witness to the lives lived. Some of the guests the house had met before, and he welcomed them back into favorite bedrooms even though they'd been gone for far too long. But as he did so he could sense the wrongness, the dual consciousness of one of the people within. It was like finding an egg with two yolks, shocking and unsettling.

"I have found your missing ghost," he sent to the attic in a sigh of settling timbers.

The attic was still in a sulk. She did not respond.

"If you would like, I will keep an eye on her."

The attic, predictably, did not answer. Not because she could not, but because she loved to gloat when she knew she was right.

There was not much that the house could do. It was, after all, just so much wood and brick. But not even the living people who crowded his rooms could have prevented what came next. Some truths, left ignored too long, had no choice but to win out.

And so Daffodil Manor did what it had always done. It bore witness to what was yet to come.

Chapter 24

THERE WERE ONLY FOUR BOTTLES OF CHAMPAGNE in the cellar, and with the Prohibition on there was no easy way anyone could run out and buy more. So Cook and Mr. Henry divided the bottles among twenty champagne flutes, and poured a measure of a bottle of Coca-Cola for the household staff, since there was no champagne left.

Ophie carried a tray of champagne flutes very carefully, holding the silver tray with both hands as the Carutherses' various cousins each took a flute, exclaiming over having champagne.

"Richard, you must have paid a fortune to have this shipped here!" a particularly wizened old woman said. She was one of the few who did not wait for Richard's toast before raising the glass to her lips and taking a smacking sip.

"You're going to have to bring me another, dear," the old woman said to Ophie, waving her empty glass at her.

Ophie said nothing, just moved through the crowd until her tray was empty. Once she was out of glasses, Mama waved her over to where the rest of the household help stood in a line nearest to the grand front door that Ophie would never walk through. She hadn't even known the fine thing opened at all until visitors had poured in through it earlier that day. She had figured it was just for show; no one had ever used it that she had seen, not even Richard, who preferred to exit through the kitchen, since it was closest to the garage.

Many things were different at Daffodil Manor, and Ophie was fearful at what that would bring out.

"I tried to save a little champagne for us, but Cook caught me." Clara, still inside Penelope's body, sidled up to Ophie and winked, handing her a half-full glass of soda pop.

Ophie took a drink of it, and Clara waved her off.

"Save it for the toast!"

"What are we toasting?" Ophie asked, stealing a sweet sip.

"I don't know, but doesn't Richard look dreamy?" Clara said, sighing with her whole body. Ophie couldn't share Clara's admiration; all she could imagine was one of the people in the room having a fight with poor, lovestruck Clara and killing her in a fit of rage, which was exactly what happened in most of the detective stories.

Richard stood on the stairs, a wide grin on his face. He wore a red rose in his lapel and a new suit. His brown hair had been slicked to the side, and Ophie supposed he must be handsome.

Mrs. Caruthers stood next to him, leaning heavily on his arm, looking just as happy. It was difficult for Ophie to reconcile the mean old woman she'd worked for the past few months with the woman wearing the beautifully beaded gown, her sparse hair combed into a gorgeous updo.

"Doesn't the missus look lovely?" Cook said with a smile.

"It took me nearly an hour to do a style she liked," Mama murmured.

The older woman clucked her tongue. "Your talents are sorely wasted here."

"She stole that dress from me," said a woman next to Ophie, and she startled to recognize the ghost from the never-ending dinner party. The woman held a glass of red wine and scowled up the stairs. "Gold was never her color."

"I'm sure it looked much better on you," Ophie said. The ghost harrumphed and moved off through the crowd, where a few of the other household ghosts had joined the group, as well as some ghosts Ophie had never seen before. A small pale ghost peeked out at her from behind a woman's skirt, its form so slight that it was hardly more than a wisp of fog. An older ghost rested his hand on the shoulder of the lady who had quickly drained her champagne, and she shivered as he did so. The dead here were following their loved ones around, restless and unhappy, just as they were everywhere. Ophie was thankful once more that her daddy had passed on. How terrible it must be to remain trapped where one had no place, where nothing ever mattered or could change anything.

"Cousins, aunts, and uncles!" Richard called over them all. "I am glad you could join us tonight for this momentous occasion. As you all know, tonight is my birthday—" At that, the white folks all held up their glasses, and there was a smattering of applause. "But that is not the only thing we will be celebrating," he continued.

A murmur went up from the group, and even Cook and Mr. Henry looked surprised by the announcement, shifting uncomfortably. Surprises were never good when you were the household help. They usually meant extra work.

"Tonight, I want to also introduce you to Miss Edwina Cuthbert—the love of my life, and, as of last night, my fiancée."

Everyone exclaimed as a plain-looking white woman dressed in a demure flapper-style dress ascended the stairs to join Richard and his mother. It was the same woman who had walked into the kitchen so suddenly a few weeks ago, interrupting Ophie and Cook's conversation.

Ophie's breath caught in her throat, and she started looking around for the form of Penelope in the crowd, terrified at what Clara would think. Everyone began to clap as Edwina stood on the other side of Richard, and even though Mrs. Caruthers looked like she'd just taken a bite out of a lemon, she managed to recover enough to smile tightly.

It was when Richard opened his mouth to say a few more words that Clara made herself known.

"No!" she said, still possessing Penelope, taking a step forward. "This isn't right. This isn't how it's supposed to go!"

The crowd began to murmur, sounds of disapproval and anger, and Ophie took a half step into the crowd. She had to get Clara out of there, and then . . . She didn't know what. But it probably started by telling her she knew she was Clara. But before she could move any farther, Mama pulled Ophie into her side, wrapping her arms around her.

"Don't you dare say a word, Ophelia Harrison," Mama said. "Penelope is your friend, I know, but she's also a dreamy girl who is about to learn a very important lesson about reality."

But that was the problem. That wasn't Penelope acting out at all. It was Clara. But Ophie couldn't say that to her mama.

"Dear girl," Richard said, his expression kind. "I know this comes as a shock. But you needn't fear, we're not going anywhere. Edwina will be moving into Daffodil Manor after our marriage. And I will be keeping the house open for friends and family to come and visit the entire year after our wedding, which you are, of course, all invited to!"

Clara jerked as if slapped, and looked around at everyone clapping and smiling and giving her looks of sympathy.

"I don't . . ." The girl inside Penelope trailed off, and then her look of confusion melted into despair as she realized the truth. Richard only saw her as the hired help. That's all he could see. Whatever he and Clara had shared during her lifetime, it was gone now.

For Ophie, who could now clearly see the ghost lurking beneath the skin of the girl, all of this was like reading a tragic pulp romance—just the kind she and Clara loved. But everyone else in the room was making the same assumption that Richard had: that Penelope had finally found a secure position working for a family of means and was worried she might be out of a job. After all, what else could a colored girl like Penelope want from a white man who was so very high above her station?

With that, Clara ran out of the room. Ophie made another move to follow her, but her mama's strong arms kept her anchored right where she was.

"You can talk to her after dinner. We're gonna be one short for table service, so you'll have to help." Mama's voice was low but firm, and Ophie nodded, her gaze on the beaming Edwina and Richard. They looked so happy. And she supposed that the worst was out there now. Clara knew about Richard's lady.

But then, she wondered, what could a hurt and angry ghost do with a broken heart?

Ophie followed the rest of the household staff as they went to the kitchen to finalize preparations for the evening meal. Her belly churned, not with hunger for the delicious-smelling beef Wellington that was about to be served to the guests in the dining room, but with dread. She had the feeling that things would get worse before they got better.

Chapter 25

THE DINNER SERVICE WENT OFF WITHOUT A HITCH, much to Mama's delight. As Ophie carried dishes to the sideboard to be served and cleared dirty plates to make way for the next course, her mama kept giving her proud looks across the room. But the plates were nothing compared to the heavy tea services Ophie was used to carrying up and down the main staircase for Mrs. Caruthers. She lifted the food-laden dishes easily and removed them soundlessly, and if the wizened old woman who had guzzled her champagne kept asking her for a refill of her wine, a request Ophie could not accommodate even if she had wanted to, then it was a small price to pay for the dinner progressing quickly, and without incident.

Penelope was nowhere to be found during the meal, and as soon as Ophie had cleared the last plate and the guests had moved on to other activities, she stripped off her apron and went searching for Clara, not sure whether to hope that she was still possessing Penelope or that she had left her body and disappeared. She couldn't imagine any good coming of her continuing to possess the poor girl, but she was also desperate to speak with her.

Ophie searched the entire house and found Penelope tucked into a chair in the library. She wasn't crying, but she turned the pages of a *True Romances* magazine disconsolately.

"I guess these were silly after all," she said as Ophie entered. It was obvious now that Clara was truly riding around inside of Penelope's body. Not just her voice, but even her movements were so much like the dead girl's. Ophie could have been excused for missing it at first, but maybe she hadn't wanted to see it. Maybe she, like Clara, had truly wanted something that she didn't quite have and was willing to let small things slide in order to get it.

But not anymore. Daddy always said you had to do the right thing, even if it was the hard thing, and the right thing was getting salty old Penelope her life back.

"I know who you are," Ophie said, voice low. "This isn't the way, Clara."

Penelope—no, Clara—tore the magazine in half. "All I ever wanted was a happily ever after, Ophie. Just like any girl. Why shouldn't I get a grand proposal and a man who loves me more than the moon? He forgot about me, Ophie," Clara said, tears streaking down her cheeks. "They all forgot about me."

"I didn't," Ophie whispered. "That's why I'm trying to help you."

She scoffed and threw the torn magazine to the ground. "I know, Ophie. But it's not enough. I was supposed to have a life, a grand one! And instead I'm . . . nothing but wisp."

"Was Richard going to give you a happily ever after?" Ophie asked. She still had no idea how to get Clara out of Penelope's body, but maybe if she could solve Clara's murder, then she could help the spirit pass on, releasing Penelope from the possession. "The night you died, you said there was a grand party. Was he going to propose to you?" If Ophie could lay out the pieces of the puzzle for the ghost, maybe she could put them all together and come to the answer herself.

Clara jumped to her feet. "Yes. Oh, yes. That was why I borrowed the dress. He told me to come downstairs right before dinner so he could announce the news to his family. Just like tonight. Only—only someone wanted to talk to me."

"Was it one of the cousins?"

"No," Clara whispered. "No. Oh. Oh, Richard!"

Clara suddenly exploded out of the room, running past Ophie and out the door. Ophie tried to follow her, but she wasn't sure which way she'd gone. It was like the entire girl had just disappeared, her ghostly abilities working even though she still rode Penelope's body.

Ophie ran through the house, searching for Clara. What if it had been Richard who'd killed Clara, not one of the cousins? Ophie had thought it might be a Virginia cousin because that was the night Clara disappeared, but now she wondered if the murderer hadn't been closer.

Ophie ran through the kitchen, down past the servants' quarters, and outside. Richard and his fiancée stood under the big oak tree and gathered well-wishes from his family. Penelope, or Clara, was nowhere to be found.

She had to be somewhere else. But where?

As Ophie turned to run back into the house Richard called her over.

"Ophelia! Would you be a dear and run up to check on Mother? Edwina took her up to bed a few moments ago; she was awfully worn out by all the excitement, but I know she likes a glass of warm milk to help her sleep."

Ophie bit her lip in frustration but nodded tersely.

That was one of the problems with living at Daffodil Manor. There was never any real end to the workday. There was always one more thing to do.

"Oh, and, um, Ophelia, is it?" Edwina said, breaking away from the group to stop Ophie as she made to enter the house.

"Yes'm," Ophie said, bobbing a curtsy. She did not know this Edwina, with her soft voice and perfectly bobbed brown hair. The woman could be nice, but Mrs. Caruthers seemed nice when company was around and Ophie knew that to be an act.

"There was salt all over Richard's mother's room. I found that curious, so I swept it up. Do you know anything about that?"

Ophie's heart thumped painfully in her chest, once, and then again. She thought back to the strange way Penelope had stood outside Mrs. Caruthers's room, and the fact that Mr. Henry had decided to salt only the old woman's room and Clara's old room.

Because he knew what had happened to Clara, how she had died.

It made sense. Mr. Henry had been with the family a very long time, even coming up with them from Virginia. There was no one Mrs. Caruthers trusted more. But it was the old woman's room he had salted, not Richard's.

Which meant that Ophie had been wrong. Again. Richard hadn't killed Clara.

Ophie ran. She sprinted back inside the house, ignoring the exclamation of surprise from Edwina and a few of the other guests. She ran through the kitchen, ignoring Mama's and Cook's yelps of surprise and shouted censure, grabbed the saltshaker off the prep table, and climbed the stairs, her short legs pumping hard up the grand staircase. When she got to Mrs. Caruthers's room she flung the door open without knocking.

"What do you think you're doing?"

At first Ophie thought the question was for her, but as her eyes adjusted to the gloom of the bedroom she realized that a figure stood over Mrs. Caruthers where she lay in her bed.

Clara, still inside Penelope's body, swayed from side to side, as though she were in some kind of trance. The curtains were still open, and the only light in the room came from the moonlight filtered in through the window. Ophie, panting after her race through the house, turned on the electric lamp nearest to the door, throwing the room into a stark relief of deep shadows and light. Behind her the door slammed shut on its own, and an icy chill ran over Ophie's skin as she realized she was trapped.

The figure stood over Mrs. Caruthers with a look of

rage twisting her features and a pair of scissors gripped in her hand. The body was still mostly Penelope's, but she could see bits of Clara coming to the surface, subtle changes that made Ophie's stomach turn. She gasped as Penelope's skin grew paler, and her features changed so that when Ophie next blinked, Penelope was gone and there in her place was Clara. Not Penelope with Clara's mannerisms, but Clara as she must have looked when she was living. Her skin rippled in an inhuman way, as though Penelope fought to reclaim her body and couldn't. For the first time since the incident on the trolley Ophie was terrified of just what the dead could do.

"Clara," Ophie said, her voice coming out in a squeak. She cleared her throat and tried again. "Do you remember what happened to you?"

It seemed like a stupid thing to ask, but the gumshoes in detective stories were always trying to get suspects to talk so they could figure out what to do next. Nothing good would come of leaving Clara in Penelope's body—as much disdain as Ophie had for the racist old woman, she couldn't let Clara kill her. But Ophie did not know how to get the ghost to leave the girl, and clearly the realization about her murder had only made her stronger. She still wore the pretty tortoiseshell comb, and Ophie's only idea was to find a way to take it out. Hopefully that would free Penelope of the possession and Ophie could help her after that. She had no idea how, but she could only solve one problem at a time.

Clara turned slowly, unnaturally, her torso finishing before the rest of her. "Chickadee? What are you doing here?"

Ophie swallowed. She dared not run up to the girl while she was holding those scissors. "I told you I would help you solve your murder. But you have to help me. Please, tell me what you remembered just a moment ago, when we were speaking." She took a small step forward, keeping her hands behind her back.

"I remember Richard," Clara said, the hand holding the scissors shaking. Her eyes darted back and forth, as though she were reading a page in a book only she could see.

"You were in love with Richard, right?" Ophie said. Another step.

"Yes! He took me to the cinema for the first time, we saw *Birth of a Nation*. I didn't much care for it, but Richard looked so dashing as we left the theater." She laughed and closed her eyes as she remembered the evening. "He said he loved me." A tear slid down Clara's cheek. "He asked me to marry him. We were engaged."

"I know who you are now." It was the absolute worst time for Mrs. Caruthers to interject, but Ophie should have expected the old woman wouldn't be able to keep her mouth shut. She rose up in the bed, pointing an accusing finger at Clara. "I knew it when I heard you laugh! You're dead, and dead you should have stayed."

What happened next felt like it took an eternity, and happened all at once. Penelope lurched toward Mrs. Caruthers with the scissors, and the woman held up her hands in defense. At the same moment, Ophie threw the saltshaker, which she had uncapped. It was the only thing she could think might help prevent the worst possible outcome.

The container burst into a shower of salt as it hit the girl in the chest. There was a sound like the room was inhaling, the air grew thick, and there was a pressure change that made Ophie's ears pop. Clara crumpled to the floor, the scissors skittering away under the bed. Ophie lunged toward the girl's inert body, pulling out the tortoiseshell comb. Her features melted back into Penelope's, and her chest rose and fell as she breathed.

Ophie exhaled in relief. Clara had left Penelope's body.

"This is your doing, isn't it?" Mrs. Caruthers demanded from the bed. "You knew Clara! You're her low-born kin, aren't you? Well, I know how to deal with uppity pickaninnies like the two of you; I always did."

Now it was Mrs. Caruthers who held the scissors, standing by the side of the bed. Her face was twisted in an ugly expression, and Ophie clambered to her feet just as the bedroom door slammed open.

"What is going on?" Richard demanded. Edwina stood beside him, and behind them was Mama. She took one look at the tableau before her and pushed her way past Richard and his fiancée to gather up Ophie into her arms, her gaze locked on Mrs. Caruthers.

"Ophelia, do not say a word," Mama said. But Ophie laid a calming hand on her mother's arm.

"No, I know what I have to do," Ophie said. She stood, spine straight. In the corner, more solid than she'd ever been, was Clara. She sobbed brokenly, her throat an ugly gash, like a second, red, smiling mouth. Ophie pulled away from her mother and went to her friend's side.

"Do you remember now?"

Clara nodded through the tears. "Everything."

Ophie reached out and took Clara's hand in hers, the ghostly fingers melting into hers just a little bit, not chilly at all but warm, as though Clara were still alive.

And finally, she understood.

Ophie turned toward Richard. "Did you love Clara?"

The man jerked as though slapped. "I don't, I . . .

yes. I did. How do you know Clara?"

"I didn't until I came here." Ophie took a deep breath. Her chest was tight, and she couldn't look at her mama where she knelt over Penelope. She'd made a promise to Mama, and now she was going to have to break it.

"Clara used to work for your mother, but you couldn't help but fall in love with her. She was pretty and bright and made everyone around her happy." Sudden tears pricked Ophie's eyes as she thought about the times they'd spent together, both in the attic and the night they'd gone to the movies. "She was like a bright sun, and you'd been in this big old house, just you and your mother, for a very long time."

"Ophelia . . . ," Mama started, but Richard held his hand up and took a step into the room.

"No, let her finish. She's right, every word of it." Richard stared at Ophie in pained shock. "I asked her to marry me. That's no secret," Richard said at the gasps from behind him. Many of the houseguests had crowded into the hallway behind and craned their necks to see what was happening in the bedroom. "Edwina knows."

Richard didn't understand why his family was gasping, thinking that it was because of the slight to his new fiancée. But that wasn't it at all.

"What you didn't know, Richard, was that Clara was a Negro," Ophie said, a heavy sadness falling over her as the rest of the pieces of the story slid into place. "She was just passing light. Your family from Virginia knew, though. Her mother had worked for your aunt."

Richard frowned, as though searching for the words to say. Ophie did not give him a chance to speak, continuing with the tragic tale of Clara's end.

"The night you went to the movies, you asked Clara to marry you, and gave her this tortoiseshell comb until you could buy her a ring."

"I was . . . impulsive," Richard said, looking at the comb Ophie held in her hand.

"But you told your mother that you were going to get married."

"And I took care of it, like I always do," Mrs. Caruthers said, coming around the bed, the scissors still gripped in her hand. "I offered her money to never see you again, Richard. To leave and never come back. And she said no. How dare she! She told me that I would never understand what it was that you shared, that you wouldn't care that she hadn't always been a white woman. As if she could just *decide* to be white!"

"You killed her?" Richard's eyes went wide. "Mother, are you saying you killed Clara?"

Mrs. Caruthers froze, looked at the group of people

gathered in the hallway—which had only grown as more people came to see what the commotion was about—and laughed. "Don't be ridiculous. In the end, she took my money, just like all the house girls your father got too fond of. This is why I loathe domestics. They are always up to no good, throwing themselves at every single man above their station."

It was at that moment Clara's sprit, unseen by all but Ophie, straightened up tall, and it was as if the whole room took a breath. Her face twisted, and her entire being went a brilliant violet. The room crackled with energy, and a deep fear twisted in Ophie's middle, stealing her breath for a moment. Ophie did not fully understand how the dead worked, but she knew that a ghost that powerful and angry could hurt those around them.

"Check the closet," Ophie blurted out, pulling one last memory from Clara through their connected fingers.

"No," Mrs. Caruthers screamed, and Clara laughed, an ugly, echoing sound. There was a creak and a crack, and then the closet door exploded off its hinges. Everyone shielded their eyes, and a few people in the hallway let out cries of alarm, but Richard ignored them all and took long strides toward the gaping maw of the closet.

There, at the back, was the large cedar chest. Just as

it had been the first time Ophie had opened the closet, the day Mrs. Caruthers had demanded she never open the closet again. Ophie moved now to stand in the circle of her mama's arms, knowing that whatever came next would be bad but necessary. Mama must have known as well, because she wrapped Ophie up in a hug and squeezed her tight. Next to them, Penelope slowly climbed to her feet, unsteady and a bit dazed.

"Did I fall asleep?" she asked, and Ophie patted her hand awkwardly as Richard and one of the other men pulled the chest out. Mrs. Caruthers by this time was just muttering to herself.

"It would have been scandal, and ruin," the old woman said, even as everyone ignored her. "Can't you see? Can't you understand?"

The chest was locked, and Richard kicked it until the padlock came free with a clank. Houseguests pushed into the room to see, all pretense of manners forgotten, and in the corner, Clara crossed her arms, watching and waiting just as she had since Mrs. Caruthers had killed her.

Richard lifted the lid to the chest, and a collective gasp went up around the room. A few of the houseguests close enough to see inside rushed away, hands held over their mouths as their dinner threatened to make a reappearance. Richard fell to his knees next to the chest and let out a single sob, and Edwina laid a consoling hand on his shoulders before looking away, tears sliding down her own pale cheeks.

In the far corner of the room, Clara's spirit smiled. The purple bled away from her form, and she looked at Ophie and gave her a wink. "Thank you, chickadee," she said. "You are simply the cat's meow."

And then she sighed in deep relief before exploding into a million golden pieces of sunshine, glittering as she finally moved on.

There, in the chest, covered in a layer of white powder, was Clara's body. She was curled up, as though she had long ago decided to take a nap tucked into the space and never awoke. Her skin had withered in the time she had been hidden, going gray and leathery, but there was no doubt who she had once been. In her hair was the mate to the tortoiseshell comb that Richard gripped in his hand.

There was a deep breath of shock, and Mrs. Caruthers fell to the floor. A moment later, Ophie watched as the old woman's spirit appeared over her body, her expression slack and confused.

"What are all these people doing in my room?" she demanded.

"You're dead," Ophie said to the ghost, as one of the party guests walked over to check the old woman's pulse. Everyone seemed to be moving very slowly, unsure what to do in the face of so much unexpected death after such a lovely party. Then, they all began speaking at once—crying out in anguish, calling for someone to ring a doctor—and no one was paying attention to the young girl speaking softly to the space above Mrs. Caruthers's lifeless body. "You can pass on or you can stick around. You'll have company," Ophie said, her heart feeling brittle as she looked at the ghost. She didn't have a chance to say anything else before her mama gently took her hand and guided her from the room, Penelope following unsteadily behind.

"Come on, Ophelia," Mama said. "This is no concern of ours."

And for once, Ophie, exhausted and somehow both happy and sad at the same time, agreed.

Chapter 26

NO ONE SPOKE OF THE NIGHT OF THE ENGAGEMENT party.

As the houseguests packed and departed—many of them doing so that very night—Ophie, along with the ghosts of the house, listened to their whispers and murmurs. None of them spoke about Mrs. Caruthers killing her son's first fiancée, a woman who had been her personal maid and a colored girl light enough to pass as white. Richard and his new fiancée, both in a daze of shock and grief, glided through the manor almost as if they themselves were ghosts, directing the house staff to this task or the next like they were only half certain that the work should even be done at all. Luckily, Cook had lived through more than one tragedy at Daffodil Manor, and she took over the management of the household as she always did, without a complaint and with an iron will.

Penelope never quite recovered from being possessed by Clara, something of the dead girl remaining even after she'd passed on. Which was, in Ophie's estimation, a bit of an improvement. The girl was happy to do her part, no longer sullen, and far kinder than she had been before the ordeal.

Richard decided not to have a funeral for his mother, and Mrs. Caruthers was placed in the family tomb with a minimum of ceremony. A small obituary in the paper was the only notice of her passing. It had been, as the old woman had feared, quite the scandal. Just not the one she had expected. Ophie was unsurprised to discover that she'd had few friends, especially after she found Mrs. Caruthers in a chair beside the gossiping woman in the dining room a few days later, each of them reenacting their ends in a gruesome fashion. You could judge most folks by the company they kept, after all.

"Honestly," said the maid who could usually be found trying to clean the high windows on the second floor. "Some people can just never be happy."

"No," Ophie agreed. "By the way, you have done a great job of keeping the windows free of cobwebs. It's hard to clean that far up, and I figured someone should tell you so."

"Oh," the girl said as she began to fade away in a

glitter of sunshine. "Thank you. I was hoping someone would notice."

Without Mrs. Caruthers to look after, Ophie found she had a fair amount of time after finishing her chores, so as Mama and Penelope closed up the bedrooms once more and emptied out Mrs. Caruthers's room, Ophie spent her time attending to her own cleaning—helping the few remaining spirits in the house pass on.

In the library, Ophie showed the endlessly arguing man how he had been right—reading him a passage in a book of history that detailed the Civil War yet to come for him, and the fact that it was caused by slavery. The man had been so shocked by the revelation that he'd exploded into blue sparkles, and Ophie couldn't help but laugh at the sight.

In one of the unoccupied bedrooms, she sat for a couple of hours with a plate of cookies. When the ghost of one of Mrs. Caruthers's sons finally appeared, in uniform with his hand tightly gripping a bottle, Ophie laid a hand on his arm, which was naught but chilly vapor. "It's okay," she said, smiling. "It's okay to be scared, but I know there is someplace great waiting for you. You should go see it. Get out of this unhappy place."

He looked through Ophie, taking a long moment before he nodded. "You're right. Thank you. Once more, unto the breach," he said before fading away into blue sparks that smelled vaguely of sulfur.

In the garden, under the oak tree, she found Colin sitting on the ground. She had not seen the boy since the night Mrs. Caruthers died. She sat down next to him, relishing the shade. Spring was sizzling into summer, and even the deepest shadows of Daffodil Manor were inhospitable.

"I can go now," Colin said as Ophie sat down.

"What do you mean?" Ophie asked. "Why couldn't you go before?"

"Because I was afraid she would hurt Henry," the dead boy said, eyes distant as he looked into a past that only he could see. "I was afraid she'd take everything out on him, the way she always took it out on me. It's why he helped her even when she did bad things, you know. He was still a little scared of her."

Ophie's breath caught as she realized that Colin was talking about Mrs. Caruthers. Cook had said once that Henry had been with the old woman since long before she came north from Virginia, and Ophie wondered if Henry had come to Pittsburgh because he wanted to or because he was property.

Ophie decided that maybe she wouldn't worry about helping the ghosts dying over and over again in the dining room.

"How do you know Henry?" Ophie asked Colin, wishing for this smallest piece of story to take with her. Not because she was nosy, but because someone should remember this boy.

"He's my baby brother," Colin said. "I have to look out for him."

"He's grown now. You can do whatever you want to," Ophie said to Colin, and the boy smiled for the first time ever.

"I know. Thank you, Ophie. Thank you for helping."

Colin faded away slowly, like Ophie's daddy had on that long-ago morning, and before she knew it she was crying, releasing the tears she'd held back for what felt like years. She cried because girls who believed in happily ever afters could be murdered in attics, and because men who just wanted to have their voices heard could have their words choked off forever. She cried for lost boys like Colin and for all the dead who still waited for someone to help them. And she cried because so many of them would be forgotten, their stories never remembered, never told. The task seemed impossible, and overwhelming, but someone would have to help them.

Someone had to try.

"Ophelia, what is the matter?" Mama said, walking out the back door and finding Ophie under the oak tree, tears streaming down her face.

"I miss him," Ophie said, forgetting their unspoken rule, breaking yet another promise. "I miss Daddy so much."

Mama's face crumpled. "I miss him, too, Ophie. Every damn day."

And then Ophie was in her mother's arms, and they were both crying, and for the first time in a very long time Ophie thought that maybe, just maybe, things could be okay.

"Ophie," Mama said after a long while when their tears had dried and the sun had traveled closer to its evening rest.

"Yes'm?"

"Tell me about the night your daddy died. And I do mean everything."

Ophie smiled, a great weight lifting from her chest.

And then she told her mama everything.

The Hill District

❦

PITTSBURGH WELCOMED ALL, BUT THE PEOPLE OF the city tended to draw lines. Lines across class and lines across race, lines between the immigrants and those who had lived in the city more than a handful of years. Lines between the Polish and Irish and Hungarians and Negroes and everywhere in between. And one of those lines was strongest around the Hill District.

Colored folks couldn't live just anywhere, but the Hill had always welcomed Pittsburgh's darker-skinned residents. First, the Free Blacks, who came looking for opportunities across the North; and later, the Haitians, who had taken their independence by force. By the time the Jazz Age marched in, the Hill was a bustling neighborhood full of music, theaters, gambling halls, and families. So, so many families. Growing and living, fighting and loving, and doing it on the Hill because it was the only part of Pittsburgh where they could do it without facing the enduring hardship of racism.

Houses were expensive in the Hill District. The Great Migration, in which Black folks took any opportunity to flee old Jim Crow and the terror of the Klan, meant that more colored folks were pouring in to the city every day. That made houses hard to find. But when the girl who saw the dead and her mother walked through the streets hand in hand on their way to the cinema, the girl nodding to the dead and her mother pretending not to notice, the Hill made note. As did the dead.

It was pure luck that a small row home, a two-bedroom with a nice garden and a large front room where a person could have a hair salon, if they were so inclined, just could not seem to stay occupied. The previous tenants said the house was chilled even with the fireplace packed near to overflowing and that there were strange sounds all hours of the night. There were whispers of spirits and haints, and even the conjure woman called in to cleanse the place said that there was nothing to be done. The house belonged to the dead.

The girl and her mother bought the house the first day it was on the market, all financed by a Good Samaritan who claimed to have their best interests at heart, but who the dead knew to be carrying around a guilt so heavy that he tried to fix it by spending his considerable fortune on good works. If some of those donations helped to keep those who knew the truth of his mother's passing quiet, well, that was just another reason to be thankful, wasn't it?

The dead did not judge. Much.

The girl and her mother made a life in that small house, the girl spending the summer painting the windowsills and doorways a curious shade of blue. And if they used a bit more salt than necessary those first few weeks, much to the chagrin of the neighborhood's ghosts, the mother did not complain. After all, she knew better than that. Everyone deserved peace in their own house, even a girl who could talk to the dead.

In the fall, the girl dashed off to school once again during the day while her mother welcomed people from the community into their front room. There she pressed and curled and beautified the hair of the ladies of the Hill. And in the evening, the dead would crowd around the back porch while the girl spoke to them, taking notes and promising to carry out one last task for those who asked. Sometimes, she would link fingers with a spirit to understand what it was that they needed, even if it was just for someone to remember who they had once been.

Other times she would have to send away a particularly bothersome spirit with the threat of iron and salt, but those times were rare.

The dead did not mind. They finally had someone who would listen.

At night, after dinner was done, the girl and her mother would sit together and tell stories about the good days, and the bad ones, too, and realize over and over again that there was nothing they couldn't do as long as they did it together with honesty and love. Together they could survive just about anything, even if sometimes telling each other the truth was hard. But they would go through whatever hardships they faced together.

And that was enough.